Implements
Of
The
Model Maker

Published by Long Midnight Publishing, 2021

copyright © 2021 Douglas Lindsay

ISBN: 979 8 5026 2292 9

www.douglaslindsay.com

IMPLEMENTS
OF
THE
MODEL
MAKER

DOUGLAS LINDSAY

1

Sitting in the car, in silence, on the way back to the station after the funeral. Early April, a pale sky. Winter lingers, cold winds from the north.

'It is a beautiful piece of music,' says Detective Inspector Kallas.

I'm driving, Kallas is sitting beside me, staring straight ahead. Expressionless, as ever.

The funeral of Constable Milburn was a quiet affair. All funerals are quiet at the moment. The DI and I were representing station management. There were three more of us in attendance, the others all staying behind to join the family at the small wake. Katie Milburn died from Covid complications, having gone into hospital in the first place because she got stabbed in the line of duty. A shitty, avoidable, awful death.

I'm not the heroic, selfless character of anyone's narrative, but I wish it had been me. There wouldn't have been half the grief, half the regret, half the determination to make sure the woman who stabbed her in the first place doesn't fall into one of the gigantic chasms that have opened up in the criminal justice system.

It's not like I was there, or anything. The case itself seemed so small, so insignificant. A woman going door-to-door, targeting the old and the vulnerable, offering a fake vaccine. There've been a few of them. Small-time, nasty little criminal ventures, featuring small-time, nasty little criminals. When cornered, this one stabbed Constable Milburn. Didn't even appear to be that serious, they said. She was hospitalised but wasn't expected to stay long. Then there was internal bleeding, and the hospital stay was extended, and then she caught the infection, and then, and then… the story that's been repeated throughout this last, godawful year.

So, it's back to work for Kallas and me, although with Milburn's assailant already apprehended and her case in the hands of the procurator, there's nothing major filling the books for the moment.

'What is?'

We're not listening to music.

'The Handel keyboard suite in D minor,' says Kallas. 'They played it at the end of Katie's funeral.'

'Yes, right,' I say.

Stopped at lights, eyes unthinkingly on the circle of red, waiting. I can still feel the tears of Katie Milburn's mother. The movement of her shoulders, the complete silence that was coming from her, yet, sitting behind, we knew she was crying. The look on her face, and in her eyes, when she turned to watch the passage of the coffin from the small church.

Lights change, traffic moves.

'What?' says Kallas.

'Sorry?'

'There was something in your voice. When I mentioned the Handel. There was something.'

Well, she is a detective.

Slowly, as the months pass, I understand her better, and I fall more under her spell. And though I may be less and less surprised by her insight, she can still knock me off guard, particularly with her phenomenal perception of nuance. The slightest inflection in the voice, and she's on it.

'Hmm,' I say.

And another red, slow to a stop behind a white Tesla.

Don't see many Teslas around, yet they say fake Bond villain Elon Musk is the richest guy on earth. How did that happen?

'Damn,' I mutter softly, tone resigned. 'You always do it, don't you?'

'What is that?'

'You half-read someone's mind. But you don't really say much, and if it was anyone else, it'd be like, fine, let's just leave it. But your silence is like this weird superpower. It's like…' We move off from the lights, will be back at the station in five minutes. 'It's like, the silence manifests itself as a vice that clamps around my chest, squeezing and squeezing until the words come out.' A beat. 'Like toothpaste.'

I glance at her, there's a small smile on her lips. God, I love that smile. Look away quickly.

'If only I had that power when interviewing criminals,' she says.

'You do.'

Another glance, the smile has gone, the steady, blank gaze has returned, staring straight ahead.

We drive on, one minute to the next, approaching the station. In my head the conversation about Handel remains to be completed, but I've no idea if that's what she's thinking. But it doesn't matter. It's like she infects me with some strange OCD, where I have to finish something because I've started it, even though I only started it with a minor voice inflection while saying *yes, right*.

'I was watching a porn movie last week,' I say, the words appearing with crushing inevitability on my lips. 'It was, I don't know, must've been a porn movie with a budget, whoever makes them anymore. Anyway, of course, I wasn't watching the whole movie, following the narrative or anything, I watched a ten-minute clip from the movie. It was a Last Supper-type situation, twelve guys at a table, and the Jesus arrives, but Jesus, of course, is a woman. And then Jesus… has sex with the disciples. All of the disciples. And it was like the porn version of a Brian De Palma shootout, very worthy and serious and aware of its own artistic integrity, even though it was just Jesus getting gangbanged, and they had this really sombre, dramatic music playing, and it was recognisable, even though I didn't know what it actually was.'

'And it was the Sarabande from Handel's keyboard suite in D minor.'

'Sarabande? I guess, if that's what they played at the funeral.'

I park in the small car park behind the station. Engine off, I turn to look at her. I'm not thinking about the funeral now.

'That is quite the juxtaposition,' she says.

'Yep.'

'I know that film, though I did not think of it at the funeral. That is an interesting scene.'

So now, here we are, sitting in a car, two feet apart, looking at each other, and I'm thinking about Kallas watching porn. God, I'm such a moron.

'Interesting's one word for it.'

'The gangbang as a pornographic trope is generally very exploitative, and unworthy of artistic consideration, but by featuring a major erotic actress in the role and investing her with the natural authority of the Last Supper situation, it allows the scene to transcend the genre's familiar lurid mire.' A pause, then, 'I like it. We should go to work.'

She gets out of the car, leaving me sitting there watching her walk slowly across the car park, having another one of those regular moments when I just want to spend the rest of the day, me and Kallas, naked in a warm bed.

As I get out, lock the door and follow the DI towards the stairs at the back of the 1960s shopping precinct that now houses the police station, the look on the face of Katie Milburn's mother comes back to me, and the juxtapositional forces of extreme grief and extreme eroticism cancel each other out, and I enter the station in a familiar state of melancholic gloom.

2

Sitting at my desk, going through paperwork. This afternoon, a case of domestic abuse.

There are few things more depressing than domestic abuse in all the world. You meet, you fall in love, you get married, you get the mental and physical shit kicked out of you. God, these people are awful.

On this occasion, the abuser is a guy in a suit. Brian Clarkson, rich as fuck. Sounds like the abuse has been going on for a while, but for years Mrs Clarkson could get out and about, avoid the worst of it. She learned to see him coming from some way off and could make herself scarce. And then, lockdown. The official stay-at-home order, bar a few fleeting months last summer and early autumn, has been in force, one way or another, for over a year. And so, the domestic abuse got an uptick. A painful, bloody, nasty, ugly uptick. That's the story.

There are a lot of Mrs Clarkson's in the world, not enough Mr Clarkson's catching covid and dying. Which is what they deserve.

As a police officer I'm not really allowed to say that part out loud. Actually, as a human, I probably ought not to say that part out loud.

I interviewed the guy at the end of last week. He gave nothing of himself, bar a contemptuous look across the desk. The look that said he shouldn't be there. The look that said he'd done nothing wrong. The look that said he knows the chief constable, or the MP, or the MSP, or, I don't know, some fucking director at Ibrox or something, and so he thinks he's immune. Laws aren't for the likes of him. Notions of decency aren't for the likes of him. The old guard. The generation who grew up standing on the shoulders of people who grew up standing on the shoulders of the generation who landed on the Normandy beaches. Basically, this fucker is the same age as me, except I'm fifty-four going on twenty-five, and he's fifty-four going on entitled-old-twat-in-a-country-club.

The interview didn't really get anywhere. He is not currently in custody, although Mrs Clarkson is, at least, staying with her sister. That's where we are, and I'm here, processing the paperwork, putting everything together to go to the procurator. Chances of this man ending up in a prison cell, which is where he belongs?

Let's be realistic.

Zero.

So, this is life at the moment. Paperwork and casework and interviews and drudgery, each thing liable to be more depressing than the one before. I work late most days, then I go home, and then what?

Sgt Eileen Harrison wants me to expand my horizons. Do more stuff. I've got lots of interests, I said. What, she said? Football. Movies. Random TV shows I stumble across, after flicking endlessly through eight hundred channels for two hours in the evening. Porn. Vodka.

Well, I'm trying not to drink vodka, lurching from one period of abstinence to the next, and Eileen is trying to help me along the way, and DI Kallas is also trying to help me along the way, and I'm trying to help them help me, because if I didn't, then I'd be an even bigger asshole than I'm naturally disposed to be.

So, there's that. Can you call the AA meeting an interest? And I'm lying about football, because at the moment there's football on television *all the time*, and it got boring months ago. There's just too much.

I wonder, when society has managed to shoehorn itself back into some semblance of the old normal, if football will return to the old ways, or whether the constant-football genie will be out of the bottle for good.

I also don't watch many movies, much TV, or much porn either. My daughter did get me another jigsaw, so there's that. Late evenings spent at the small dining room table, eating a microwave meal, drinking Coke Zero, and looking at the slowly assembled image of Gertrude, Lady Agnew of Lochnaw, one-time poster child of the National Gallery in Edinburgh. So far I've done the edging, her face, top of her chest and her breasts. Struggling with the rest of her dress and the blue background. Every time I sit at the table, I can feel her looking a little more contemptuously at me for my lack of progress.

DI Kallas has been trying to get me to go out running, and

—

6

that happened once about two months ago. And that's about that.

'Hey,' says DC Ritter, who sits across the desk, slumping down heavily into the seat.

A good friend of Katie Milburn, this is her just getting back to work after the wake.

'You all right?' I ask.

Gradually, as the weeks turn into months, and the days become never-ending, we speak to each other a little more. We never didn't get on, we never argued, but we operate on different planes of existence, our identical worlds of crime and punishment viewed through polar opposite prisms.

Polar opposite prisms? Is that a thing? Is that science?

She lets out a long sigh, shakes her head.

'Shit,' she says. 'That was shit.'

She's been crying, although maybe not in the last half hour.

'You don't have to be here,' I say.

'What else is there?' She nods to herself, staring vaguely at the desk. 'Just using it as a crutch. Likely won't get much done.'

'Better to be here than sitting at home watching celebrity cooking fail videos on the Internet,' I say.

She stares blankly across the desk.

'Because that's what I do when I'm not at work.'

That's what you get for trying to be funny in a literal someone-just-died situation. I hold up an apologetic hand, take the hit, then glance at my monitor.

'Sorry, Sergeant,' she says quickly.

'No need,' I say, shaking my head.

Another look across the desk, nothing more to be said, the mild awkwardness disappears quietly into the ether, and we both go about our business.

*

Don't get very far.

'Tom?'

Turn away from the monitor, where I've just been struggling to not call Brian Clarkson a cunt in my report, look past DC Ritter towards Kallas, who is walking past.

'We are in with Chief Inspector Hawkins,' she says, without slowing, and I nod and am up and out of the chair.

A quick knock, we're obviously expected, and then we're into the office. Hawkins is on the phone, and she gestures for us

—

to sit in the two seats by her desk.

I try not to look at Kallas. I pretty much spend my working day, trying not to look at her, apart from the obvious exceptions, such as when we sit in a car and talk about Christian gangbang cinema.

Sometimes it feels like she's too beautiful to look at, that's the trouble. Six months ago, she undressed in front of me and went swimming naked in the Clyde. The same week her husband left. Being the mush-hearted romantic fool that I am, the combination of events immediately made me fall in love with her. But, of course, she got dressed again, and her husband came back. That's what happens.

Those feelings haven't gone anywhere though. Here for the duration, I'm afraid, until one of us leaves. Even then, it'll take a while to clear from my system. It's the very essence of true romance: like sepsis, but with better skin tone.

The phone clicks off, and I'm back.

'Everything all right?' asks Hawkins.

We stare at each other across the desk while I compute the reason she's asking me that question.

'Sure.'

'You've been writing the report on Mr Clarkson?'

'Yep. It'll be a slow grind, but hopefully we can nail him.'

She looks at me curiously, and I find myself saying, 'Nail the fucker,' and nodding.

'Mr Clarkson?'

Ah. That tone. The one that says Brian Clarkson is an upstanding member of the community, or Brian Clarkson does wonderful things on behalf of the children, (whoever the children are), Brian Clarkson votes Conservative, Brian Clarkson wears a suit. Surely we're not listening to his obviously hysterical wife? She probably just needs a long weekend at Dunblane Hydro. A series of spa treatments will do her the world of good.

'Yes.'

'I thought perhaps there'd been a misunderstanding.'

'There's audio,' I say.

'Well, I…,' she begins, but there really isn't a lot she can say. She hasn't heard the audio, and if she had, we wouldn't be having this conversation. 'I'm sure it can't be that bad,' she says anyway. 'Is there… will it be admissible?'

'Mrs Clarkson has hours *and hours* of audio. For the last

—

few months, she had Alexa record everything in the house. There's a lot. Obviously, I haven't listened to it all, but there's no…' Swallow, take a moment. This guy makes me spit with fury.

'Are they so bad?'

'He's a thug, all the worse because he hides behind the suit and this veneer of respectability. If he had a tattoo on his forehead and he came from, I don't know, fucking Westburn or something, you wouldn't…'

'Tom.'

Kallas, soft and quiet, wielding my name like an off-switch. I don't look at her, keep my gaze on Hawkins.

'Listen to the tapes,' I say. 'You won't be able to look at him.'

My tone of voice seems to be getting through to her, which doesn't normally happen. Probably because I'm usually so glib. Usually. Deadpool levels of glibness. Not when talking about this guy.

'I will.'

She swallows, looks at Kallas, who remains, as ever, completely taciturn, then she nods, glances at her computer screen, and puts herself back into the right place from which to dispense whatever executive instruction she's summoned us in here for.

'I need to send you into Glasgow,' she says. 'Obviously I'd rather not, I'm not sure we can afford one, never mind both of you, but what Glasgow asks for…'

She looks back at us, one to the other, perhaps waiting for the question, but she ought to know that Kallas never speaks unless she really has to, and I'm still processing visceral anger, and couldn't care less about getting dispatched to Glasgow. It happens, or it doesn't, I don't care either way.

'You'll be aware of the body that was discovered a few days ago. A woman near the Barrowlands. There's been another one today, another body, another woman in her forties. Body found in Glasgow Green this morning.' A pause, she glances at her computer, turns back. 'A Church of Scotland minister, which I suppose might be ironic, given some of the things that have gone on here, but really, it's no one's irony. It's just sad.' Another glance at the screen, acquainting herself with the facts, then when she speaks, she's not looking at us. 'Name of Julia Wright, forty-one.' She swallows. Not as tough as she wants to be, Chief Hawkins. Don't suppose any of us are. I've cried like a wean a fuck-tonne myself on this job after all, though often enough just because I've run out of vodka. 'Similar method of murder to the first victim. Stripped naked, arms and legs bound with the same thin, brass wire, incisions made with an unknown instrument to the neck and groin, precipitating rapid bleeding and death. Again, the pathologist, a name I don't know, Dr Wendall... Dr Wendall describes the method used as fastidious.'

Another swallow, she turns away from the screen and looks back at us.

'We have a repeat killer,' says Kallas.

'Yes. The body was found at nine a.m. this morning, so this is very early days. But the full details of the first murder had not been made public, so this cannot be a copycat. This is a repeat killer, and so... and so, everything needs to be thrown at it. All hands to the pump.'

She glances back at the screen.

'You will be there as long as you're needed. Once such a full-scale investigation is up and running, it may be that it can be quickly concentrated into certain areas, it may be that by going full steam, they get a quick result.'

'Who's the lead?' I ask.

'DCI Eurydice Hamilton.' A pause. 'You know her?'

Eurydice? Really?

'That is an interesting name,' says Kallas, filling in the gap left by my silence.

'Yes,' said Hawkins. 'Sergeant, you seem struck dumb. I do hope you haven't slept with her.'

Ha! I mean, I bring that kind of cheap jibe on myself, after all, I can't be complaining. And it's a stupid, ill-timed joke, for which she will immediately apologise, but it's a good atmosphere snapper, a saviour from the funk brought on by talking about that bastard Clarkson. Good on her for cutting through it, by reducing the conversation to my more familiar level of innuendo and inanity.

'I'm sorry,' says Hawkins, looking at Kallas as she makes the apology, 'that was not appropriate for the moment.'

'We should get going,' says Kallas. 'We will hand off any necessary outstanding business and get into Dalmarnock as soon as possible.'

'Thank you, Kadri,' says Hawkins, and then I get a look from her, and a nod, and that slight shadow across her eyes that says she hates herself for regularly saying the wrong thing in my presence, as though the very idea of me discombobulates her, and then I'm following Kallas from the office, closing the door behind me.

'Do you have much to pass on?' asks Kallas.

'A couple of things. Mainly Clarkson. I'll speak to Eileen.'

'Let me know if you need any help sorting everything out.'

'I'll be good. Fifteen minutes?'

'Yes, fifteen minutes.'

She nods and walks to the far end of the open-plan to her desk, and I can't stop watching her for a few moments, then with a shake of the head I give myself the metaphorical kick up the arse, and off we go.

3

What's the collective noun for a crowded room of detectives? A posse? A crime scene? A scrotum?

Scrotum sounds about right.

At least thirty detectives in one room, having arrived in ones and twos. Some conversation floating around, casual, wary, not wanting to be overhead. It's not like we're all jockeying for position – albeit there'll be a few of these bums looking to be the top dog – but still, in a room of one's peers, in what is a pretty unusual situation for everyone, there's inevitable conversational caution. No one wants to be overheard sounding like too much of a dick.

Kallas and I, sitting together, in silence. On the wall, blow-ups of the two crime scenes. Early spring in the parks, grass beginning to grow, trees and shrubs slowly coming to life. Five photographs from each murder, emphasising that the victims were bound in the same way, the arteries in their necks and groins were severed in identical places, and the bodies were left lying in precisely the same position.

On the left, this morning's victim, Julia Wright. First, an overall view of the scene, taken from about thirty yards away. The body on a patch of ground, in the middle of a small copse. The body, cold and white, stands out against the fresh green of the grass, though people might still have easily walked past it, the corpse in the midst of the trees in the grey light of dawn.

Second, a head shot. How often we've seen this kind of picture. The still of the dead. Eyes open, face in repose, she looks pale and cold and beautiful.

Third, incongruous with the others, the living head shot. An attractive woman, though somehow the peace of death suits her. Perhaps I'm just assuming that because she was a minister.

Fourth, taken from above, looking down on the naked corpse, blood having seeped into the grass around the head and neck, and around the thighs.

The fifth, the corpse back at the lab, laid out on the bench, cleaned up, legs slightly parted, the wounds in the neck and groin cleared of blood and on display.

On the right are the photographs of Jennifer Talbot, whose body was discovered on Saturday morning. A woman of a similar age, a more toned, muscular body, but the surroundings aside, in death the photographs look almost identical. Saturday was colder, frostier, icier, and the grass is tinged with white.

'Do you notice the minister's expression?' asks Kallas.

The like-minded genius of silence.

'What d'you think?' I say, with a small nod.

'Dying at peace, knowing she was going somewhere better,' says Kallas. 'Or an accident of death, and we are projecting something on to her that could not possibly be there. She is dead. Her face is in repose. What we imagine to be a lightness of spirit is merely, however, the skin tissue arranging itself in the middle of a cold night.'

'I'd go for the latter. It's tough to believe that someone started to drain her of blood, and she was suddenly overcome by serenity.'

'Hmm,' says Kallas.

'How's the religion in Estonia?' I ask, which is a very roundabout way of asking the great Glasgow question, *which school did you go to?*

'There are churches, there are congregations, but they are small. By church membership, Estonia is the least religious country in the world.'

'Really?'

'I have not personally done the research, but that is the received wisdom.'

'Wow, virtually no religion. That's amazing. Everything you say about Estonia sounds perfect. I think I might move.'

'It is very flat. And we can be quite racist. The winter lasts for six months.' A moment, then she says, 'And there is no word for excited.'

You see, there she goes. We're just having a conversation, pointless words filling the gaps between the last thing that happened, and the thing that's just about to happen, and then she tosses in one of those pitch-perfect, dry jokes, and they're *so* perfect and *so* dry I have to look at her just to make sure, and there's the slightest of smiles on her face, and it feels like drowning in a bath of warm chocolate sauce.

Yeah, whatever.

I smile ruefully, then turn away, and look back at the gallery of gruesome on the wall, and then the door closes on the room, and DCI Eurydice Hamilton is walking to the front. No podium, no microphone, instant silence.

She takes a moment, assesses what she's been given in terms of manpower, nods at a few people, sends nothing the way of the Cambuslang branch naturally, as she knows neither of us, and then she turns to look at the photographs, her way of getting everyone else to look.

'You've all had a few minutes with our victims,' she begins.

A pause, making sure that Julia Wright and Jennifer Talbot have our full attention, and then she turns back to the room.

'This is a highly unusual situation, and I know it's not as though you all had nothing else to do. Our thinking, however, is that this has the possibility of being long and ugly. This kind of behaviour screams repeat pattern. We need to swarm all over this. In the next twenty-four hours we need to interview every single person who knew the victims. And Rev Wright... well, she did what ministers do. She knew a fuck-load of people.

'And look, I don't know how long this'll last, regardless of the result. For now, though, we just have to throw the kitchen sink at the wall, and hope something sticks.'

Throwing the kitchen sink at the wall? I suppose we've all done that.

'The Talbot investigation is obviously three days old already, but as we all know, three days is just getting started. Three days is just beginning to kick the tyres. So, the team and I have done the preliminary work on that, and this morning we've interviewed Rev Wright's husband and a couple of her colleagues at the church. There has been no narrowing down, far too early for that. This is where that starts. Today I'm going to ask you all to concentrate on Rev Wright. The list of all church members, regardless of whether or not they attended church regularly, or at all, has been split up between you. We've also got the breakdown of friends and colleagues from the wider church community. I want an initial interview done with everyone on the list by close of play tomorrow.'

She turns for a quick look at the photographs, then she's back round.

'On the way out you'll be given the preliminary report, everything you need to know about the victims, and then you need to go and start tracking down those on your list. I'll want it all written up, but of course, anything your gut tells you should be flagged up, anything that demands instant attention, I'll ask that you call Sgt Blumenthal.' She indicates a large guy in his thirties sitting by the door, and he raises his hand just in case anyone missed her pointing to the biggest guy in the room by twenty-five stone. 'This is a fucking shitshow, people, so no fucking about.'

Eurydice Hamilton claps her hands like she's just exhorted us all to get out there and overturn the 2-1 deficit to Rangers in the second half, and then she heads to the door and is gone.

I've honestly never met anyone called Eurydice before. I'm not entirely sure what one expects from someone with that name and a Scottish accent. Posh, probably. Not such liberal use of the f-word.

Oh, you know what I hate? When people call it the F-bomb. I mean, what the fuck is that? The F-bomb? Fuck off, you overly dramatic cuntweasel. It's just a word, like every other fucking word. F-bomb. Jesus.

Still, didn't see it coming from DCI Hamilton. Although, perhaps she got it from her more famous namesake. As the Eurydice of myth was about to break free from the underworld, escape to the surface, and go and live a happy life of wine and sex and swimming naked in warm Mediterranean waters, that tube Orpheus turned round, and perhaps, at that moment, a well-placed, 'Oh, for fuck's sake' escaped Eurydice's lips. Certainly what I would've said.

Blumenthal, in position by the door, has a pile of thin folders to distribute amongst the scrotum, an orderly queue of whom has already begun to form.

'I see a problem coming in the same car, if we get sent to opposite ends of the city,' I say.

'We will return to the office to read through the details and make plans. The task, wherever it leads us, will start with phone calls.'

Good point.

'Ma'am,' I can't help myself saying.

4

Me and Sgt Harrison having a quick bite to eat, sitting out on a bench in five-degree weather in the precinct, watching the world go by. Not that there's much of the world going by. Still pretty quiet out here in the world.

The afternoon has turned beautiful, nevertheless, and well worth sitting out in. The air is crisp and cold, the sky a gorgeous pale blue. We both have a cup of warm soup and a cup of coffee to follow. Even so, some of us, on missions of the greatest import, do not have all day.

'So, today's victim was a minister, right?'

'Yep.'

'Where was her church?'

'Partick-ish,' I say. 'Not far from Byres Road. Not sure if it's officially Partick at that point.'

I take a glug of soup. Chicken and vegetable. Generic and basic, but tasty nevertheless, can feel the warmth of it all the way down my throat.

'There's something about ministers and murder, isn't there?' says Eileen. 'You keep getting sucked in. I think the universe might be trying to tell you something. You're getting to the stage where seven out of every eight crimes you have to investigate are related to the Church of Scotland. You should set up in your own specialist unit.'

'Funny. This is, what, like the third in twenty years.'

'Seems like more. You could have your own badge. You could be the maverick cop who all the rest of us view with suspicion, but who does amazing work fending off the evil that lies at the heart of Christianity. And wouldn't it be great if it turned out that all the stories are linked, and there's some nefarious mastermind behind it all? Some quiet old minister, preaching to five or six octogenarians in a wee kirk in Applecross, or something, and it turns out he's Moriarty.'

We're staring at each other from a couple of feet apart on the bench.

'And you'd get to bring him down in an intense firefight,' she adds, with a smile.

'What did you eat for breakfast? Nicholas Cage?'

'Where did *that* come from?'

'I don't know, sounds like the kind of shit film Nicholas Cage would make these days.'

'Well, I think I'll skip eating Nicholas for breakfast, thank you very much. Anyhoo, tell me everything?'

I down the rest of the soup, take a napkin to my lips, and then a sip of coffee.

'Minister. Woman in her forties. Married, knows literally everyone. I mean, that's the trouble with ministers, they're connected to like everyone within ten miles. But then, there's the other side of the coin, and such is the way of these things, our minister was a bit of a looker. So, there's always the possibility someone, you know, had a romantical interest.'

'You're so shallow,' she says, through a mouthful of soup.

'What?'

'It's not like it's just attractive people who have relationships, is it?'

'Good point,' I say. 'I'll add that to my developmental database, try to factor it into the investigation.'

'You're a cheeky sod. Keep talking.'

'Just at the outset here, there are no specific leads, husband aside. And the husband is only a lead in that he was her husband. They seemed, far as anyone could tell, to have been happily married.'

'And the first victim, was she also attractive?'

I smile at that, take some more coffee. Mouth quickly adjusting, able to take a little more this time.

'Good coffee, by the way,' I say, tipping the cup.

'Thanks.'

'A round-the-world yachtswoman. Jennifer Talbot. Yes, attractive, and as an added bonus, she was pretty fit. I mean, physically fit.'

'I don't recognise the name.'

'No, doesn't look like she made a thing out of sailing round the world. Didn't race, didn't write books about it, or anything. It was just something she did.'

'So, what was she doing in Glasgow?'

'The last time she sailed around the world was three years ago. Since then, she's been staying in a small boathouse on some guy's property down by Helensburgh. Some rich bloke she used to be married to, but who's now married to someone else.'

'That sounds like a story.'

'It does, but the likes of me and the boss won't get anywhere near it. We get all the noise on the periphery, though there's not much periphery with this one. She was repairing her boat, one plank of wood at a time by the sounds of it, and was aiming to head back out on the waves at some point.'

'Dead now.'

'Exactly.'

'Any detail about the last time the victims were seen alive, that kind of thing?'

'The vicar had been doing the rounds. Looks like she didn't really stop during lockdown, but had been doing more, now that we're opening up a little, touring the neighbourhood, visiting her flock. Church has only just restarted, not many people attending. She was out most nights. Husband had no idea which congregational sheep she was seeing on any given evening.'

'Same murder weapon?'

'Too early to say.'

'Don't have the results back from the second murder?'

'Nope.'

'And the first, it was what?'

'They don't know exactly, but it was small. A small tool of some sort.'

'A small tool?'

'That's all they've got.'

'Hmm.'

She takes a long drink of soup, staring straight ahead. I give her a quick glance, at her profile, with blonde hair falling over her forehead from beneath a maroon, knitted hat, the collar of her thick coat pulled up high. She looks like the gorgeous blonde one out of Abba in some snowy video or other. I mean, I'm fucked if I know if Abba ever made a video in the snow, but you'd think they did, right?

'I think I'm as caught up as I need to be,' she says. 'So, what's on your plate this afternoon?'

'I'm speaking to some parishioners,' I say. 'Average age, one hundred and twenty-nine.'

'Lucky you.'

'I mean, one of them is literally in a home and has dementia, and the people at the home are like, what are you thinking, but we all had Eurydice telling us not to fuck this shit up, no stone unturned, so I'm out there, booked in an hour from now, to speak to old Margaret about the dead Rev Wright. And I have another interview before that, a few more afterwards.'

'I'm jealous.'

'No, you're not.'

'I mean, you always luck out, Tom. You get to be at the cutting edge of the biggest investigation of the year. How cool is that?'

'I'm not at the cutting edge. You know where I'm at…'

And with the thought that comes into my head, another bleaker thought immediately follows, and I feel the arrival of the dark shadow, and I take another drink of coffee, and stare ahead at the crisp cold day, and try and hold on to that.

'What just happened?' she asks, looking at me now.

'It's cool.'

'What just happened?' she repeats, though she's trying to keep a little lightness in her voice. 'Tell me, or I won't sleep with you again.'

That's funny, can't help smiling. Eileen, crime fans, has never slept with me. And never will.

'I just thought, I'm like Bond in *Thunderball*.'

'Go on.'

'The nuclear weapon's been stolen, shit's hitting the fan, everyone's in a mad panic, and all the big-balled agents are being called in. Bond's one of the main guys, so he expects to get sent to Moscow or Vienna or some shit, but M has this hunch and sends him to the Bahamas, and Bond's like, you're kidding me. It's the biggest case on all the earth, and you're sending me on holiday. That's what this is like, except I'm not Bond, and I'm quite happy to be on the outskirts. Of course, he got to go and have sex on the beach, while I get to go to a care home and interview Margaret.'

'That's a shit analogy, by the way,' she says.

'Why?'

''Cause M was right. The nuclear bombs were literally in the Bahamas.'

'Suppose,' I say.

A long drink of coffee, nod to myself, time to switch on and get going.

'So, what was the dark shadow?' she asks. 'It wasn't just that you don't get to go to the Bahamas.'

Look around the precinct, as quiet as ever, the odd person here and there, a couple of women talking a little too loudly, a guy pushing a pram, a kid on a bike. The day still cold and beautiful.

'Taylor always used to do the Bond references.'

'Ah,' she says. 'Well, my friend, there are plenty of positive things to think about DCI Taylor, if you have to think about him, but better still, think about your case. You being you, we can be fairly confident you're going to end up on the wrong end of the nuclear weapons.'

I nod, take another moment, another look around, then I smile at her, we share the look, and I'm on my way.

'Call me later, if I'm gone when you get back,' she shouts after me, and I lift a hand in response.

5

'We'll never get another minister now, we really won't. People talk about how hard it is to maintain a congregation, but it's nothing compared to actually getting a good, long-term minister. Like gold dust. Took us almost three years when we got Julia, and it wasn't as though the decision to accept her was unanimous. But I mean, I said to Frederick at the time, we are not going through all this nonsense to say no to the woman. She was going to be our minister, come hell or high water. You're sure you don't want a cup of tea? I got fresh biscuits in Aldi this morning.'

'No, honestly, I'm good, thanks, I really should get on.' This man could talk all day and all night. I need to be prepared to wield the metaphorical elbows of impatience. 'You can't think of any reason why anyone would want to murder Julia?'

'God, no, of course not. She was lovely, very giving of herself. And don't think for a second that that's a given. There's plenty of ministers quite capable of being a cunt.'

You see, that's why it's a good reason not to have tea. Otherwise, I might have sprayed him with it while trying to stop myself bursting out laughing.

'No internal church politics that might have driven someone to extremes?'

'There are always internal church politics, but really, there was nothing like that.'

'What about the people who'd objected to her appointment in the first place?'

'I didn't say people had objected to her appointment.'

'You just said it wasn't unanimous.'

'I suppose I did.'

A moment, he conjures up the image of all the objectors, perhaps he tries to place them in a murder-type scenario, and then I can see him mentally step back from the image, his head shaking. 'No, I really don't think there's anything that you could hang a murder investigation on. There is, and you must find this in your line of work, quite the step from petty grievance or small argument, to murder.'

'Not as big a step as you'd like sometimes.'

'Well, that's intriguing.'

Not really.

Look at my watch. Time to crack the fuck on.

'Thank you, Mr Williams, you've been very helpful,' I say, and his face sags a little at the thought that the highlight of his week, being interviewed as part of a murder investigation, is over so soon.

*

You know, I like the sound of the round-the-world yachtswoman a bit more. In fact, a lot more. She was going to have stories to tell, and sure, she's dead, and wouldn't get to tell them, but someone will know, and it's going to be a lot more interesting than this.

'Did you go to church every Sunday?' 'Yes.' What was that like?'

Eileen has a point, however. It's not as though my previous interactions with church congregations have ended up with me falling asleep with boredom. Any group of people doing literally any old shit on earth can end up in some sort of murder-type situation. It's what people do, thanks to that innate human capacity to fuck shit up. And these old people, I really shouldn't be so judgemental. They have stories to tell. A tonne of them. They've done shit. They may be old and slow and incapable of starting a riot in a Russian prison, but fifty years ago they were the people on the front line of life. They've been there, they've done it all.

Last visited a home in the course of my duties in October. Six months ago, seems like a gazillion years in this brutal winter. So cold, so endless, so much dying. I expect there to be hardly anyone left in the home that I've now come to, but it transpires to be full.

'No one,' says the manager.

'No Covid deaths at all?'

'We were on top of it throughout,' she says. She's young. And I mean, like, *holy shit, you're the manager, you look like you should be in the crèche*, young. Straight out of university with her first in Old People Studies. 'Obviously we've had deaths during the course of the last year, but interestingly, perhaps with all the added protections, lack of visits, and overall standards of cleanliness, fewer than normal. Impossible to know if there's a correlation, but that's one for the future. We can look at it when we get out the other side.'

She doesn't say it, or even demonstrate that she's thinking it, but I see the quick tap of the wooden desk. *If* we get out the other side.

'Well, that sounds like a success story,' I say. 'Well done.' She makes a small gesture of appreciation, although there's something just a little condescending about it. Perhaps she thought I said *well done* like I was talking to a six-year-old.

'What can you tell me about Margaret Allan?'

'Oh, Margaret's been terrific,' says the manager. 'Every day is a little adventure.'

'What does that mean?'

'It's not like she moves off her chair, or goes anywhere, or *does* anything. It's like her mind has run away from home, and every now and again it sends in a report from some faraway land. There's… there's a certain romance in it, as though she's permanently trapped in a nineteen-thirties drama in Rangoon or Saigon or in the jungles of South America. A world conducted in black and white, where everyone still speaks with the accent of a Pathé News voiceover.'

My mind runs a little at that, a flight of fancy, and so don't immediately respond.

'I'm really not sure the point of you talking to her, but obviously we're not going to stand in the way of a murder inquiry.'

'You know the last time she went to church?'

'Oh, she hasn't been to church in the four years since she came to stay here. That was a while before I arrived, of course, but I've obviously checked.'

'Did Rev Wright ever visit?'

'She came once a quarter. I think that was good, it's certainly more than any other minister visits the home.'

'Was she visited by elders, anyone else with a church connection?'

'I mean, now you're getting into the specifics of Mrs Allan's life here, detective, and it's not her that's under investigation.'

'I'm just…'

'I really don't know the job description of everyone who visits our residents.'

Yeah, fair enough. If I'm James Bond in *Thunderball*, this isn't even the Bahamas, this is, I don't know, it's so far away from the nuclear weapons, it's Pluto. It's one of the moons of Pluto. Wait, does Pluto have moons? Pluto's a pretty small-ass planet after all. Hang on, it's not even a planet anymore. It's an ex-planet, voted out of office by an electorate of scientists.

'Sergeant?'

'Sorry, you're right,' I say. 'If I can just go and have a quick word with Margaret, I shouldn't be too long.'

'You're all right if one of the staff sits in?'

'Of course.'

'Keep the mask on, and no closer than two metres,' she tacks on, with a hidden smile.

*

'Do you remember her?'

Margaret is in her room, which isn't the worst room anyone ever spent their life in, but still the outlook from the window is meagre, the room decorated in uninspiring magnolia – as opposed to that inspiring magnolia you get in fancy schmancy establishments – a couple of pictures on the wall that speak not of travel and bygone romanticism, but of adequacy and doing the least that can be done.

'Yes, of course,' comes the reply. 'Now listen, I won't hear a word said against her, no matter what anyone else says. She's very strong, very capable, very determined. Very happy… You know what I mean when I say that?'

One arrives with presumptions, but people will always knock those presumptions out of the park. Margaret Allan, at least to listen to, is switched on and strong. No wizened old lady, words dribbling softly from her lips, the last vestige of logical and coherent thought.

'How do you mean it, Margaret?' I ask.

'Happily married. Very happily married. Frank is a lovely man. Really lovely.'

Rev Wright's widower is called Benjamin. Works in marketing. Now I don't know if she's just getting Benjamin's name wrong, or whether she's picked me up wrong and is talking about a completely different woman, who happens to be happily married to Frank.

It's going to be a long day.

'Can you remember the last time you saw Rev Wright?' I ask, dropping the name again, just to be sure.

There's a clock on the wall. One minute past four. I need to keep an eye on that, make a quick call on just how much I'm wasting my time here, and then get going.

'No,' she says, and her voice has a heavier tone, as though she's been reminded of something bad. Her eyes drop, she stares at the floor, her hands meet in her lap, long, thin, bony, yellowing fingers entwine.

I wait for a moment, hoping she'll continue, hoping the explanation for the darkness will be forthcoming, but she appears to have shut down. Quick glance at the nurse by the door, whose upper face creases in a small smile at my look, and I turn back to Margaret.

'She came here last month,' I say. 'You don't remember?'

She's staring at the floor. Mottled beige carpet, the kind that's less likely to show spills and stains.

'Rev Wright was killed last night,' I say.

She's been told already, so this isn't me dropping an uncomfortable truth, unaware of what the reaction will be.

Nothing. Margaret stares at the floor.

I try to relax. Straighten my shoulders, stretch, aware of the comforting crack of neck bone. Slow breath. Ignore the nurse at the door, she's bored and disinterested anyway.

'There's a darkness about everything,' I say. Not entirely sure where that came from. I sound like Batman. But I need to not speak to her like she's ill, or like she's a five-year-old. 'And there's certainly a darkness about this. But it's rare for the darkness to come out of nowhere. It happens, of course, but not here. We don't think Rev Wright was selected at random.'

Searching her eyes for light. There's something in there, something reacting to what I'm saying, I'm sure of it. Yes, I could be imagining it, I'm looking for it, after all, I *want* to see it, but the eyes are so expressive, the slightest awareness can show.

'There was another murder three days ago. Not someone that you would know. Not someone involved in the church, even, but there must be some link. The deaths were so meticulous, so precise, it doesn't feel like they would be random. That's the darkness we need to unearth.'

—

The fingers have started working, the smallest of movements, almost indiscernible, but present, nevertheless. A flutter in the air of this still room.

I give her the space now, a few moments' silence, hoping she'll fill it. But all there is, is the insignificant movement of the fingers, the distant light in the eyes, the face turned towards the floor, the gentle movement of the head, the sound of her breathing.

'I need the essence of Rev Wright,' I say. 'Who was she? What was it that would have brought the darkness?'

Margaret's head snaps up, her eyes are on mine. A sudden movement. Scares the shit out of me, to be honest. Manage to keep my mouth shut, reaction limited to a small backwards movement of my head. I swallow.

'She was a whore,' snaps from her lips, the same as her head snapped up, and these four words it seems are the sum of what she has to give, because I can see the snap leave her as she speaks. As though, in the conjuring of the sentence, she gave everything she had to give, all her power invested in one sudden, explosive delivery.

She was a whore. That's all.

Well, no one saw that coming.

Of course, the woman is riven with Alzheimer's, and a minute ago she wouldn't hear a word said against her, and that Julia's husband was called Frank. So, is it Frank's wife who's the whore?

'Rev Wright?' I ask. 'You're talking about Julia?'

'Talking,' she says, her voice softer than it was before. Her eyes are still on mine, but there's no longer any depth there. The life behind them has suddenly been hidden, or perhaps has just gone altogether. 'Talking,' she repeats, her voice that bit thinner than it was the first time she said it.

And that's all I'm going to get. *She was a whore.*

I relax again, rest back a little in the seat, and look at Margaret. Margaret stares at the floor and thinks of who knows what.

*

'It's not what it used to be. Used to be full every Sunday. You should've seen it. Couldn't find a seat some days. People standing at the back. And the singing.' She clasps her hands

---

together, smiles at the memory. Uh-oh. I've inadvertently done that thing where I've transported an old lady back to her happy place. Church, sometime long ago in Neverland, and I don't doubt for a second that the number of people in the building in her memory grows every time she thinks of it. 'The rousing hymns, *Mine Eyes Have Seen The Glory… Be Thou My Vision…* a full church, full voiced. Oh my…'

I could still be here tomorrow morning.

'Had Julia visited you recently?'

She gives me a curious look, unsure perhaps why I'm intent on dragging the conversation back to the present, because who really wants to live in *this* present? She stares deeply into my eyes for a while as she readjusts, perhaps tries to concentrate on what I actually asked, then slowly shakes her head.

'I thought she'd tried to visit most of the congregation in the past year?'

'I was out. When she came, I was out.'

'She only came once?'

'Far as I know.'

'Where were you? You've not really supposed to have been out in the past year.'

Now the look is perhaps a calculation. Is it OK to tell a police officer you've been hanging around with your best friend Agnes, or will I arrest her on the spot? And obviously, I'm kidding. I couldn't care less where she was.

'We're investigating a murder, Mrs Helmsley, it's all right to admit you went next door for a cup of coffee. I'm not going to charge you.'

The gaze remains, then slowly the eyes cloud over, the look becomes more distant, the concentration slips, she looks away. Gazing at the floor now, but really seeing nothing, while looking far into the past.

'You should've heard it. You should've been there.' A moment, and then, even more plaintively, 'I don't know what happened.'

*

'These people live in cloud cuckoo land, they really do.'

Last interview on the list. Been a long afternoon. Sitting in a small office just off Byres Road. This guy is some sort of vague management consultant, running the kind of business that will have the word *solutions* in all their blurb. The office is small, nevertheless, so he obviously doesn't know anyone in the Tory government. He didn't manage to turn his small consultancy firm into a supplier of ridiculously large amounts of PPE.

So far, seven interviews, no one with anything useful to say. Rev Wright was popular, doing her best under trying circumstances. I was regularly told about all the aged members of the congregation who'd died in the last year, with no acknowledgement that quite a lot of them would have likely died anyway, given the demographic. And, of course, people don't die any more, do they? They *pass*. I don't know if this is because dying has become too intimate, too personal, or too vulgar a concept. Nor, let's be blunt, do I care. But there certainly seem to be a lot of people called Margaret who have died in the last year. The Margaret Epoch must be on the wane in Scotland, the coronavirus its meteor, hastening the end.

'The golden age they talk about? I mean, seriously, when were these people alive? Eighteen-fifty-six? There's no way churches were as booming after the war as they all make out. I mean, sure, they were better attended, but it was hardly Scotland-England at Hampden levels for crying out loud.'

'Everything grows in the memory,' I say, sounding for once like the voice of reason. Surprised myself by quite enjoying listening to the reminisces of the venerable collective as I went round. It's not like anyone thinks I'm going to stumble onto anything significant here. Not even sure I'm in needle/haystack territory. It's more, needle in a field of haystacks, where the field stretches off into the far distance, a Constable painting multiplied by a thousand, and there might not even be a needle anyway. So, I may as well enjoy it. Enjoy the talk of the old days, the grumbling about the new. And, unsurprisingly, no one had anything bad to say about Julia Wright, and despite me probing with expert finesse and delicacy, no back-up for old Margaret's *she was a whore* remark.

'I suppose,' says the management guy. 'The good and the bad.'

Ain't that the truth?

'How many of *you* are there at church?' I ask.

'How'd you mean?'

'You're what? Late forties?'

'Ha!

—

'You seem young.'

'Aye, whatever. Most parishioners my age get roped into some committee or other, they're always looking for folk to do *something*. But I couldn't. Just up to my eyes in it here. Always am. So, I'd spoken to Julia a couple of times about it, but not for a while. So, you know… you're speaking to me, you're here 'n' all, but I doubt there's a lot I can tell you.'

Oh, tell me about it, Mr Management Guy. That's the very reason it's me who's interviewing you.

'So, what were your impressions of Julia?'

He smiles, that knowing acknowledgement of the question. The guy who knows the script. The guy who thinks he could be here, sitting in my seat, doing my job. He's seen the shows, he knows how this works.

'She was great. Great with the kids, great with the old yins. This past year… I mean, it's been a shitshow for everyone, right? She did what she could. Filmed her little sermons in the church on a Sunday morning. Visited members if they wanted her to, and of course, most did. I mean, that wasn't legal, was it? She shouldn't have been doing that, but they all appreciated her for it.'

'D'you know of any reason why anyone would want to harm her?'

'Julia?' he says, with bemusement.

I give him the well, obviously Julia look, and he quickly nods, masking his defensiveness behind the movement.

'She was murdered, so someone wanted to do it,' he says, nodding, gracefully acknowledging my right to ask the question.

'Yes, they did.'

'Isn't it possible she was selected entirely at random?'

'Of course, but at the moment we have no idea, so we're exploring everything.'

'Aye, right, fair enough.'

'And…?'

He holds my gaze for a moment, then lowers his eyes, nodding again. There's something there, at least. Something he's reluctant to tell the investigating officer. I'll give him the space, see if he can bring himself to blurt it out without me having to handcuff him to the chair and flay his arms, like we're trained to do at police school.

'I heard a thing once, but it was just something someone said. I mean, people talk, right, and really, when they do, it's best not to listen.'

'Well, Julia is now dead, and so…'

'It still feels wrong to put salacious gossip into the hands of the investigating officer.'

'Salacious gossi –'

'All right, that's an exaggeration. It was just a thing.'

'Tell me the thing.'

'Someone said she was having an affair,' he says quickly, as though speed of delivery will expedite the end of the conversation.

'That's a start.'

'And an end. It's all I've got.'

'Who was she having an affair with, and who told you?'

'I don't know, and I don't remember.'

I give him the derisive look that frequently substitutes as a question.

'I really don't. It was just something someone said at a thing. I'm not going to… really, I'm not going to say, go and speak to x, or you should ask Benjamin about it, or anything. That's all I've got.'

He looks at his watch.

Well, that ended quickly.

Now he lifts his hands in that sort of papal gesture that people use, the one that says, are we done here?

It's been a long afternoon, and I'm tired, and you know, I think we are.

*

And so, a nothing evening, sitting at home, alone.

I returned briefly to the office, Kallas was not around, I wrote up a summary of the afternoon. Little to report from my interviews with Julia Wright's people. Yes, there's the idea she might have been an adulteress, and that's always going to play into a murder investigation, but I bring the rumour of it, and no substance. And half the rumour comes from an old lady who has, literally, lost her mind, and who might not even have been talking about Julia in the first place.

And so, here I sit on a Tuesday evening, the half-assembled Gertrude for company. Two small lights on in the sitting room, curtains open, sitting at the table beside the window. I scroll through my phone while I eat an M&S oven meal for two.

Cottage pie. I mean, seriously, I should be able to make my own cottage pie, it's barely more complicated than making toast, but here I am, paying M&S for their efforts. Drinking Coke, after the familiar wrestle with not drinking wine.

Not that I have wine in the house. If I had wine in the house, I'd be drinking wine. The wrestle was with whether I would take myself to the off-licence. It feels like the start of the meal is the finish line. Get to that, start to eat without cracking, then my brain is like, fair enough, you win, no point in going to get wine now, your factory-made cottage pie will get cold.

A chill, dark evening. Dank. Somewhere down the road there's an ambulance or a police car or a fire engine, and the light, in circles of blue, travels along the length of the road to illuminate the damp pavements, merging in rapid cycles with the orange of the streetlamps.

At some point Kallas calls, and the familiar awkwardness ensues. We manage to navigate our way through the conversation, detailing our days such as they have been, while I convince her that I'm not drinking.

And then, too soon, she's gone, and Gertrude and I are alone again, and I go back to scrolling through the phone, but now my heart is not in it, and I turn it off, push it away across the table. I unthinkingly finish eating dinner, tasting nothing, while Gertrude and I forlornly talk of the old days, whenever they were, when everything seemed a lot less shit.

6

Wake up early, can always feel it the following morning when I don't have alcohol the previous night. I don't bound out of bed like I'm on an episode of Dancing With The Fucking Stars or anything, but it's just there. The feeling in my head, in my mouth, in my guts. An indefinable quality of well-being. Another day successfully managed, set against another day beginning, when alcohol can await at any moment.

At least I'm not tipping out of bed, wanting to put vodka in my cornflakes. Those days will likely come again, but not this month. Not today, anyway.

Instead, two slices of toast, coffee, water, orange juice. Sit in silence. Quick look at the news on my phone, drawn into reading about the civil war in Central African Republic, realise that I probably couldn't find the CAR on a map, look at Google Maps, have the mundane thought that as a country it may be a shitshow but at least it was reasonably accurately named, then I turn my phone off.

I finish the toast; I have a second cup of coffee. I go to work.

*

I have to hand it to Detective Sergeant Blumenthal, Eurydice's ADC. Man is totally on top of things, and has, for eight-thirty in the morning, produced an excellent brief, summarising the first full day of the investigation.

In summary, however: no breakthrough, no obvious link between the two victims.

I was, as it transpired, not alone in getting rumours of the minister's infidelity. However, despite several people mentioning it, there was nothing concrete. No names, no detail on which to hang the idle gossip.

The husband denied any possibility of the idea. The motivations for that could, of course, be legion. The weakness of the cuckold. The weakness of being the last to know. Perhaps he genuinely believed in the purity of his marriage, and of his wife. Or perhaps there's the basic survival instinct. Acknowledging his wife was having an affair would acknowledge he had a motive.

I mean, let's be honest, we're not living in the Middle Ages. It's not like anyone's thinking, the wife's having an affair, she deserved to die! However, it plants division, it starts a narrative, it's a narrative that leads to argument and hurt and jealousy and anger, and from there the path to murder is, if not exactly short, not outrageously long either.

A crime of passion, however, does not explain the calm meticulousness of the murder, nor does it explain the killing of the yachtswoman a few days previously. For that, there would have to be some link between the minister, her husband and the first victim, and there's nothing there. So far.

There's something about the careful planning and the precise method of murder that suggests there ought to be a link, that suggests these women were selected for a reason, yet everything about them, the orbits in which they moved, say they were unconnected.

Julia Wright kept a list of every time she'd visited parishioners and had a programme of forthcoming visits. Her husband, who had up until she died, paid no particular attention to it, had had to admit that she was generally out more often than the list of visits suggested. While all of her most recent movements are accounted for, beyond the last couple of weeks memories get sketchy. That is itself not unreasonable. This last year, all our days have blended into one another, evenings and weekends a bland custard of nothingness.

If Julia was having an affair, there is no proof, and no one knows with whom it would've been. Why then the suspicion? This is addressed in DS Blumenthal's notes, but there is no answer. It appears she gave off an aura of it, that was all. Something about her. Some vague suspicion of it stuck to her. Perhaps men and women got the vibe. Men that she was available, women that she was a threat.

I look at her photograph for a while. Try to draw something of the woman from the picture, as though the essence of her is in there. Hair cut short to her neck at the back, short dark curls on top, a relaxed attractiveness about her face, and in the eyes. Welcoming. But then, this was the picture used on the church website. They were unlikely to have a picture of her when she was wantonly, and obviously, looking for sex.

Other players in her story, the husband aside: the church officer, the session clerk, the church elders who make up the session, though they are many. If one was to search for affair potential, the session clerk is a guy in his early fifties, there are five others under sixty in the session, though three of them are women. For the women to have been her lovers wouldn't have been unheard of, though we may just be getting into my sexual fantasies there. No other players under fifty. Julia Wright was forty-one, although, of course, age really doesn't say anything, as anyone will have sex with anyone else, if the moment grabs them. Take me, for instance.

Yeah, all right, let's not bother.

The yachtswoman's is an interesting story. Her father was a consultant cardiologist at the Queen Margaret, part-time sailor with his own yacht down at Rhu. Month-long sailing holidays every summer on which the family was obliged to join him, whether they liked it or not.

This did not go well, although it did instil in the young Jennifer Talbot a love for the sea. Her mother hated it, drank heavily on board, fought regularly with her husband through sailing trips, and was lost overboard one night in the Pentland Firth. The accident at sea was more of a suicide.

Jennifer's younger brother killed himself when he was sixteen, rather than go on another sailing trip. That is some major aversion to sailing, though possibly he had other mental health issues. That summer, a week late, Jennifer and her dad went sailing anyway.

She left home, she went to university, she continued to sail, although no longer with her father. Dr Talbot downsized yacht and continued to sail solo. He died in a storm off the coast of Brittany seven years ago.

Jennifer Talbot took to the waves. She sailed, she would stop off somewhere, occasionally she worked, raising enough money to finance the next leg of her journey, and on she went. At some stage she met Marc Johnson, a wealthy American Scot. Well, a Scot, in that his family had left in 1789 on one of the ships the Proclaimers sang about.

They got married, they did not have children, they lived in a large house on the Clyde, near Helensburgh. Marc Johnson talked of the romance of sailing, the joy of it, the air whistling through your hair, the freedom of the high seas, the wonder of being unable to see land. In truth, though, he hated it, every minute out on the waves.

The marriage lasted two years and one month, at the end of which, Jennifer Talbot once again took to sea. Five years later, she limped into the Firth of Clyde, her boat in need of repair. With no friends and no network at home, all she had was her ex-husband, who was still living in the large house near Helensburgh, now with his new wife, fellow American, Daisy.

Marc Johnson told Jennifer Talbot she could stay in the boathouse at the bottom of the garden while she repaired her yacht. The boathouse had been made habitable during their marriage and had been little used since.

That was three years ago. As of the end of last week, there was still no sign of Jennifer Talbot going anywhere. The boat was in the process of being slowly stripped back and reassembled. On the assessment of DCI Hamilton, it was nowhere near seaworthy. They are due to get a more professional assessment today.

An ex-wife living on the same property as the current wife, a stay that goes far beyond what might first have been agreed, is exactly the kind of thing that rings bells. Motive written all over it, in fuck-off capitals. Nevertheless, after a long chat with both Mr and the current Mrs Johnson, Eurydice took away no impression of any ill-feeling.

Mr Johnson said he barely saw her, even during this year of lockdown when no one could go anywhere. (The Johnsons sound like the kind of people who were going places regardless.) Daisy Johnson sounded almost enamoured of her marital predecessor, and her life on the sea. There was a light in her eye when she spoke about her, wrote Eurydice, and nothing about her demeanour to suggest resentment about the ex-wife living on their property. Rather, a genuine sadness at what had happened.

Still, the final note was, *Or she could be a hell of an actor*, and that further investigation of her background was required.

As for the murders themselves, there is little to be known of the victims' movements on the nights they were killed. The same murder weapon used each time, a small, sharp blade of indeterminate origin. Both women bound by the same strong, slender brass wire, both women killed in situ, their bodies left lying where they bled.

The only thing that might have helped identify the

—

movements of the perpetrator on either evening, was a CCTV camera near Barrowlands park, where Jennifer Talbot's body had been placed. The camera, it transpired, had been disabled sometime that evening, not long after midnight. Our killer planned ahead.

Accompanying the rundown of yesterday's progress, such as it was, was the list of people of interest I was required to speak to today, and the reasons for doing so, each one a natural progression of a development from yesterday, and I note, not at all related to anyone I previously spoke to.

Perhaps they want to move people around, utilising this grand detective task force to get as many different perspectives as possible.

'What have you got today?' asks DI Kallas, stopping by, hesitating, then sitting down, straight-shouldered, in DC Ritter's seat.

'Morning,' I say.

'Morning,' she throws belatedly into the conversation.

It's pretty much only this on-going covid-shitshow that's stopped me moving to Estonia in the past six months. If they're all like Kallas, I would love the use-no-words-unless-they're-absolutely-required approach to conversation. Plus, she's gorgeous, and since I don't know any other Estonians, all I can do is take her as representative of her tribe.

'I have a list of eight people to interview,' I say. 'Haven't quite processed it all yet, but most of them seem speculative on first viewing. On the other hand, some of them are connected to the yachtswoman, so there's that. You?'

'I have a similar list. I spoke to DCI Hawkins to ask that she agitate for our removal from this investigation. This does not seem like a good use of the time of a detective inspector and a detective sergeant. She does not want us to absent ourselves, however, regardless of the level of work required. She wishes us to play our part, so that the station is seen to be pulling its weight.'

Suddenly realise that I'm leaning forward, elbows on the desk, chin resting in my clasped hands, staring at her. Like a psychopath. Straighten up, lean back, try to get myself together.

'The higher up the chain you get, the more you need to toe the line,' I say. 'You'll be doing the same yourself soon enough.'

'I do not aim to go any higher in Police Scotland. Detective

Inspector is the correct level for me,' she says, true to form playing a straight bat to my glib throwaway.

I nod at that, because really, what else can I do, and then we sit across the desks and stare at each other for a few moments. I have nothing. I mean, if this was Harrison, I'd be gibbering away like a flatulent goat, spouting all kinds of shit.

'I should get on,' she says, abruptly bringing the latest non-conversation in our working relationship to an end. 'Perhaps we will bump into each other at some point today.'

'I'm down the river, speaking to some people beyond Partick, way beyond, down towards Bowling. Then a couple in the city centre later on.'

'And I am in the West End, so perhaps not. We may see each other this evening. Have a successful day and let us hope at least there are no further murders.'

She nods, I nod in response, and off she goes, to be sensible for an undisclosed amount of time back at her own desk, before heading off out into the wilds. I turn back to the report on my laptop, start reading through it again, making sure I've got everything that might be relevant appropriately logged, and then I lift the phone and start the process of making sure people are going to be where I need them to be when I get into the area.

7

The day begins with a mundane chat in an office in Clydebank with a woman who supplied Jennifer Talbot with navigation equipment for her yacht refit.

She's kind of busy, as I sit on the other side of the desk. Writing an e-mail on her computer, talking to me at the same time.

'She was interesting, I'll give her that. Plenty of stories to tell. Well, she would've had, I'm sure, if she'd wanted to tell them.'

'How d'you mean?'

She pauses to focus on her e-mail, then says, 'You could tell she wasn't used to conversation. A solo life on the waves, and all that.'

'So, she never told any of the stories?'

Another moment, now finally she looks at me, taking a second to acquaint herself with the question.

'Pretty much. She'd mention some drop-dead detail, like colliding with a giant blooper fish off the coast of Palau, and you'd be like, holy shit, what was that like, and she'd be like, you know, it happened, and you could see… I don't know, like a shadow would cross her face. Maybe short of her actually saying, shit I've said too much, but there was something there.'

I've no idea if there's such a thing as an actual blooper fish, or whether she just said blooper fish as an example of a generic big-ass fish. Not about to ask, what with it not mattering at all.

'She'd said too much?'

'Yeah, like… I don't know.'

She holds my gaze for a moment, as though she's considering saying something else, then she waves it away, and looks back at the screen.

'Hey,' I say, though there's no admonition in my voice, 'I've got a tonne of these interviews to do, and really I'm not going to take long. Maybe you could just do one thing at a time, and I'll be out your hair.'

'You think I can't multitask?' she asks, without looking at me.

Bit of a tone. Contemplate some bullshit police authoritarianism, but decide to wait until she looks at me, then I just give her a classic deadpan stare, and she instantly folds, and says, 'Whatever,' and turns to give me her full attention.

'What d'you mean, like she'd said too much? She had something to hide?'

'Yeah, like, look, I'd developed this theory. I said it to Ian. Like, she ha –'

'Ian?'

'Partner. Like I said to Ian, it was almost like, I mean, I'm not basing this on *anything*, but it was like she'd, like, *never* sailed around the world, *ever*. Like she had all these bits of stories but with no detail.'

'How'd that tie in with the damage to the boat?'

'I've no idea about damage to the boat. I've never seen the boat. You?'

'Nope, not yet. But they say it was damaged.'

She shrugs.

'So, how does your theory tie in with what she was looking to buy off you?'

'Pretty well. I mean, on the one hand it could be she just wasn't ready to fit it to the craft, or she didn't yet have the funds to pay for it, because, of course, it's pretty expensive these days, but really, under my theory, the reason she hadn't actually got around to buying all the equipment she'd been talking about for the last year and a half, was that she wasn't going anywhere. Because she never actually went anywhere.' A moment, while she thinks about it. 'That's all. I have no proof, so, you know, don't put me on the stand, because I'll deny everything.'

She smiles.

*

This is why we hate ourselves.

In a small clubhouse, overlooking the Clyde, down beyond Clydebank. The home of The Old Clyde Rowing Club, where Jennifer Talbot used to come. She didn't have her own equipment. Used the club boats and oars, came here once or twice a week for training. Kept herself to herself, really didn't have anyone here she could call a friend, and so there is little to be gained.

Nevertheless, here I am, talking to the club captain, Alice Rowe, and I have self-loathing. How weak I can be.

She's in her late-thirties, very attractive, very fit, dressed and ready to go out on the water, wearing Lycra shorts and a black, zipped crop-top. Really, who invented the zip-at-the-front crop-top? Must have been a man, right? She has an athletic, slim physique: small breasts, flat stomach. She's not wearing anything on top other than that zipped top. That zip just calls out to be pulled down, those small breasts waiting to be revealed.

Get a grip!

Jesus.

I was a few minutes' late, and she looked like she was just about to head out onto the water assuming my non-arrival. When I got here, I got the wry smile, an acerbic remark or two, and she let loose her long hair which she'd tied back for the sports part of her morning.

The hair thing was as flirtatious as it sounds, including a couple of moves straight out of a shampoo advert. Or a porn movie.

First thing she said was, 'I'm bored,' as though in explanation for the hair moves, then she offered coffee.

And so here we are, standing at the window of a well-to-do clubhouse, looking out on the river. There are three sculls on the water, two singles and a double, serving to further elevate the scene above yesterday's procession of dour laments on the state of the church and its place in society.

There's something beautifully evocative about the smooth passage of the boats, and with the cold water warmed by the mid-morning sun, the prow of the boats cuts through a faint layer of steam rising from the river. It's wonderful, augmented by the open windows of the clubhouse, allowing us to hear the sound of the oars in the water, and the voices of the pair in the double scull travelling far along the river.

I try to focus on that, rather than on the presence of the woman standing beside me. The clubhouse is not officially open for members to come and sit and do whatever it is members of a sports club do when they're not doing sport, and so there are no staff, she had to make the coffee herself, and the two of us are alone in the building. Standing in companionable silence by the window, watching the scene play out before us.

The only thing taking the edge off this idyllic Wednesday

---

morning setting – aside, obviously, from the fact I'm investigating an horrific double murder here – is that across the river is a derelict brownfield site.

'Dreadful, isn't it?' says Alice Rowe.

'Yeah.'

'These fucking people. The council offered to buy the land, and they were going to do some low-cost landscaping. No big deal. Bit of grass, some trees, borderline rewilding. Everyone likes trees. And look, surprise-surprise, they've done nothing. They're holding out for the developers, and those fuckers haven't got to this point on the river yet. But they will, of course. I mean, they're everywhere else, aren't they? Absolutely atrocious, it truly is.'

I indicate the land with my coffee cup.

'You lot must be rich, aren't you?'

She smiles. 'Us lot?'

'The club members. This is a nice clubhouse, the whole set-up reeks of money, like you've all come here straight from rowing in the Boat Race, and long summers drinking Pimm's on the Thames at Henley.'

We share a look. Of course, she has nice eyes. Green. Seductive. Lovely smile.

I never understood why women find me attractive, why they bother with me at all. Maybe that's just because I don't find men attractive, so I've no idea what it is women see in them. Maybe it's because I know what a fuck-up I am inside. Nevertheless, here we are.

'I thought you said you were a detective?' she says with a laugh.

'You could all chip in together and buy the land for the club.'

'Well, I shan't pretend the money wouldn't be there to do it. But the will? You have not met our club members. And I shan't lie, my money currently comes from Desmond, several years yet before I get it from mummy and daddy, and Desmond is exactly the kind of person who looks upon that land over there and sees a selection of luxury apartments for the young professional.'

Mummy and Daddy… God, I love posh people.

I smile, take another drink of coffee. This is good shit, by the way.

We look at each other. Definitely something in the look.

Jesus, focus, you prick.

But really, her husband is some old snark called Desmond. I could be wrong, she could be an Olympic athlete in training, but there's just something that says bored housewife. She's come from money, has never had to work, Desmond is doing whatever he does, kids are finally back in school, or maybe they're with grandma or they're doing something, and she's here, doing this. Talking to me, toying with me, amusing herself.

'I just spoke to someone,' I say, making some attempt at business, 'who wondered if perhaps Jennifer Talbot had never, in fact, sailed around the world at all.'

'Really? Who said *that*?'

I answer that with the closed lips of a true professional, and she rolls her eyes.

'Well, I hope it wasn't one of our lot. What utter nonsense. Good grief, some people are absolute cunts, aren't they?'

Ha! You know, there's just something funny about people using the word cunt. There just is. Bite me, I don't care. And it's always even better when it comes from the mouth of someone who went to Miss Penelope's School for Girls, Cheltenham Ladies' College, Finishing School in Zurich, and Oxford.

'Of that, Mrs Rowe, there is no argument. People are most definitely cunts.'

'Alice,' she says, touching my arm. *Fuck.* 'I have no doubt that Jennifer sailed around the world. She had led a rather wonderful life.'

'Did she talk about it much?'

'No, she did not, but that was who she was. She was quiet. Kept her own company.'

'Did she have any friends at the club?'

'Not really. She spoke to people when she was here, if we spoke to her first, but she didn't go out of her way.'

'She never competed?'

'Never.'

'Never rowed in a double scull?'

She gives me an amused look, shakes her head.

'Are you listening?'

'Did you speak to her?'

'I speak to everybody.'

Another smile. The *I don't just speak to them* smile of the true flirt.

'Did she ever speak back?'

—

She laughs, shakes her head, takes a drink of coffee.

'Jennifer had been coming here, twice a week for, what, three years? I spoke to her every time I saw her. I'm always here, I have nothing else to do. What would you like, Sergeant Hutton, that I recorded every conversation?'

'Wasn't really expecting that, no.'

'On fifth of January, twenty-nineteen, the deceased informed me she'd had unexpected fuckery with a gentleman named Roger, a man with a prodigious cock, who suggested that he may, one day in the future, wish to end her life.'

'You're finished, right?' I say, smiling, and she laughs.

Dammit. She just completely unnecessarily introduced sex into the conversation. There's literally only one reason why people do that in life.

I may be speaking for myself there.

She catches me looking at her. And not at her eyes. I get a pair of raised eyebrows in response, but the eyebrows are saying, yep, the zipped crop-top. Invented *by* men, *for* men.

Shit.

'Was there anyone she paid any particular attention to; anyone she gave even the time of day to?' I ask, forcing the words, forcing the questioning. 'Any time where she might have mentioned someone in passing, and you thought, now who might that be, or that's weird, she doesn't usually talk about *anyone*?'

'And so he persists,' she says smiling.

She sighs lightly, then looks out on the water. Dutifully giving it some thought. Coffee cup to the lips. The cup rests there. It could be she's been distracted by some thought, useful to the investigation. More likely, it's the pose. She knows I can't take my eyes off her.

Fuck it. I'm losing the battle. Not that there was ever much of a battle.

Well, this is probably round about the time Bond would have sex on the beach after all.

She turns, glances around the room, her eyes settle on something for a moment, then she looks at me as she lowers the cup. We stand a couple of feet apart. Her eyes, her lips are intoxicating. She swallows the coffee which has been sitting in her mouth for a few seconds. I automatically swallow too.

'Are you sure you're a police officer?' she says. Tone slightly different this time.

'What d'you mean?'

'You've not been sent here by Desmond to test me?'

'I really don't think I'm that much of a test.'

She holds the look. Maybe this is part of her game. Toying with me, playing whatever part comes to mind at any given moment.

'You have something about you.'

'Everyone has something about them.'

'Not like you.'

I defensively lift the coffee to my lips, take a drink. The coffee has cooled too much, and I wonder how long we've been standing here. How long have the occasional silences actually been lasting?

'You really think there's anything here related to a double murder?' she asks, vaguely indicating the clubhouse.

'The police are interviewing pretty much everyone who ever met either of the victims, and this is my place in the investigation. On the periphery of the periphery.'

She smiles at the line, then nods to herself.

'Lucky for me, though,' she says, and again she touches my arm.

We share the look. I think we've both already gone past the *is this really going to happen* stage of the pre-sex ritual, moving on to the *who's actually going to make the move* part of it. At least, that's what's happening in my head.

My eyes drift down her body again, no attempt to hide the look, partly because I enjoy looking, and partly to make sure she also enjoys me looking. Her nipples are now pushing against the fabric of the top. And there's the zip, the invitation, down the centre of it.

She takes the coffee mug from my hand and places it on the window ledge, laying her own mug beside it. Then she lightly puts her hand against my chest, and I take a step or two back, so that we're now away from the window.

Another hesitation, another moment, the pause before stepping over the threshold, and then she puts her fingers to the zipper and slowly lowers it. The zip is undone, the sides of the top fall open, revealing her breasts, small and firm, dark pink nipples hard with anticipation.

Our lips meet, I take her left nipple lightly into the fingers of my right hand, and she gasps quietly into my mouth.

—

I have guilt.

Look at that. I have guilt. And it's not guilt about having sex on the job. I'm Bond in this scenario, after all, I get to have sex on the job. The guilt is all about DI Kallas. Even though we're not a couple, even though there is nothing spoken between us, even though she is married and, presumably, sleeping in the same bed as her husband every single night. Even though, even though, despite it all and everything after, I feel guilty. Like she would disapprove. (She *would* disapprove.) Like she'd be upset. Like she'd feel betrayed.

We're standing in front of a trophy cabinet, Alice Rowe and me. A grand, if traditional looking, sports club cabinet. The top two shelves are trophy-laden. The third shelf has a model double scull. The bottom shelf a large model of a yacht. But one of those fancy-ass yachts, that don't have sails, the type the rich have. So, it's only a yacht in the way that the Royal Yacht Britannia is a yacht.

To be honest, I have no idea what the actual definition of a yacht is.

'Malcolm had the –'

'Malcolm?'

'The chairman. Malcolm had the idea of commissioning a bespoke model of the double scull in which two of the club members won a gold medal at the 2018 Worlds in Plovdiv. You can read the plaque. He searched around, found this guy locally. I mean, Glasgow, local, not exactly just around the corner.' She indicates the yacht, the plaque of which states 'La Sultana', Bulgaria, 1962. 'Having seen the model maker's work, Malcolm decided he wanted something else, something more elaborate than a scull, though he still ordered the scull, of course. Kept the Bulgarian theme.'

She smiles.

That was great sex. No need to go all literary about it or anything, it was just great sex. And the woman can use her tongue.

We look at the Sultana for a while, which is a beautifully-executed model, but really, just looks like a bit of a boat to me.

'I'd've gone for some old sailing ship myself,' I say.

'Hmm. Me too. This was used as a spying vessel by the Soviets in the North Atlantic during the Cold War. Malcolm has something of a Cold War fascination, the most niche little bits of its history of interest to him. That, at least, is something in his favour.'

I give her a quick glance to see if she's being facetious, but she does appear to genuinely appreciate niche intertest.

'So, how does this relate to our murder victim?'

'Yes, sorry. The model maker was called Crispin Thebes. Dr Thebes. Interesting guy. He came here to look at the cabinet. He likes to get a feel for where his models will be placed. The setting, the light levels. There may appear to be something fundamentally trivial about making models, and yet, the man is without doubt a master craftsman. An artisan. Very old school. Entirely meticulous in every part of the process.' A beat, another, her eyes on the models the whole time. 'One must also respect that.'

'How many times did he come here? I mean, it's just a cabinet, right?'

'Oh, just the once. A very singular man. Striking. Not necessarily in appearance, though I will say he is very handsome, but he has… presence. A man of note. No idea why, now that I think of it, but he…' She gives the model maker some more thought, now looks at me as she speaks of him. 'He owns the room, you know the type, but without projecting himself in any way whatsoever. Very interesting. And Jennifer was here the day he was here, and they got talking, which seemed odd in itself. And they talked for a while.'

She indicates a table by the window, overlooking the ramp where the sculls are pushed into the water, presumably the place where they sat and talked, then she turns back to the cabinet as she thinks of them.

'Maybe not so remarkable. Jennifer had stories to tell, and there's just something about the doctor.'

She shivers, shakes it off, then gives me a look.

'So, I don't know, you could speak to him. That's really all I've got.'

'What's he a doctor of?'

'No idea. He's young, I mean, fifty maybe, but he'd be young if he was a medical doctor and had retired already. I presume something maritime-related. You can ask him.'

'What was the shiver?'

'The shiver?'

'You were standing there thinking about him and you

shivered. What was that?'

Almost asked if she'd had sex with him as well, but that would've been very cheap. Very, very cheap.

'Someone walked over my grave, that's all,' she says, and she turns away, last look at the cabinet, and she moves back to the window, and the view out on the river.

Our time is up, I believe. Probably for the best. The half-life of male post-sex disinterest grows longer with age, but this woman is still delicious, she has the same eyes, and she's wearing that same zipped top, although now the zip is not done all the way up and is even more alluring.

I need to get on.

'Thank you,' I say, walking up beside her, taking a last look down on the river.

'You're welcome, Sergeant.'

We glance at each other again. Ah, there's the look in her eyes. The same one I'm wearing. Guilt. Regret. Melancholy. The offer was made, and it could not be turned down.

'I should leave you to the river.'

She nods, smiles, manages to pull her eyes away, and look back down on the water.

'I hope you find… I hope you catch who did this. Jennifer was lovely. Not great with people, you know, but she was interesting and full of life. And now… Just, just catch him. That's all.'

I look down on the river, not sure what to say to that. It feels false to make any kind of promise, so little part will I play in whether or not the killer actually gets caught. My part as Bond in this situation ended with her sitting astride me, as I lay on the clubhouse floor.

Outside the day continues, the River Clyde winding slowly past, on its way to the sea and the far horizon.

8

Another day around the houses, little of note to record. (Now that the sex has been recorded.) A couple of other people whose orbits Jennifer Talbot briefly flitted through, plus another four who'd had dealings with Julia Wright, all church-related though not members of her own kirk. I have nothing to report, bar the passing reference to the model maker. It all feels like what it is, playing the smallest of bit-parts in the blockbuster movie. Not even the guy in the red uniform who gets killed in the first five minutes of Star Trek. I'm the guy in the red uniform who walks past Kirk and Spock as they're walking along a corridor chatting about which one of the crew Kirk's going to make a move on that night.

Four-forty-seven, one more person on my list to see. I have a five-fifteen appointment with him. Reverend Bill Yorke. Worked with Julia Wright on a study paper on youth engagement for the Glasgow Presbytery. That must've been a thrilling read. One wonders if they allowed themselves any practicality in the answer. The straightforward 'we can't engage the youth, we're screwed' of it.

Sitting in a small café near Royal Exchange Square, taking a coffee and a doughnut, while I wait. The place is relatively quiet, as almost everywhere is at the moment, the cafés not long reopened. Not many people having coffee at this time of day anyway. Home time. Getting ready for dinner time. Whatever time.

There are two women sitting at the window. There always are. I call it Hutton's Law. At any given point in time, in any café, anywhere on earth, there will be two women sitting at a table by the window. Is it 100% accurate? Perhaps not, but few scientific laws are. I might write a paper on it one day. Perhaps I could get a commission from Costa or Starbucks.

Hutton's Law also states that there's a high degree of probability that I'd sleep with one of the women, but not both of them. I'll probably omit that from the official paper that gets submitted to the *Coffee Journal of Great Britain*, or the coffee equivalent of *The Lancet*, whatever that is. Probably *The Cafetiere* or *The Grinder*.

Flicking through my phone, looking for mentions of Dr Crispin Thebes. I mean, really, what a weird name. This guy sounds so palpably creepy he can't possibly be guilty of anything. It's too obvious. It's a name thought up by a screenwriter, or a random name generated by one of those Internet memes like, *your serial killer name is the saint on whose day you were born, plus the name of the first Greek city you can think of.*

That might be a little contrived. Likely wouldn't get shared enough on the Internet to gain meme status.

Regardless of the origins of the fellow's name, he's nowhere to be found online. However it was he received his PhD, there's no record of it anywhere. Of course, if he's my age, or thereabouts, it's possible he earned his doctorate before the times when absolutely everything went online.

Kind of curious to meet the guy, but we have our strict instructions from the top. We've to meet our brief, speak to the people they request us to speak to, then report back. If there are any solid leads we think need to be followed up, that's not a decision for us to make. They are to be reported to Eurydice Hamilton, and she will decide whether she requests the officer to take action, or whether she intends taking it on herself.

Perhaps it's just trying to keep control of a huge operation. Perhaps it's a power play, cementing her position, making sure no one else pulls something out of the bag, threatening her place as Glasgow's preeminent detective.

Not sure what the take should be if one knocks on a door, then some chap jumps from a window, shouting, *I did it, but you'll never catch me!* Are we allowed to pursue, or do we have to fill in a form first?

I was going to ask that in the meeting, but I didn't want to be seen as *that* guy, so kept my mouth shut. We must all have been thinking it. Would've said something to Kallas in the car on the way back to the station yesterday, but it sounds kind of trivial, and Kallas has that way about her.

I doubt, regardless, that there's anything to be gained from speaking to Dr Thebes. He was just a guy who chatted to our victim over a year ago, yet it is what they're looking for, so it gives me something to write in my report. I can be Employee of

—

the Day! I can win a ten-pound Amazon voucher!

Shake my head to clear the meandering monologue, take a look around. There are the two women by the window, there's a mother with a baby asleep in a pushchair next to her, the mother making the most of her ten minutes of peace.

Two tables along, a young guy on his own, typing away on a MacBook. Doesn't have the hipster beard or the top-knot, but still, he's got the vibe. Fucker's probably writing a book of vegan recipes, which he'll publish himself on recycled toilet paper.

At the back of the café there's another guy sitting on his own. There's an interesting looking bloke. He has a coffee, an empty plate, and he's doing a jigsaw that covers most of the table. I'm a newly-designated expert in the jigsaw field, being on my second in twelve months, so I'm automatically curious about the guy doing a jigsaw like this. In public.

What did he do? Bring it in here, and has spent the entire day drinking coffee and doing a jigsaw? That seems kind of a weird way to fill your time. Or maybe this is his spot, like, in the whole city. He comes in every day for half an hour to work on his jigsaw. No one else is allowed to touch it. Or wait, maybe it's on one of those jigsaw mats, and he rolls it up and takes it onto the next place.

Look at my watch, puffed cheeks, exhaled breath, lift the coffee, drain the cup, settle it back on the table. A last look around, establish which of the two women at the window I'd sleep with if there was a gun at my head – note to crime fans, I clearly wouldn't need a gun at my head, just an offer – then I pull my coat on as I stand up. Ten minutes to walk up the road to the church where I've arranged to meet Rev Yorke.

Get to the door, just as the young woman who's been running around clearing up tables passes by, and we both pause as we make sure to not come too close to one another.

'Thanks,' she says.

Lovely eyes.

Yeah, that's all. Lovely eyes.

'What's the story with the guy in the corner?' I ask, not looking over as I speak.

'The Jigsaw Man?' she says.

Can't help smiling at that.

'Is that his name?'

She gives a quick glance, I mean, super-quick, but long

---

enough for anyone to realise we're standing here talking about the jigsaw guy.

'He owns the café,' she says, then she lowers her voice even more, and looks a little sheepish. 'I don't even know what his actual name is. Everyone just calls him the Jigsaw Man. It's kind of cute, really.'

'And he just sits there all day, doing jigsaws?'

'Pretty much. He talks to people, you know, like if they want him to. He's wise.'

'Wise?'

'Aye, like a sage.'

Now I can't help glancing over at him, and this guy, the sage, informed by the fates that he's being discussed, looks up. He smiles, nods – something of the John Lennon about him, maybe – I nod back, and he returns to his craft.

The girl and I share a look, a well-there-you-are kind of a look, and with that my short time in this café is done, and I head out into the chill of a late Wednesday afternoon in April.

*

'As if this past year hasn't been bad enough.'

I'm sitting in an office behind the church nave. A church like any other. I wonder if Jesus has noticed I've become a regular these days. I mean, given that no one's been able to go to church in Scotland for the better part of a year, I've got to be in the top 0.001% of attendees. Perhaps it will earn me forgiveness for all the shit I've inflicted on people over the years.

I like the cut of Bill Yorke's gib. An honest, sincere, practicality about him. A decent man, looks like he knows how to laugh. Yet, for now, he is a decent man, laid low. Everyone who had any affection for either of these women has been laid low.

'Church congregations have been ripped apart. Who knows how many will be left to return on the other side, how many will even want to? How hollow the phrase *the Lord works in mysterious ways* sounds this year. How hollow… And now this. I really don't understand.'

He's been staring at nothing, his eyes lost in the middle distance, then he looks at me, manages to focus.

'You'll know about the case in Cambuslang last year?' he asks. 'The minister who took her revenge on the town?' Know about it? I lived it, my dog-collared friend. 'I mean... oh, dear Lord, that was such a terrible business. That she could think of doing such things. Something else to be added to the list, and it wasn't as though the Church came into the pandemic from a position of strength. And now Julia...'

I have questions to ask, and one should never rush to judgement, of course, but there's nothing for us here. In the law of things coming in threes – which is obviously not as scientifically on point as Hutton's Law of women at café windows – I'm due, in the course of my career, to come across another Church of Scotland minister who's guilty of murder. But not today. Not this guy.

Sure, people lie, and people affect personas, and people morph into various shapes to fit whatever position they need to take at any particular moment, but that's not him. This is a good man, brought to his knees in sadness. That sadness perhaps exacerbated by questioning his faith.

My phone pings in my pocket, the noise loud in the confined space of this quiet backroom. We look at each other across his desk, and then he offers me the chance to check the text.

'Really, we all have work to do, Sergeant, it's fine.'

'Sorry,' I say, cursing myself for not turning the sound off before I came in. It's rude, that's all. Nevertheless, now that I know someone's looking for me, I have to check.

It's from DS Blumenthal. The thought flashes through my head that it might be all over, as I click open the text. But no, nothing so final, nothing so complete. Instead, a request to go and see one more person this evening because they think I might be in the vicinity. And they're right, I am.

I stare at the phone, reading the name. No such thing as coincidences in police work, right? I should call it in, of course. I mean, they've just asked me to go and see him, so when I report back, it'll be on the basis I was doing as instructed. However, when I toss in the fact that we now have a link between this man and both murder victims, DCI Eurydice Hamilton is going to be spitting blood. My blood.

Slip the phone back into my pocket. I can't just dismiss Rev Bill Yorke because something more interesting has come up. Plenty of crimes are solved by the boring lead, the interview that didn't seem to be going anywhere, the player in the narrative who seemed to have no recognisable part. So, I need to complete

—

52

the job here, and then I can make a decision.

'Can you tell me about the paper the two of you worked on together? How did that work, exactly, in terms of writing the actual report?'

He nods, accepting the need for the mundane, the dull, the straightforward questioning. I try to pay attention to his answer, but my mind is already jumping ahead.

9

There was an old guy at Julia Wright's church by the name of Jeb McDonald. He was an elder there for literally sixty-five years. Jesus Christ. Sixty-five years doing that shit, watching the decline and fall. He finally retired just over a year ago. Two and a half months later he died in hospital, alone, infected with the covid virus.

As a parting gift on his retirement the church got him a handmade model of the yacht on which Jeb had spent all his weekends and all his holidays, up until about ten years previously, when he'd grown too old for the hardships of the sea. The model was made, in the kind of knockout, drop dead happenstance on which investigations are founded, by Dr Crispin Thebes.

This is exactly – exactly – the kind of thing that should be reported back up the chain. Initial contact with the first person, as far as I'm aware, to have potentially known both victims, is definitely the kind of thing Eurydice is going to want to be in on. And she's right, she should be.

So, logically, the next step is obvious. They may have asked me to go and see Dr Thebes, but I should call and let them know about Thebes and Jennifer Talbot, in which case there is no doubt I will be stood down, and Eurydice will take charge.

On the other hand, logic and what should happen can back off. It's not even that I want the glory. I don't want to be the breakthrough guy, I don't want to be the guy strutting around, balls out, taking all the credit for saving humanity. I don't even really care whether this goes anywhere.

So, why am I sitting in the car, on my way to the building where Dr Thebes lives by the Clyde? Partly I'm curious. That was some recommendation he was given by Alice Rowe. That level of charisma, she made him sound like Barack Obama multiplied by George Clooney. So, that's kind of intriguing. And what with him being a man, 'n' all, there's inevitably a little jealousy there. Can't help it. What is it about him that makes him so attractive to people? What made him stand out so much to Alice, what made him the only guy in three years that Jennifer Talbot bothered to speak to? I'd like to know. Should I pass this up the chain, I'll never get anywhere near him.

So, that's part of it. But then, there's the other, larger part.

Why would I do this thing I'm not supposed to? Because I'm not supposed to.

That's all.

Come to the rear of the building, down by the river. Park the car, look up at the three floors of the small block. Cold, early evening, sun now masked by low cloud. Lights on, few curtains yet closed. There's a woman right in front of me, standing at a sink, speaking over her shoulder to someone out of sight. The next room along, there's a TV on the wall. Other lights on in the building. I look up at the third floor, wondering which apartment will be his, but it's useless speculation for now. Out of the car, blip it behind me, up to the building entrance, press the buzzer for apartment 3/6.

Take a step back, look through the glass door at the small foyer. Low lit in blueish purple, mailboxes, large mat just inside the door, linoleum tiles over the rest of the floor. On the wall to the left, a large painting of this part of the Clyde, the Finnieston crane before a late evening orange sky.

Do I have the feeling? You know the one, the premonition of what's to come, the gut police instinct that cries danger, or at least, cries moment of some significance. I think I do, but then it might just be because of how Alice Rowe described him. Or maybe it's because I know I shouldn't be here.

A slight crackle, then, 'Yes?'

Swallow, aware of a certain, and unexpected, feeling of nerves.

'I'm looking for Dr Thebes.'

'Yes?'

'Detective Sergeant Hutton, Police Scotland. I wonder if I might have a word.'

'Third floor, end of the corridor on the right.'

The crackle clicks off, the door clicks open. Inside, just as I'm getting to the lift, the door opens, and a young couple emerge. Holy shit, they look miserable. Just had a fight. The guy looks mad, the woman has the look of someone who's done something wrong, knows it was wrong, but is steadfastly going to stick to her position without apology, because admitting wrongdoing would be, in some way we spectators can only speculate, catastrophic.

I step back, let them pass at a safe distance. The guy and I exchange a look, which means I take the brunt of his ire. Whatever. Don't know what she did, but I'm on her side.

Into the lift, third floor, the scent of the women still here. Something woody.

Something woody. Jesus. Listen to Sherlock Holmes here.

Yes, Watson, this is the butt of what is known as a cigarette.

Good God, Holmes, I don't know how you do it!

Ping!

Out the lift, onto the third floor. Directly opposite the door, a narrow floor-to-ceiling window looking down on the river. Well-lit hallway, a few small paintings of Glasgow along the wall. The University, Kelvingrove, the Cathedral, the Necropolis. The familiar suspects. Along the short corridor to the door at the end.

The door has been left open a fraction. I wipe my shoes on the mat, knock, enter. Take a moment just inside the door, then close it behind me.

There's a small vestibule area, with a mat and a cupboard on the right and a couple of coat hooks on the wall, then the room opens out into a large open-plan kitchen, dining, lounge area. Perfectly ordered and proportioned, like it's come straight from the IKEA factory.

By the window on the left, which is wide and looks directly across the river to the BBC's Pacific Quay, there's a man sitting at a table, working on a model ship. He eyes the model through a magnifying glass, which he wears strapped around his forehead.

Around him are a series of drawers and standing shelves filled with various implements, making this the workshop part of the open-plan. But it's not like anywhere that any normal person has ever worked in. So neat, so methodical in its order, it could be tidied away in less than a minute. Knife blades, knife handles, drill bits, hammers, a vice, screws and nails, tweezers, wax and sandpaper, planes and what look like razor blades, and all sorts of other small tools the names of which and the uses for which I have no idea.

A veritable – *yes, Watson, veritable!* – collection of potential murder implements.

On the table beside the model, there is an easel on which sits a black and white photograph of an old ocean liner, the vessel that Dr Thebes is currently working on. Directly in front of him, on another larger stand, is a schematic drawing of the deck of the ship. There are other drawings tucked in behind.

'Detective Sergeant Hutton,' says Thebes, without turning. 'Do not linger. There's coffee made if you'd like to help yourself, though I sense you have recently been in a café.'

Jesus.

I walk further into the living area, watching him all the time. The mainframe of the model ship is complete, he's currently working on the top deck. He hasn't turned to look at me yet.

I stop about two yards from him, keep watching him for a moment, realise I could get sucked into it, sucked into the warm silence of watching a master craftsman at work, and I force myself to look up, across the river.

Lights on at the BBC, people in offices, the end of the working day. The river below is still, barely a ruffle of wind on the water, no boat traffic to speak of. I doubt there's ever much.

'What was that?' I ask. 'The coffee line?'

He finishes what he's doing, connecting a single piece of rigging using a small pair of pliers and a knife, then he removes the magnifying glass, places it on the worktop, and turns to face me. There's only the barest of red marks on his forehead where the strap had been.

'I can smell it on your breath,' he says.

I hold his gaze for a moment, turn to look at the door, the distance, then turn back. Take another look around the room. I suppose that's interesting. The room does not smell of anything, even though it's open to the kitchen. No food smells, no cooking smells, no obvious smell from the materials he's working with here, as though there's a giant aroma-eater hovering in the middle of the ceiling, absorbing it all.

In such an uncontaminated room, perhaps the smell of coffee really would project quickly and far.

I'd say he was a little over fifty, but he has a shock of white hair. Not long, but thick, nevertheless. And his eyes. Holy shit. *Yes, Sergeant, he has eyes...* Kind of a Paul Newman blue. Yep, that's who this guy is. He's fifty-year-old Paul Newman with seventy-year-old Paul Newman's hair.

'Dr Thebes?'

'Of course.'

'We're investigating the murders of Julia Wright and

Jennifer Talbot.'

No question having been posed, he doesn't have anything to answer.

'I believe you might have known both victims.'

'Yes.'

'You knew them both?'

'Yes.'

'You don't seem surprised at my presence. You've been expecting us?'

The grandiose *us* for this one-man team.

'As you say, I was acquainted with both victims. Although neither relationship was widely known, I presumed there would be sufficient resource thrown at the investigation for the police to become aware of my existence. Your visit was only a matter of time.'

That's all. I wait for something else, but there's nothing coming.

That moment becomes a sudden silence, and he controls it. He commands it, but in a completely different manner to Kallas commanding a silence.

'Relationship?' I say, forcing the word out, so that the silence doesn't engulf the room. Then I feel stupid, because this man demands a certain quality from the people he's talking to. He demands respect and demands that you know as much as he does, and there's me grasping at the word *relationship* because in a tabloid sense it implies something. Yet, this man will not speak in tabloid, and there's no reason why it should imply anything. I, for example, have a relationship with the girl behind the counter at the Haddows that's a six-and-a-half-minute walk from my apartment, but it doesn't really amount to much.

'I would have thought they would send someone more senior,' he says.

'Really?'

'It's hard to imagine that there were many people who crossed the orbit of both women. I may well, indeed, be the only one who did. As such I will immediately be put at the forefront of the investigation. I have seen DCI Eurydice Hamilton on television. I expected her call.'

'What exactly was your relationship with Julia Wright and Jennifer Talbot?'

The cold blue eyes burrow into me again, and then, without moving, without his face changing expression at all, it's as though he turns off the laser, and the look relaxes. He has accepted the question; he's finished reading my mind for now.

'I met them both through my work, though that is something of which you must already be aware. Julia and I stayed in touch. There was a certain mutual attraction there, though it was something with which she was uncomfortable given her position.'

Honest and forthright, or at least the appearance of it.

'You mean as a minister, or as a wife?'

'More the former than the latter, I feel.'

'And did the mutual attraction lead anywhere?'

'We'd been having an affair for the past six months.'

Holy shit. Well, this guy isn't worried about being judged, is he? Nor is he worried about placing himself firmly at the heart of the investigation.

'Did Julia's husband know about it?'

'Julia did not think so.'

Another moment, the next question not appearing instantly on my lips. Jesus, Eurydice is going to be so pissed off.

'Exactly why are you here, Sergeant Hutton? I'm curious by what means you come to my door?'

'And Jennifer Talbot? Were you also sleeping with her?'

The question feels cheap and leading, a boring, unimaginative and obvious inquiry from a boring, unimaginative and obvious detective.

'Yes, of course,' he says. OK, there's that. Shit. 'It started just over a year ago. We met at her rowing club. A chance meeting, but often enough that is how these things begin.'

'Jennifer Talbot was not married, so you were free to conduct any kind of relationship you wished to.'

Again, since there was no question, I get no answer.

'Was there a reason to keep it a secret?'

'You are confusing something being kept secret, with something that people just don't know about. I do not have friends. Jennifer did not have friends. We had no reason to broadcast the relationship to anyone. The relationship, in any case, was hardly worth broadcasting. We had sex, here, in this house, once or twice a month. Would you have had us place an advert in the Herald?'

God, this guy is so damned practical.

'Was Jennifer having a relationship with anyone else?'

'That was not for me to know.'

'Did Jennifer know about Julia Wright?'

'Not as far as I'm aware.'

'Did Julia Wright know about Jennifer Talbot?'

'Yes.'

'Why?'

'I told her.'

'Really? It doesn't sound like the kind of thing she needed to know.'

'I decided she did at the time.'

I nod at that, try to slow it down. Usually one wants the questions flowing, because the interviewee is liable to say something they might not otherwise have done. Dr Thebes, however, seems completely in control. I'm going to have to report back to the centre what I asked him and what he said, near as dammit as I can remember, so there has to be some thought put into it.

Won't lie. He's completely thrown me with the blunt (apparent) honesty.

'The feeling seems to have been that Jennifer Talbot was in no rush to get back to sea, despite having spent so much of the previous fifteen years there. She loved the sea. Her life was on the sea.'

He stares at me. There I go, not specifically asking a question.

'Is it possible she wanted to stay here, on land, near Glasgow, because of you?'

'No.'

'How would you know if you didn't talk much?'

'We talked enough.'

'So, what was keeping her here?'

This time he pauses. He's assessing me. Deciding whether I'm worth talking to. He already knows, after all, that others will come later, regardless of what he says now.

'I still wonder why you're here, Sergeant. They say that a great police task force has been sent out into the field, the net thrown wide. Speak to everyone who was known to ever have had any contact with either of the victims. Clearly, however, they would not delegate this – me – so far down the line.' He stops for a second, the look this time saying *no offence*, without him actually saying *no offence*. 'You must have been asked to contact me because I'd popped up on radar central because of one of the women. Julia seems more likely, that was more widely known. So, DCI Hamilton, or perhaps, whoever is running her operation on the ground, asked you to see me. Meanwhile, you discovered of your own accord that I had met Jennifer, which means this afternoon you visited the rowing club at Clydebank. Regardless of which piece of information came in first, this afternoon you learned that I knew both victims, and yet you did not call it in.'

He pauses, but with the kind of authority that says he's not finished talking yet. Jesus, this guy probably knows what I did at the rowing club.

'Normally,' he continues, having given it precisely the right amount of thought, 'one might anticipate such action would be as a result of grandstanding. Detective of the month, centrefold.' A long look, the burrowing into the eyes. 'But that's not who you are. The detective sergeant in his mid-fifties. And DS Hutton at that. I think I may have heard of you. Not a grandstander.'

'Tell me about Jennifer. Why wasn't she going anywhere?'

How narcissistic of me to allow him to keep talking like that. *Read more of my mind!*

'We're all naughty at heart, aren't we, Sergeant? We all want to be the one to turn our backs on authority. To do what we want. No, to do what we're not supposed to do, regardless of whether it's what we want or not.' A beat. The cold look lingers on. 'And that's why you're here.'

I find it a regular feature of the police interview, the interviewee deciding to talk about me and my motivations. I wonder if other police officers get this, or whether there's just something about me that invites it. The haunted cop.

There I go, making it about me. Again.

'Jennifer Talbot?'

'I appreciate that, Sergeant Hutton. You will have an entertaining conversation with DCI Eurydice Hamilton once you have left here.'

'Really?' At some stage, the sophisticated and urbane will get under your skin, and you crack. 'If you don't tell me why Jennifer Talbot was delaying having to return to sea, then I'm going to assume it was because of your relationship, which will mean you have been lying, which will only exacerbate how –'

'She was scared.'

Three words tossed quietly into the room, stopping me in my tracks, and although he spoke over me, I heard them clearly enough.

'What does that mean?'

'Before she returned home the last time, she had been at sea for a long time, stopping off on land only occasionally. It was a bad trip, with a lot of wild, inclement weather. She got into trouble in the Pacific, not far off the coast of Chile. She thought she was going to die. When she made the Chilean mainland, she thought she might stay awhile, but she decided she should face her newfound fear, or she might never go back to sea. She headed for Scotland. She feared the passage around Cape Horn, though those fears proved unfounded. Nevertheless, as the journey continued, she found herself beset by trepidation. And then, when she was on the final leg of her journey, in the North Atlantic, her vessel was battered by the worst storm she had encountered in all her years of sailing.' A pause, one moment, one minute to the next. 'She was terrified. She got home, barely, and she knew she would never go out again. However, she did not know what else to do with her life. In truth, Sergeant, she was lost. She hid behind the illusion that she would repair her boat, and once more take to the sea, but her murder has not robbed her of that dream. It was no dream, and it was never going to happen.'

'Will others corroborate that?'

'What others?'

'Those who knew her at the rowing club.'

'No one knew her at the rowing club.'

'Marc Johnson?'

'I do not believe she confided in Marc Johnson. Perhaps she had done so in Daisy Johnson.'

'What was their relationship like?'

'You would put stake in hearsay?'

'It's background.'

He smiles. How chummy of us. DCI Hamilton would not be happy if she was watching video of this police interview event.

Outside the sky has darkened a little, the lights of Pacific Quay shine on the still waters of the Clyde. Dr Thebes has conducted the entire interview with a small pair of pliers in his right hand, and now it is as though the pliers are projecting. *It's time for us to go back to work.*

'You would have to ask Mrs Johnson,' he says.

'Have you any idea why someone would want to kill either

---

of the women? Or both of the women?'

'The motivations of much of mankind are quite beyond me, Sergeant, and I do not know anything specific.'

The held look, the burrowing of the eyes, eventually the nodding head.

'I believe it may be time for you to go and report back to headquarters. I, meanwhile, really need to get on with the job in hand.'

I hold his look for a moment, then glance quickly at the model.

'Which vessel is it?'

'The Andrea Doria, the nineteen-fifties ocean liner, sunk off the coast of Nantucket after a collision with the Stockholm in thick fog.'

'A commission?'

'Yes, of course.'

'Who commissions a model of a nineteen-fifties ocean liner?'

'I would rather not discuss my clients.'

I take a step closer, look down at the work he's doing. Fair play to the man, as they'd say on the sport, that is an extraordinary job by the way. The detail, the colouring, the precision. A thing of beauty.

'How much do you charge for something like this?'

'Twenty-nine thousand pounds.'

Holy shit.

I give him another look, his eyes look back, once more burrowing right through me. Cold. Piercing. Blue.

*

When I get outside I call DS Blumenthal and tell him I need to see DCI Hamilton straight away. He says she's gone home for the night already, and that I can come and see her first thing in the morning. I say I reckon she'll want to know this evening. What is it? asks DS Blumenthal. I tell him. For a moment I get silence, then he says he will call back, and hangs up. Less than a minute later he calls. Come to Dalmarnock right now. DCI Hamilton will be waiting for me.

Sounds like she lives quite close to the station. So, there's that.

10

'What the fuck were you thinking, exactly?'

Hmm, that's funny. One tends to think of sentences that begin *what the fuck*, particularly when delivered in a stressful Glasgow work situation, as being quite aggressive. Angry, accusatory, that kind of thing. Despite this, as I stand in the middle of DCI Hamilton's office, and she sits behind her desk in a white blouse, sleeves rolled up, looking like she's at the arse end of a long day at work, she looks curious rather than annoyed.

'That's reasonable,' I say.

'Oh, thank you, Sergeant.'

So, I'm fifty-four, and still finding new women younger than me to take me to the cleaners. Exactly the career path my parents would have dreamed of for me when I was a young bastard running wild on the streets of Uddingston.

'I knew I shouldn't,' I say. 'So, I did.'

I get the look. The long, slow look of incredulity. I'm familiar with that look.

'You knew you shouldn't, so you did?'

'Pretty much.'

'Am I to respect your honesty?'

'I won't... I don't know, I won't tell you how to take it, that's just what happened.'

'Jesus fucking Christ.'

That, one should note, is an exasperated *Jesus fucking Christ*. This woman's pretty damned attractive, by the way. And yes, I know, I find all women in power attractive. Fuck off.

'So, the bottom line is that we have a suspect who was having an affair with both victims,' she says.

'No one said he was a suspect.'

'The man was sleeping with two women, and the two women have been murdered. He's a suspect. Did you ask if he's sleeping with any other women?'

'No.'

'Did he tell you anything that he might not tell me when I go round to interview him now?'

'He said the reason Jennifer Talbot hadn't gone back to sea was not related to the repair of her yacht. Said she was burned out. She'd had a few too many bad experiences and had discovered fear along the way.'

'That's not what anyone else says.'

'If he's telling the truth, they were sleeping together. Perhaps she talked more to Dr Thebes than she talked to anyone else.'

'Dr Thebes is a man, right?' she says. Funny. 'For men, having sex and talking don't necessarily go hand in hand. My husband can't talk after sex because he's already got a mouthful of sandwich.'

I laugh. I mean, I think that was appropriate. She's pretty funny for a detective chief inspector.

'Anything else?'

'Well, like I said, he's a model maker, so he has lots of small tools. Some of them looked sharp. And there's rigging and wire and the like.'

'OK, that's positive,' she says, though her voice is dripping with sarcasm. 'So, we have a suspect, who not only was fucking both victims, but who literally works using implements that were potentially used in the murders.'

I nod.

'And you, what? Left someone else in his presence? Tied him up to make sure he couldn't go anywhere?'

'He'll still be there.'

'He'd better be.'

'He's blunt,' I say. 'I didn't at all get an impression of guilt from him. He seems willing to talk about anything. However…'

I weigh the words. How to describe the guy?

'I'm sure this'll be good.'

She gets up from behind her desk, goes to the coat hanger in the corner of the office, takes a jacket and throws it on.

'Well, I'm not sure how to put it,' I say. 'You'll understand when you meet him. He's… something.'

'He's something?'

'Yeah.'

'Huh. Insight much?'

Wait, she just said *that*?

'You're going there now?' I ask, so that I don't curl up into

---

a scrotal ball of discomfort at that abominable use of the English language.

'Yes, of course.'

'Would you like me to join you?'

'Jesus, you've got balls. No, Sergeant, I would not. Look, maybe I'm showing you some respect because you've obviously been on the force a long time, maybe I'm just respecting my elders, but I'm pissed at you, Sergeant Hutton. I cannot have *anyone* on this investigation who decides to do their own thing, and certainly not someone who intentionally does the opposite to the right thing. You're done here. Go back to Cambuslang. I shall be expressing my unhappiness to your chief, and I will leave it to her to sort you out.'

We stand a yard or two apart in her office, a weird kind of a staring match. Tension in the air, yet neither of us has expressed any actual anger. Other than her saying she's pissed, like she's an American, though the tone was wrong.

'OK,' I say.

'See yourself out the building,' she says, and then she walks quickly from her office, leaving the door open behind her.

11

Who was the first person to use the word *much* at the end of a sentence like that? A social media thing, maybe, given it's an abbreviation. Rather than writing, *Well President Trump, you incontinent piece of racist shit, I think you might be projecting there when you accuse the Democrats of being corrupt…* they write, *Donald Trump, projection much?*

Who did that? I mean, I know the person themselves isn't entirely to blame. If, the first time it had been done, everyone had just ignored it, apart from maybe one or two people who'd had a quiet word, then we need never have heard it again. Instead, weirdly, other people read it and thought, wow, what a great way to use the word much. And so, this affected linguistic aberration was born.

Nevertheless, that very first person needs to be found and punished. I'm not for violence generally, but they need to be flayed. They need some *Game Of Thrones* level of shit inflicted upon them.

With such trivial thoughts do I sit and eat dinner.

I didn't go back to the office. I presume the report on my misdemeanour will not yet have made it to the station, so I would have had to be the bearer of ill news, and I couldn't be bothered with another telling off. One an afternoon is quite enough. So, I came straight home, and here I am, darkness having fallen, sitting at my small dinner table by the window, looking out on the street below.

I drove past the off-licence. Booyah! Felt a tangible pain in my gut as I did so. Everything crying out to me to stop. But in the next couple of days I'll need to go to a meeting, and I don't want to go in there stinking of drink, and I don't want to not even turn up, and I don't want to walk in sober and clean shaven and looking OK, and have to say, it's been zero fucking days since I had a drink.

Maybe I can drink afterwards. Wouldn't be the first time. We'll see how the coming days look. See how much humiliation

DCI Hawkins wants to lay on me.

This is just classic. I'm not in the slightest stressed. There's a big case going on, but I was barely this side of the boundary rope, and now I've been dispatched to the pavilion, and I couldn't give a shit either way. As dressing downs go, that was pretty mild there from Eurydice. Maybe Hawkins will be more on top of it, maybe instructions will have been passed along the upper chains of command that I should be appropriately dealt with, but I won't care about that either.

The things that get to me, that affect me, that fuck with my mental health, like remembering the past, and being forced into corners, being led astray by the wrong women, and getting into huge fights with upper management, none of those are happening. Maybe the being led astray thing, but then I don't even consider Alice Rowe the wrong woman. That was just something that happened, having no bearing on any other aspect of my life, or on the investigation.

But none of that matters. I want a drink, because that's who I am. That's where I am. I don't *need* a reason.

Nevertheless, tonight I've made it. Here I am, sitting at my table, eating an elaborately prepared pasta dish. And by elaborately prepared, I mean a jar of green pesto, a couple of chopped up mushrooms and a few small tomatoes, parmesan grated on top, some fresh parsley. Some fresh parsley that I bought ten days ago, but it's survived.

It counts as cooking in this house.

Food schmood. The main thing is I'm drinking Coke Zero. Dinner plate on a mat, beneath which lies the unfinished Gertrude, Lady Agnew of Lochnaw. Her come-hither look is a little more judgemental this evening. She knows I betrayed her.

As a work of retrospective, contemplative art, my assembling of the jigsaw is progressing slowly. I think of the Jigsaw Man, sitting in his café every day. Being sage. What a guy. Wonder what his story is. Somehow, I imagine he's lived a hell of a life. Drugs, partying, women, drink. Prison, maybe. This is his calm after the storm, this is him stepping back from the brink. Maybe he was pulled back from the brink, saved by a friend from the demonic pit.

Fuck do I know? Maybe he did a philosophy degree at Glasgow and this is his way of monetising it. He sits in his corner pretending to be sage, people are like, who's the wise guy over there, I mean, an adult doing a jigsaw every day in public, that's so fucking sage, and he has his website and merchandise, sweatshirts with a single jigsaw piece, and some catchphrase such as, *Think like the Jigsaw Man, one piece at a time*, or some shit like that.

The Jigsaw Man. That rings a bell. Right, the forensic pathologist who fooled people into thinking he could identify everything about a killer from what he had for breakfast.

Phone starts to ring, saving me from the random inanity that plagues my waking hours, the mind that never shuts up, and I lean over behind me and lift the phone off the small table with the lamp by the door to the kitchen.

Kallas.

My heart does a thing, because that's how much of an asshole I am these days. I'm a guy whose heart does a thing.

'Inspector,' I say.

'Good evening. Are you all right?'

'Never been better.'

'You do not sound as though you have been drinking, at least.'

Why madam, my reputation precedes me!

She must've heard the news.

'I had to drive past the off-licence doing about fifty, but I made it,' I say. 'You heard, then?'

'A report was sent to me and Chief Inspector Hawkins about ten minutes ago. The chief is no longer at work, although I know she checks her e-mails at home, so she will likely see it this evening.'

'And what did the report say?'

'That you were being removed from the investigation for insubordination and not following orders.'

'Really? Insubordination is harsh. What a bitch.'

'Interesting. It is true that no specific instance of insubordination is detailed. Perhaps it was intended that it was included within the blanket of going against direct orders.'

'Definitely harsh, then. Does it say what I did?'

'You spoke to someone who had been romantically involved with both victims, instantly placing him at the centre of the investigation. You ought to have informed DCI Hamilton before you made first contact. It would appear that when she went to talk to him, she found him unwilling to engage. She is putting this down to you having spoiled the ground.'

'Ah.'

—

69

'What does that mean?'

'Well, she didn't seem too mad about it when we spoke. However, having spoken openly to me, if he then chose to be taciturn with her, I could imagine she's going to be pissed off.'

'It is apparent she is pissed off.'

'That's the way it crumbles, cookie-wise, right?'

'That is a reference to the film *The Apartment*?'

I smile down the phone. Well, look at us. This is a much easier conversation than normal. It's because we have something specific to discuss. We have an activity.

'Yes.'

'While acknowledging that it is not within her purview, she has requested that you be suspended.'

Can't help laughing. I mean, not like a hyena or anything. It's not hilarious, and I'm not laughing hysterically at the injustice. It's just, I don't know, stupid. I guess there are pension questions around me getting punted out the door, but it's only money, right? Hopefully I'll have had the balls to drink myself to death before I need much money.

'I'm sure the chief will be delighted,' I say. 'Nice to bring a little light into someone's life.'

'She will be torn, certainly. She will appreciate the opportunity to suspend you, pending possible ejection from the force, given your history. However, I suspect she will not enjoy being told how to handle a disciplinary matter by a fellow chief inspector.'

She pauses. At least, I think she's paused, then it becomes apparent that she's just finished, and suddenly there we are, standing on the other end of a phone, in awkward silence.

'What did you –' I begin, heading the elephant off at the pass, but she starts speaking at the same time, and I shut up first, allowing her to continue.

'What did you do exactly?' she asks. 'Who is this Dr Thebes?'

Work, work, work. I should enjoy it while it lasts. The conversation, I mean. I love talking to Kallas, and the conversations about the other stuff, the non-work stuff, always end up stilted and uncomfortable.

'He's a guy who makes models. Replica ships and the like. He was in the middle of it when I turned up at his house. I mean, on the one hand, it seems kind of trivial, but holy shit, he's good. And he's got something about him. There's something… I don't know, it's like he's the really cool assassin in a movie. Good-looking, but terrifying at the same time. Just, something exceptional. The kind of guy who will own the room without having to open his mouth. They asked me to go and see him because they'd heard he'd met Julia Wright. I, meanwhile, had just become aware that he knew the yachtswoman.'

'You should have reported that.'

'And I didn't. But straight off the bat he told me he'd been sleeping with both of them. Quite open about it.'

'Was either relationship over before the women were murdered?'

'We didn't get to that, but I didn't get that impression.'

'Is he sleeping with anyone else who ought now to be looking over her shoulder?'

'Good question.'

'You did not ask it?'

'Didn't think to.'

'You perhaps could have done a more thorough job,' says Kallas, not so much being blunt, as ramming the truth up my arse. 'On the other hand, you would have known that DCI Hamilton would soon follow in your wake, and so perhaps you were slightly off your game.'

'That'll've been it,' I say, glibly.

'Why did you not call it in as you should?'

I let out a long sigh. Well, I was already downright blunt about that with Eurydice, so there's nothing left to hide, is there?

'Naughtiness,' is, for some reason, the word that comes to mind.

'Like a child.'

Thanks, boss.

She's not wrong.

'I will, as always, be on your side, but one day I will not be able to protect you any longer. Perhaps tomorrow will be that day.'

Her tone never changes, every word just delivered as if she's a not very good actor, reading a fairly bland script. And yet, her words cut me in half. Maybe I'm projecting, because I imagine she's disappointed in me, but there she goes, putting her neck out for her wastrel sergeant, and there I go, not giving a fuck about anyone other than myself.

I hesitate before the apology, although it is there, on the tip of my tongue, and she fills the gap with, 'I will see you

—

tomorrow morning. Good night.'

She hangs up without waiting for anything further. In her quiet, undemonstrative way, she sounds way more pissed off at me than Eurydice Hamilton.

Bollocks. Toss the phone onto the sofa and return to the dining table. There's the half-eaten bowl of pasta, and there's the glass of Coke fucking Zero – huzzah! – and there's the half-finished Gertrude, looking even more disappointed in me than she was before.

I talk of my alcohol addiction, and I talk of my sex addiction, but they both pale next to my hating-the-fuck-out-of-myself addiction that will one day lead to me stepping off the ledge.

12

I'm sitting at my desk, drinking coffee, staring blankly at my computer. Of course, there's work to be done, but here we are, seven-thirty-eight in the morning, and my brain is yet to get out of first.

Knowing I was going to be in a spot of bother with the boss, I obviously felt some primordial need to get into work early, rather than pitching up at around nine. Yet here I am, present in body, utterly lacking in motivation.

This is the perfect time of day for some idle chatter. That's what most people would be doing at a time like this. DC Ritter is right there, across the desk, in her usual position, but I said good morning, and she smiled in reply, and then started working. Eileen's not in yet, Kallas is not in yet. I sit and stare at my screen, seeing nothing, thinking even less.

Across the office, Chief Inspector Hawkins enters, walking quickly through, looking at her phone. She does not acknowledge anyone, does not look up from her screen. She is holding a Costa coffee in the other hand, a bag hooped around her bent elbow.

She looks like an American TV actress. Not anyone in particular. But you know that American TV show look. Attractive, slim, great teeth. They all kind of look the same. Plastic. Though I don't mean she's had work done. That's a different kind of plastic. Just that special American TV kind of plastic beauty.

She's in her forties, perhaps at some point made the decision to not get married, to not have a family, concentrate on her career. A career woman, scaling the heights of Police Scotland. Perhaps the decision was made for her. Perhaps she can't have children. Perhaps she'd love to have children but has never met the right partner. Perhaps all kinds of shit. Her heart was broken, never to recover. Man A, the Mr Right of romantic fiction, died six months into their marriage. No, not that. She'd still be wearing the ring, in memoriam. Perhaps he died before the wedding. Perhaps he left her for her best mate. Perhaps she's a lesbian and feels she can't come out. Though, seriously, why? Perhaps she's a lesbian, has come out, and I know nothing about her private life. Because, after all, I do know nothing about her private life.

Coffee lifted from the desk to my lips, take a drink, tastes great but the movement is automatic and I'm barely thinking about it, so drinking it without even really noticing, cup back down on the desk, still holding it in my right hand, fingers warm on the cup, staring idly at the closed door of Hawkins' office.

'Tom.'

I turn. Heart does the thing.

Yada-yada-yada.

'Inspector,' I say.

I wonder if anyone other than her realises that I'm a bumbling, lovesick moron in her presence. Do all the young 'uns in the office regard me with even more disdain than before?

'The chief inspector would like to speak to you. I insisted that I be present.'

Notice, from the corner of my eye, DC Ritter looking over. Wondering what I've done this time.

'Are you sure? She didn't say anything when she walked past?'

Kallas stares at me, the familiar look to accompany the glib remark.

Last slurp of coffee, then place the cup back on the desk, get up, follow the inspector across the open-plan. She's wearing jeans, smart and stylish, naturally, but jeans all the same, the round collar of a plain white T-shirt showing above the crew neck of a maroon, cashmere jumper. Simple, right enough, but Jesus she's gorgeous.

Head's not really in the game, is it?

Snap of the fingers, and we're in the chief's office, the door's closed, and we're not sitting down because we're not staying.

'I think I might have had enough of you, Sergeant,' says Hawkins as an introduction. This obviously isn't to be a trial of any sort, with an explanation and an examination of the facts, and a reasoned decision arrived at. It's more like a Trump impeachment trial, verdict already decided before kick-off.

I'm going to take a leaf out of the book of my new nemesis, Dr Thebes, and only answer actual questions, although now that my crush has inserted herself in the drama, I'm less likely to say something outrageously stupid in any case.

New nemesis. Fuck's sake.

'This seemed a relatively simple task. This, in fact, was really a task that ought to be have been done by constables. But we all understood the reasoning from the centre. Bring experience to the party, perhaps the vital clue was less likely to be missed. All you had to do was do your job. Do your job. Interview some people, and report back. One would've thought that the worst that could happen was you missed something. And you know what, Sergeant Hutton, I'm not sure you would miss anything. You seem, against all the odds, to be a decent officer. When you function, that is. Then you do this, and I'm getting e-mails from this Eurydice woman, for goodness' sake, telling me how to do *my* job, and I'm of a mind to tell her to… well, frankly, she can fuck off, even if she does have a point. And then, *and then*, at five to seven this morning I find myself just out the shower, standing naked in the middle of the bedroom, getting absolutely eviscerated by the chief constable of all *fucking* Scotland.'

'Not on Zoom, I hope.'

Couldn't help it. We were all thinking it, right?

'Oh, my fucking fuck,' she says, and she looks helplessly at Kallas for support. Kallas has her face on. The same face she has on in literally every single circumstance. Not really sure what Hawkins was expecting.

'Can you just,' she says, turning back to me, 'shut up. Just shut up, Sergeant. Whatever any of us think of this, Eurydice Hamilton is the current face of crime investigation in Glasgow. Probably in the entire country. I, like you, have no idea whose dick she sucked in order to get there, and you know what, maybe she didn't suck anyone's dick. Maybe she's there because she's the best fucking detective in all fuckdom. But what it means is she has dominion. She can do what she likes, and when she's pissed off about something, everyone gets to hear about it. And she's pissed off at you, and the chief constable got to hear about it.'

She takes a breath, sits back, lets out a long sigh. Shakes her head, as though clearing away all the malign thoughts of her defective detective sergeant, she stares at the desk for a moment or two, then she shrugs and returns to the fray.

'Jesus,' she says. 'This is it. This. We're done. The chief

constable deeply wanted me to suspend you, but he's aware of the optics of the day. Suspending an officer for interviewing a suspect won't look good. So… this is it. My instructions were to give you a bollocking.'

We hold the stare, one moment to the next, my face blank – I think – hers exasperated.

'How'd I do?' she says.

I think she's joking.

I almost say that she blew it by introducing the image of herself naked in the bedroom, but a man must know his time and place, and this isn't it.

To be honest, that line definitely only stays in my head because Kallas is in the room.

'Good use of the phrase *oh my fucking fuck*,' I say, instead.

'I'll try to use it more often. Go, leave, I'm sure you have work to do.'

I nod respectfully in response, look at Kallas, and then she turns with me and we head towards the door.

'A word, Kadri,' says Hawkins, and so I'm back out into the open-plan on my own, door closed behind me.

Work awaits. Regular, boring-ass work. It was, after all, what I was doing two days ago. And those last two days were also pretty boring, anyway. Well, apart from meeting the mysterious doctor. And having fabulous, illicit sex on a floor.

Back to my desk, sit down, hand goes straight to the coffee, take a drink, make something of a face, set the cup back down on the desk.

'Everything all right?' asks DC Ritter.

'Coffee's too cold,' I say.

My spider sense tells me to look across at her, rather than at the computer. She's giving me the well-practiced *seriously?* look of the youth.

'You didn't mean the coffee, then?'

'Everything all right?'

'Yeah, it's fine. In a shock turn of events, yesterday I went off-piste, upsetting DCI Eurydice.'

'Uh-oh.'

'Everyone is upset. Apart from me, as it turns out. So, I'm off the exciting double murder case, and back to this.'

I indicate the computer.

DC Ritter, apprised of all the facts, has nothing else to say. We don't really do conversation, but we don't do conversation in a completely different way from the way in which Kallas and I don't do conversation, and with a mutual nod we get back to work.

*

So goes the day, round and round the buoy. There's nothing major on the books, which was why Hawkins was cool with both Kallas and I being dispatched to the investigation in the first place. Indeed, it appears she offered up someone in my place, but they didn't want anyone else from Cambuslang. I have blighted the reputation of the station. Only the fact that Kallas is demonstrably, and obviously, my polar opposite in almost every way, meant that Eurydice did not insist on her also being ejected by association.

To be honest, I could do with more days like this. Going through the motions, one day blending into the next. Nine-to-five, or six, or seven, or eight, Monday-to-Friday, one week, one month at a time. Just over five years from now I'll hit retirement age, and I can go quietly off into the sunset, move away from the west of Scotland, go somewhere no one knows me, and drink myself slowly to death.

I could do that now, of course.

No one knows why I don't.

*

I get home at some time after seven-thirty. Was clearing up years-old paperwork by the end of the day. Could've reasonably left at five had I chosen, but an evening with an unsweetened soft drink and Lady Agnew didn't really appeal so much. Stuck it out as long as possible, then it got to the stage where I knew the Champions League would be on TV by the time I'd got home and made dinner.

'You cool?' said Eileen, as I walked past, which was code for, *you're not drinking this evening, are you?*

'As a little Fonzie,' I said, and she smiled, and she knew I was telling the truth, and she allowed me on my way, unmolested.

And so, here I am, sitting at the table rather than on the sofa, Bayern versus PSG on the TV, no shits to give about the game, but trying to pay attention.

Dinner is a single chicken breast. Cooked it in butter, with a little mustard, onions and mushrooms, lid on. There's probably a word for that. I mean, cooking a bit of chicken in that way. I don't know what it is. And I'd usually have white wine in it. I mean, when you hear chicken, butter, onions and mustard, you think, white wine, right? So that was just me taunting myself. Briefly considered buying one of those wee bottles of wine to use in the cooking, but really, there's no one in my position *that* stupid. Like, *I'll just stick a little of that in the chicken, and not drink the rest of the bottle.* Along with that, made some rice and peas. Rice and peas don't really count as cooking, particularly since I ended up doing them together to cut down on the washing up.

Didn't see Kallas all day, and so did not hear tell of the double murder investigation. I'm left to wonder how Eurydice is getting on with Dr Thebes. I doubt there's really many places for her to go. Hard not to imagine a guy like that completely on top of every interview situation he's ever in, regardless of the circumstances. I doubt he has anything to hide, and he won't be fazed. And you know, even if he killed them both, I kind of suspect he'd still be completely unfazed. There would not be a careless fingerprint, nor a blood-soaked shirt stuffed in the back of a wardrobe.

It gets me thinking, as I stare vaguely at the television. Dr Thebes. Everything about him is meticulous. The flat was the most orderly looking flat ever witnessed in bachelor-dom. Not, of course, that I actually know he's a bachelor. Or he may have a girlfriend who comes over. But everything about the way his work area was set up, the perfect order of it, the everything-in-its-place of it, combined with the neat perfection of what he's actually doing there, points to his almost compulsive level of fastidiousness. Guys like him aren't on the scale: they *are* the scale.

I look deadpan at my reflection in the window. Really? I just thought *that*? *They are the scale.* What a prick.

Whatever. The guy is who he is. Meticulous and precise. Perfect. Exact in every measure. And then what of the murders of Julia Wright and Jennifer Talbot? The duplication of corpses. The wrists and ankles perfectly bound. The cuts in the neck and groin, the accuracy of the insertion of the blade in relation to the artery, to the exact millimetre identical in both victims.

Sleeping with both victims, and the presence of all those

small tools aside, isn't Dr Thebes just what we're looking for?

Bayern score, the commentator gets excited. Sound is on super-low, as I don't like listening to them anyway, so the TV holds my interest long enough that I watch the replay, but I couldn't care less.

Isn't the football commentator the most redundant person in television? What purpose do they serve?

'X passes to Y.'

'That's a great ball, Brian.'

I fucking know it's a great ball. I can see that.

'That's a mile over the bar, he lifted his head at the last minute.'

Yep, saw that 'n' all, mate.

The reason football's the most popular game on earth is because it's so simple. Consequently, there's very little for the football commentator to explain. They exist entirely as a result of having been there, out of necessity, when football was on the radio, and then they switched to TV. And they're still there now, decades later. Maybe there's a button, in this high-tech age, where you can silence the commentator, but still get the sound of the crowd, so you've got the atmosphere. Of course, there is no crowd at the moment, but the sound of twenty-two guys shouting *fuck* at each other is still atmosphere of a sort, and preferable to Middle Aged White Man Y apologising on behalf of the entire television industry every time a profanity emerges from the flat screen.

Dammit, I was constructing a thought before. Don't remember what it was. There was no need for it, anyway. I was thinking about Thebes, and what does it matter? I'm off the case, and Eurydice is unlikely to want my input. Time to switch my brain off.

Shit, that's not even a switch. Not thinking about work is my brain's resting face.

I glance at the football without really looking at, watch a guy pass a ball to another guy and him pass it to someone else, then look back at my dinner. Chicken not in white wine. Rice. Peas.

The new law of my brain is that a vacuum is automatically filled with the vision of DI Kallas walking naked into the Clyde. In fact, not so much the walking naked into the Clyde, more the getting undressed in the first place. That perfect body.

I don't even masturbate thinking about her like that, as

though the act is too cheap for it. Unworthy. And so there is no reset button of the male orgasm, and the soul-crushing, melancholia of the thought is allowed to continue unabated.

Time passes. I finally take myself to bed at ten-forty-five.

*

At eleven-thirty-one the phone rings, the object of my desire, sounding as wide awake as she always does, requesting my attendance in DCI Eurydice Hamilton's office immediately.

'She says you have ten minutes,' says Kallas, 'although obviously if you take longer, she is still going to need you.'

'Why does she *need* me exactly?'

'You will learn more shortly.'

Kallas hangs up. I lay the phone down on the side table, then swing my legs over the side of the bed and sit in classic fifty-four-year-old man position. Butt naked, feet flat on the floor, elbows on my knees, head in my hands.

Buckle up, boogaloo, there's a storm coming.

13

Showered, didn't shave, teeth brushed, in position. And by in position, I mean waiting outside DCI Eurydice Hamilton's office.

She went round to see Dr Thebes last night. She had, unsurprisingly, the same thought I had about his meticulousness. Also, unsurprisingly, she had that thought a lot more quickly. This morning she got a warrant and took a team to his apartment. A tooth and nail search. Ultimately, they took away all his model making equipment. All of it.

They have already ascertained that the wire used in the murders was the same as the thin brass wire Thebes had as part of his supplies, and that cuts in the neck and groin were made with a 0.2mm razor saw. Thebes, unsurprisingly, has such a saw amongst his tools. They have been unable to specifically connect the wounds with the exact razor saw they found amongst Thebes' equipment, but that does not mean, of course, that it was not that saw which had been used to commit the crimes. The saw, certainly, had been very recently cleaned and polished. They did note, somewhat reluctantly, that all his tools had been recently cleaned and polished. The latter point could just as easily indicate Thebes' habits as a model maker, or Thebes' habits as a serial murderer.

What Eurydice needs, of course, is DNA, or traces of blood. She has none of that. Just the model making implements of the model maker, who happened to know both of the victims.

Nevertheless, and I don't blame her, she considered this enough to bring Thebes in for questioning. We have him, at most, until Saturday evening. He is refusing to speak to her. He hasn't engaged a lawyer, seeming to be well aware of his circumstances and his rights. She has to face up to the fact that he can just sit there in silence for as long as it takes, and then she'll likely have to let him go. All she has is the possibility he makes a mistake, says something he shouldn't, inadvertently opening the door.

He doesn't strike me at all as the kind of person who ever makes mistakes. There will be nothing inadvertent. Keeping his mouth shut will be one way, which is interesting, but I would have thought he hardly needed to hide behind silence. Even if he is guilty, he will control the narrative.

None of which explains why I'm here, and in giving me the rundown when I arrived, DI Kallas was none the wiser. I thought maybe we'd get to sit in awkward silence together for a while, but after giving me the download, she headed home. It's now gone one o'clock, after all. Maybe she was just making sure I turned up.

I'm sitting in a deathly quiet open-plan office, one other person here – she's sitting on the other side of the room, and even though my back is to her, I can feel her presence, aware that I'm not alone – and the only sound is a low, electrical hum. Lights and heating.

Tiredness has, inevitably, kicked in. I yawn, long and satisfyingly, leaning forward, head down, elbows resting on thighs. God, I could sleep now. The stimulating effects of shower and Listerine have worn off.

The door to Eurydice's office opens, and a woman in a grey suit emerges. She doesn't look at me, even though I look at her, examining her with the trained eye of the libertine. Yes, libertine.

She's a grown-up. I mean, sure, we're all grown-ups. But she's focussed, and, based on my ten-second appraisal, I'd say humourless. Whatever. I'm the king of instant judgements.

She nods at Eurydice, then takes her phone from her pocket and is reading as she walks to the elevator. We're only on the second floor, but it's harder to read walking down stairs than it is in a lift, so that's that decision made. She could be checking the Champions League scores or reading a message from her kids or her husband or her wife, but I know she's working. She's the type.

I watch her to the lift, then look back at Eurydice, who's standing at her door, looking at me. Watching me watch the lawyer. Not that I know the woman who just left is from the procurator's office, but I'd take the bet.

'Thanks for coming in, Sergeant,' she says, and she indicates her office, then walks in, not waiting for me.

I follow her, closing the door behind me. She doesn't sit at her desk, instead going to stand at the window. Little view from here, just the lights of Dalmarnock stretching to the lights of Rutherglen. Down below, the broad, dark expanse of the river.

She stretches, arms bent above her shoulders, eyes closed. I watch the movement of her breasts in the reflection in the window, then look away quickly, before she opens her eyes. Unexpected direct eye contact can be one level of discomfort. Eye contact via the window reflection is another matter. There's innately something surreptitious about it.

I'm not really sure what she wants me to do, so I go over and stand beside her. The entire wall is floor to ceiling window. The kind of thing people get thrown through in action movies. And we stand here, looking out on the world. I put my hands in my pockets, she finally lowers her arms, emits a gentle sigh from the back of her throat, and does not look at me.

The town at night. There's nothing to it, really, but I'd love an aspect like this. There's something wonderful about the night, the lights and the dank darkness. All I have from my window is the building across the street, one road, orange lights. It's enticing enough in itself, which is why I never close the curtains when I sit at my small dining table. But a broad cityscape at night would be amazing.

Hmm… maybe when all this virus madness has settled down, I can take myself to some city for a while. New York or Tokyo, somewhere that's just bustling. Get a nice room with a big window on, let's say, the twentieth floor or thereabouts, and spend all my time looking out on the world. While away the minutes and the days and the weeks of my life. A drink in my hand the whole time, no responsibilities to fuck up.

'Where are you, Sergeant?'

Now she's looking at me in the reflection, and I shake my head to bring myself back.

'Tired, sorry,' I say.

'You're a dreamer, eh?'

I don't know what to say to that, so I smile ruefully and nod. The only weird thing there was that I wasn't dreaming about sex. Of course, there was at least a drink in my hand.

'Well, I had hoped not to see you again. No offence. But we are where we are, as people say nowadays.'

'And where is that?'

'We have Dr Thebes in custody. He's refusing to speak.'

'I heard.'

'However, he says he will speak to you.'

Having let my eyes wander away across the dark of night, I now turn and look at her, eye-to-eye, rather than via the reflection.

'Why?'

'Perhaps you can ask him. What exactly did you have to say to each other?'

'I wrote it all in my report.'

'No detail left aside?'

I don't want to answer too quickly, not wishing to give the impression of having something to hide. But really, I did write everything that needed to be said.

'He's an interesting guy,' I say. 'One of those people who... who owns the space he's in. I'm not saying he's narcissistic or anything like that. He's completely in control. You feel like you're talking about what he wants to talk about. If you manage to change tack, or in some other circumstance, manage to do something unexpected, it's as though it's with his tacit acceptance. You may think you're in control...' Finish the thought off with a shake of the head, then, 'I did feel like we had a connection, but then, if he wants it, everyone will feel like that when talking to him.'

'And I didn't,' she says.

We hold a look for a moment, and then turn back to the nightscape.

'You want me to go and speak to him now?' I ask.

'That was why I called you in, but I want to listen in, and I'm tired. I'm going to go home. You too. Back here at eight, and then we'll go over the plan.'

'You really think he killed those women?'

'I'm 100% sure of it,' she says. 'I feel it right into my bones. And I'm going to get him. You?'

'My guts are neutral on the subject.'

'Maybe your guts have had too much alcohol,' she says, giving away the fact that she will have asked, and been told, all about me. We catch eyes in the window, and she instantly shakes her head. 'Sorry, Sergeant Hutton, that was completely inappropriate.'

'That's OK.'

'No,' she says, as she turns away from the window, 'it's not.' A deep breath, another shake of the head, she glances at her computer, which has shut itself down, and doesn't bother reactivating it.

84

'Look, Sergeant, I know this is a little left field, and I hope you don't mind me asking…'

She looks at me with hesitation, surprisingly waiting for approval before asking the awkward drink- or (possibly) sex-related question. Eurydice is not all that she appears. But in a good way.

'Go ahead.'

'Do you think there's some kind of a connection between you and Dr Thebes?'

Not sure exactly what she's saying, but get the sense she's not finished saying it, so don't immediately answer.

'I mean… Jesus, one gets so tongue-tied these days trying not to say the wrong thing, people are so –'

'Really, you can say anything.'

'Fine. All evidence to the contrary notwithstanding, do you think perhaps it's a gay thing?'

'A gay thing?'

'You and the doctor. Did you get the sense of that? Of mutual attraction?'

I raise my eyebrows at her.

'Didn't see *that* coming,' I say.

'Like I said, all evidence to the contrary notwithstanding…'

'Hmm.'

I look away, turning back to the night, although we're both now standing further away from the window, and the view is more reflection than the awe-inspiring beauty of Dalmarnock.

'What does that mean?' she asks.

'Well, I'm trying to give it some thought, rather than just throw it out the window.'

'In case I think you protest too much?'

'You're determined to see through me, right?'

I turn to her, sort of smile.

'We're all detectives, detective.'

'No, I really don't care about being seen to protest. I think there can be connections between people that aren't sexual. I'm not sure, on this occasion, there's any connection anyway. Perhaps it's just that he feels he can control me in a way he can't control you, that's all.'

'I hadn't thought of it that way.'

'So, I have no idea. I will speak to him tomorrow, and we'll take it from there. Will you sit in, or watch from the other room?'

'To begin with, I think the latter will be best.'

'Roger that.'

'I apologise for dragging you in this evening. Ultimately, it hasn't proved necessary.'

'It's cool.'

Another look, the mutual decision that everything that needs to be said has been, and then we start heading towards the door. Out into the open-plan, she closes the door behind her. A glance across the room at the lone officer still working, but whoever she is, she is presumably not involved with Eurydice's business in any way, and so there is no exchange between them, and then we're standing together at the lift, turning out to be just as cat-lazy as the lawyer who didn't bother walking down the stairs.

'You have quite the reputation, Sergeant,' she says.

'I do what I can,' I say, drily. 'It's been hard-earned.'

'I had a quick look at your file this evening.'

'Is that legal anymore? GDPR and all that.'

'I'm not particularly well-versed in privacy law. Your file is rather extensive, however, so you might want to make sure it didn't get into the wrong hands.'

Into the lift, she presses for the ground floor.

'I don't care.'

'There's video.'

I don't reply. A small bump marks the passage past the first floor, before we smoothly arrive at the ground. The doors open to the foyer, to the low lighting and the quiet of night, one man, one woman behind the reception desk.

'There's video?'

'As an attachment to your online file.'

'What's the video?'

She glances at me. A moment, I role my eyes.

'Really? Back garden sex?'

'Yes.'

'That's on my file?'

'Yes.'

She gestures good night to security. I ignore them. We get to the door, and it fizzes open to the night and the rush of cold air.

We stand outside for a moment, the chill of the middle of the night in early April, poised to head off in different directions. I have no idea where she's going, who she's going home to. She, it would appear, knows everything about me, including how I look mid-orgasm.

Let's not think of such things.

'I have no idea how you're still in a job, Sergeant Hutton,' she says.

Nice. She has a way about her, though, I'll give her that. A tone. She says things like you'd imagine a critical senior manager saying, yet she delivers them with an almost rueful amusement. I really don't know what to make of her.

Perhaps she and Thebes are more suited than she acknowledges.

'Me neither,' is all I've got in response.

She nods, the words *good night* flash across her face, but she decides not to bother saying them, and then she turns away and heads towards the small car park, while I head for the gate, and my car, parked out in the cheap seats.

14

'Have you established my motive,' asks Dr Thebes.

Eurydice set the room up with some intent. There are two screens up on the wall, and since we sat down, they have each been showing one of the victims, in situ, a pale, dead corpse in a background of blood. If our man here is guilty, then he deserves it, of course. But what if he's not? Then we are forcing him to sit with the images of these two women, with whom he was involved, perhaps even loved for all we know, brutally murdered.

Eurydice will know he will not complain, and neither has he. Indeed, he has not even noticeably looked at them.

'Where there's love, there's motive for murder,' I say.

'What a romantic notion, Sergeant Hutton. Do you live in a world where only couples in love sleep together?'

'Your relationships with both women spanned some time. It's human nature, regardless of who any of us are. Attachment grows, often despite ourselves.'

He rests his elbows on the table, entwines his fingers, then rests his chin on his hands. His eyes are as cold as they were on Wednesday. He has the impression of not being in the least discomfited by his arrest. On Wednesday he was at home making model ships. Today he is doing this.

'Love finds a way?' he says, a smile in the tone that finds itself neither to his eyes nor lips.

'Usually,' I say, taking the question seriously. 'Did you ever tell either of the women you loved them?'

'Is that of significance?'

'Establishing the exact nature of your relationships is of significance.'

'No. In the case of Jennifer it would have been a lie. I found her interesting, her actions suggest the feeling was reciprocated, the sex was highly satisfactory.'

Highly satisfactory? Jesus, calm the fuck down, mate. Highly satisfactory sounds like he filled out a questionnaire.

Was the sex *Highly Satisfactory*, *Satisfactory*, *Average*, *Disappointing*, or *Like Mouth-Fucking A Sabre-Toothed Tiger*?

'Nevertheless,' I say, trying to ignore the internal comedy sidekick narrative, 'that is exactly the kind of relationship that turns to love.'

'Not this time.'

'How about Jennifer?'

'How about Jennifer?'

'Did she love you?'

'I'm not entirely sure where you would go with that as an idea, but no, she did not.'

'She never said?'

'No.'

'Maybe she loved you and never said.'

'Had I neither spoken to her nor seen her, then perhaps that might have been possible. But, as I told you already, we met and made love two or three times a month. I would have known.'

'You have that superpower?'

'You are less of a man of the world, Sergeant, than your demeanour indicates? I think not. If it is a superpower, it is one we all have. One always knows. One may be in denial, one may lie to oneself because one does not want to believe it or cannot hope to believe it, but we all know. It's in the eyes, it's in the tone… it's in the availability. There are few emotions easier to read in human nature.'

Don't internalise! Don't think about DI Kallas!

'What about Julia?'

'Very good,' he says, although I'm not entirely sure why. It was hardly a great deductive leap. *My God, man, what made you ask about the other victim?* 'Julia loved me, but she never said, and she was tortured by it. I should have ended it, but the sex was good. I allowed myself to be ruled by desire.'

'Did you ever talk about ending your relationship?'

'No.'

I take a moment. There are a few ways in which the interrogation can go. I'm aware that Eurydice, and two others from her team, are watching me at work. Spending most of my life as a lone wolf, I don't really appreciate the audience. That probably comes from a painful awareness of my own inadequacy.

'Do you know if either woman was involved in any other similar relationships?'

Eurydice gave me my brief this morning. The directions in which she wants me to take the conversation. She has already made up her mind, and she's very focussed. As far as she's concerned, Thebes is our man. So, talk of the women having relationships isn't about bringing other potential suspects into play, it's about establishing motive for why they might have argued with Thebes.

'Julia was prone to falling in love. She told me she'd hoped it would end when she married. That Benjamin Wright would be the one. The last one. It did not turn out that way for her. She had fallen for others during the fifteen years of her marriage.'

'What others?'

'Names?'

'Yes, names.'

'She never gave me names.'

'That seems like quite an intimate conversation.'

'Yes, I can see that it does. Nevertheless, I did not look to draw that intimacy from her. I did not want it.' We hold the gaze across the desk, a brief silence which he unusually ends. 'She did not mention names, I did not ask for names.'

'Did she imply she was in love with anyone else at the moment?'

'Perhaps. Such infinite capacity for love,' he says. 'Perhaps that's why she went into the ministry. Their message is one of love, after all.'

'Are you being facetious, or do you think she had such an infinite capacity?'

'Both,' he says.

'And Jennifer?'

'I doubt it.'

'You doubt she was seeing anyone else?'

'That's correct. Possibly Mrs Johnson. You will have to ask her.'

'You think Jennifer might have been bisexual?'

'Daisy Johnson was the only other person she ever mentioned. She spoke fondly of her. On one occasion I drew from it that they were in a relationship that went beyond friendship, but I do not recall exactly what was said.'

'And how about you? Were you involved with anyone else?'

'Was I having an affair with anyone else?'

'That's correct.'

He stares across the desk. Face absolutely expressionless, eyes cool. For all the air of authority, command, and guarded mystery, the look still has guilt written all over it.

Fuck it, this is not a normal guy. It's not guilt. He doesn't feel guilty about anything. There's just something to say, that's all.

'One other,' he says.

'And what is her name?'

'I'm not going to tell you that.'

'Yes, you are.'

I mean, I say that, because it sounds like the kind of thing the investigative officer would say at a time like this, but really, no, he's not. We all already know he's not. But the hoops have to be gone through. This is how the game is played.

Silence.

'If you did not kill the other women, and someone is perhaps targeting you through the women with whom you were involved, this other woman you mention could be in jeopardy. You cannot help her. We can make sure no harm comes to her.'

'I will speak to her when I get out of here.'

'That's bold.'

'You cannot charge me because I knew two murder victims, and I work with tools that could have been used in those murders,' he says coldly. 'We know this, Sergeant.' He nods in the direction of the large mirror, without taking his eyes off me. 'DCI Hamilton knows this. By Saturday's end I will have been released, and I will contact my other lover, and I will make her aware of the situation.'

'She might be dead by Saturday evening.'

'Let us hope not,' he says.

'Do you care?'

A moment, he considers his candour, then says, 'Not really.'

'Did you care about Julia and Jennifer?'

'No, not really.'

'Are you, you know… have you been tested? Are you on a scale somewhere? The lack of empathy, weird genius scale?'

'Do I have Asperger's?'

'Yes.'

'I have never been diagnosed. I do not consider that I do. I am not a genius in any facet, weird or otherwise, and while I may be lacking in empathy, I don't believe that is a trait solely held by the Asperger's-afflicted.'

I tap my fingers, as we hold each other in a familiar stare across the desk. The eyeball wrestle, which doesn't really have anywhere to go as a concept.

There's a crackle, as Eurydice checks in from next door, then her voice comes through the small speaker in the desk.

'We need to know this woman's identity, Dr Thebes. She cannot possibly be safe at the moment. If you are sure she is safe, then it can only be because you know that the man who murdered the other two women is currently sitting right here.'

The static stays online, as she has not yet turned off her microphone, though she has said what she has to say. Waiting to respond to anything Thebes might say in reply.

He turns slowly and looks at the mirror wall. Now, for the first time since we came into the room, his face changes slightly. The expression hardens imperceptibly, the cold blue eyes narrow just a fraction, the lips tighten. He looks at the mirror and through into the next room with a look that is as near as dammit the equivalent of stretching out a long arm, through the glass, then putting his fingers tightly around Eurydice's throat, and squeezing until the eyes pop out of her head.

He holds the look, and I can almost feel Eurydice shiver.

'Tough guy,' I say, to break the moment.

Should've said it sooner, but he is captivating.

He turns back, his face changing as he does so.

'We need to know the woman's identity, Dr Thebes,' I say.

He holds my gaze across the table, and I can't help the shiver that courses down my spine. Although he must notice, and he must know the effect he has on people, his face remains impassive.

'I believe she is quite safe,' he says.

That's all.

15

There are four of us in the room. Blumenthal, Kallas, Eurydice and me. Seems odd that Kallas is here, not that anyone is complaining. Either Eurydice has realised she is the kind of clear-thinking detective you need on any investigation, or else she's here as the Hutton-whisperer. To keep me under control, or maybe to translate my wildest impulses.

There I go, making it about me again.

We're in the main ops meeting room, where the team meets, but everyone else is out in the field, continuing to gather information. Now, of course, many of them have been assigned to Dr Crispin Thebes, the same wide net thrown around his life, as has been thrown around the lives of the two victims.

Thebes, unsurprisingly, has refused to give us a list of his previous commissions, and so that's the first roll of the detective dice. Contact museums and art collections and sailing clubs, any kind of organisation that might have the model of a ship on their premises. And, of course, it's a big world out there, and there's no reason why he couldn't have sent his work overseas. However, who we really need to find is this third woman, and in the first instance, it makes sense to keep it relatively local. Or regional at least, to the west of Scotland.

He doesn't have a website, all his commissions appearing to come via word-of-mouth. Desperately old-fashioned. Perhaps he was a man of connections before he started in this line of work. The police squirrels are out there trying to find out.

'This is fucking hopeless,' says Eurydice.

The four of us, sitting around the same table, four coffees at various stages of consumption, Kallas the only one not to touch hers yet. Eurydice has almost finished hers. She's a consumer. She gets on with shit.

You can tell stuff by the way people drink their coffee.

Really? *You can tell stuff by the way people drink their coffee*? Fuck off. You can tell stuff by the way people do all sorts of shit, like wash up after dinner, and keep in touch with old friends, and murder their parents.

Nevertheless, what the great detective here deduces about Eurydice from the way she drinks her coffee, factoring in everything else I know about her, is that she's a roll your sleeves up, get on with shit, grab what's in front of you by the balls, type of a woman.

'I'm not casting aspersions, by the way, Sergeant,' she says, directing the comment at me rather than Blumenthal.

'It hadn't occurred to me that you were.'

'I don't think anyone's breaking through this man, not unless he wants them to.'

'Do we even know what his doctorate's in?' I ask.

Eurydice nods at the question, but doesn't answer, choosing instead to lift the last of her coffee to her lips.

'History of Art,' says Blumenthal. 'Keeble College, Oxford. Was an undergrad at St Andrews. It takes effort nowadays to have no online presence. Particularly being a tradesman, artisanal or otherwise. But it's noticeable there's absolutely nothing. No mention of Thebes anywhere on the Internet. Whenever he completes a commission, it must be part of the deal that there be no mention of him online.'

'There are plenty of private people in the world,' says Kallas, the first time she's spoken. 'We should not confuse a need for that kind of privacy, with necessarily having something to hide.'

'I'm not giving him that,' says Eurydice. 'Not yet. Let's not get away from the basic fact. Two women have been murdered, they were women who moved in completely different social circles, and this man was having an affair with both of them. If he's not guilty, it's an extraordinary coincidence, and I'm not big on extraordinary coincidences in the world of police work.'

'So how about someone setting him up?' I toss onto the park. 'It would explain the otherwise pointless, precise replication of the two murder scenes. That could be intended to implicate the doctor. The crimes were carried out using the implements of a model maker, so that it all points in his direction.'

'Why these two women?'

'Revenge?'

Eurydice questions revenge as a motive with her eyebrows, puts the cup to her lips, looks slightly annoyed that there's only the frothy dregs.

'We know nothing about his past life,' I say.

'The dark world of art history, eh?'

'At least there's a tonne of money in it, and its regularly associated with laundering. And where there's money and money laundering…'

'So, by this measure, someone killed Thebes' two lovers in order to punish him, and chose to further punish him by framing him for the murders?'

'I'm not saying this is where we are, but as a theory it ticks the boxes of everything we know, and without being too outrageously far-fetched.'

'Hmm.'

'Or, we could have the familiar tactic of committing one crime for a reason, and then another to obscure the reason for the first,' says Blumenthal.

'Yes,' says Eurydice, 'perhaps. However, in itself it feels like a fiction. How often have we come across such subsidiary crimes in our working lives?' She looks around the table. None of us have an example to hand. 'Murder like this involves planning, it involves elaboration and pieces in a puzzle. The more you do, the more chance there is you leave something behind. It's why it generally doesn't happen in real life. As a way of deflecting attention from oneself, it's one of the more dangerous methods.'

She lifts her coffee cup again, abandons the movement with an annoyed shake of the head before it reaches her lips.

'I need to get another one of these,' she says. 'Anyone else?'

Blumenthal and I lift our cups to indicate we're good, Kallas sits impassively quiet, feeling presumably that there's no need for her to reply as she obviously hasn't even started drinking the first one yet. Eurydice walks over to the machine in the corner, sets the same cup in the slot, and presses the cappuccino button.

There's her problem. The cappuccino button is a one-way ticket to froth overload.

'Look,' she says, continuing to talk while the machine spits and splutters, 'I'm not solely focussed on this guy. Sure, I think it's him, but I'm not so close-minded that I'll be ignoring evidence if it points to anyone else, or if it proves his innocence.'

A pause, the last hurrah of the coffee machine, she waits for it, she lifts the cup, takes a taste where she stands, and then, addiction in hand, returns to the table.

'But just as far-fetched plotting and planning is the work of fiction… the straightforward and the mundane, the everything-being-as-it-seems, is the work of fact. This is how it usually goes. Does all the circumstantial evidence point to Thebes being guilty? Yes. Then chances are he's guilty. So we need to do a good job, and we need to get the evidence that goes beyond the circumstantial.'

She looks around the table, her eyes finally settling on Kallas

'It's Kadri, yes?'

Kallas nods.

'I'd like you to sit in with Sergeant Hutton. We have no idea if Thebes will speak to you, so I won't ask you to lead the questioning. However, feel free to test the water whenever's appropriate. If you think of something the sergeant isn't asking, then go right ahead.'

'Yes,' says Kallas, nodding.

The two women sit and stare at each other across the table, on the diagonal, from a few feet apart. Interesting dynamic, but there's no tension there. That's not the dynamic. There's just something not being said, though I don't know what it is.

Eurydice, to her credit, is not someone who leaves anything unsaid.

'You may be curious why I'm asking you to do this. I will be blunt, and I hope this isn't over-generalising, but my experience with the Baltics suggests bluntness will be appreciated.'

'Yes,' says Kallas.

'If you don't approve of my reasoning, I will still insist upon you sitting in on the questioning, but you can of course pass any complaint further up the chain.'

Kallas, this time, acknowledges that with a tiny head movement. I'm hooked. I mean, I have no idea what's coming. Blumenthal, more used to his boss's methods, is running a pen over a list of names, possibly just establishing the known whereabouts of all the officers currently dispatched around the city.

'You're beautiful,' says Eurydice. 'And you give off the same kind of organised, taciturn vibe as the doctor. It's like when you hear that Alicia Vikander and Michael Fassbender are a couple, and you imagine that they sit quite comfortably in total silence at breakfast because nothing actually *needs* to be said, and you understand how well they'd go together.'

'You want me to seduce Dr Thebes?' asks Kallas, her voice absolutely flat, no judgement whatsoever in the question.

'No, of course not,' says Eurydice. 'And I mean, *of course not*. This isn't me asking that in any coded way. I just wonder how the doctor will react to having you in the room, and a big part of that is that you're strikingly attractive. Which sounds like an absolutely fucking awful reason to put a woman in a room with a suspect, but I thought of it, and here we are.'

'That is all right,' says Kallas. 'I do not have the same opinion on my beauty, but it is what my husband says, so I will accept that perhaps others think it too. I do not mind. I will happily sit in on the questioning of Dr Thebes.'

Eurydice puffs out her cheeks, letting out a long slow breath, eyebrows raised at both Blumenthal and I across the table.

'Gentlemen, anything to add?'

Well, I would have something to say about the viability of Kallas and Thebes as a couple, because I'd like to object, but you know, she's not wrong. It makes a hell of a lot more sense than Kallas and me as a couple, that's for sure. When the movie gets made, I sure as fuck ain't getting played by Michael Fassbender.

Both Blumenthal and I reply with the generic lifted hand of acceptance.

'OK, good. For this next session, I'd just like you to concentrate on general specifics of the case. Let's see if we can lead him into any mistakes. Alibis, where were you on Monday evening at blah-de-blah, the usual kind of thing. You have all the details of the crimes to hand?'

I tap the slim brown folder in front of me, although I know this stuff well enough now.

'Right then, ladies and gentlemen, off we fuck.'

I can't help smiling at that, Kallas and I share a look, and we're on.

16

In the interview room, waiting for Thebes to be brought back in, Kallas and I side by side. The third time speaking to Thebes. Feeling unusually uncomfortable. The man gets inside your head, insidious, dangerous, controlling. It feels like the whole thing, each interview from start to finish, is a performance, and he's the writer and director. Perhaps, as a player in his show, one has some minor capacity to improvise, but it feels like he knows what you're going to say every single time. On top of all that, add an audience.

Everything, like literally everything, is so much easier when you don't have your superiors in attendance. Usually, this wouldn't apply to Kallas, but that's the effect of Thebes. I don't even want her here. Nevertheless, here she is, and Eurydice and Blumenthal are in the other room, and I think there might be one or two others as well.

'Alicia Vikander,' says Kallas, and I give her a little sideways glance. 'I had not thought of that. That is funny.'

Typically, she says this without any amusement whatsoever.

'I said as much to Eileen one time,' I say, feeling that I can't just ignore her, but wary of the microphones being on.

Perhaps Kallas too is a little apprehensive talking to Dr Thebes. Impossible to tell. Perhaps the trivial conversation is her shot of vodka, her slug of espresso, her draw of the cigarette.

'You did?'

'Yes.'

'When was that?'

'The time you did the thing.'

I'm staring at the table, the closed slim brown folder in front of me. Kallas is staring straight ahead, at the blank wall opposite. I know she will be looking through the folder of all the times we've worked together in the past nine months, and that she will arrive shortly at the right moment.

'The day in Troon,' she says, not even questioning.

'Yes.'

'You thought of Alicia Vikander?'

'Yes.'

This is the kind of conversation we have. I wonder if anyone's listening in the other room, or whether they're chatting amongst themselves, sorting shit out, making plans. Or perhaps Eurydice and Blumenthal have the same kind of awkward, stuttering conversations as Kallas and I, borne of unspoken attraction.

Nah. No one's attracted to Blumenthal, bless him.

'Thank you,' she says. 'That is a nice comparison.'

Well, I've got nothing to say to that. I mean, were I drunk in a bar I'd be saying all kinds of shit. I'd be a fool. But here we are, in a cold interview room, being overheard, and about to interview a double murder suspect. Let's leave the foolishness out of it.

The door opens, Dr Thebes enters, led in by Eurydice herself. So, she at least was not in the next room.

'Sergeant,' she says, with a nod, Thebes walks around the table and takes the seat opposite, Eurydice closes the door on her way out.

No point in dicking around. Press the record button, say, 'Interview recommenced, twelve-thirty-eight, DI Kallas and DS Hutton present.'

We hold each other's gaze for a few moments, then he breaks it to look at Kallas. The familiar cold-hearted look, then he turns back.

'DI Kallas will be sitting in on this session,' I say. 'She may have questions, as and when.'

Thebes looks back at her and the two engage silently across the table. I guess this was the kind of thing Eurydice was looking for. Not really sure where it will get us.

'Is that Kallas with a K, or with a C?'

'K.'

'You have the same name as the Prime Minister of Estonia. It is not a common name outside of there. You are Estonian?'

'Yes.'

'You have the Nordic look, certainly.'

Kallas, as usual when not actually asked a question, says nothing. Time for the lead interrogator to get to work.

'Can you tell us what you were doing last Friday evening?' I throw into the ring, and Thebes slowly and deliberately turns his head back.

He looks at me, he looks at Kallas, he looks back.

'You display interesting body language,' he says.

Oh, please. We're just sitting here at a table.

'I presume you have worked together previously,' says Thebes. 'You are a team.'

'Friday evening, between the hours of seven and twelve.'

Stay cool, my man. He's trying to mess with your shit.

'A very attractive woman, Detective Inspector Kallas.'

'Oh, fuck off.'

Oh. That wasn't very cool. I await the teacher's voice over the intercom, but she's obviously giving me a little more time. 'Friday evening between seven and twelve.'

'Let's make a deal,' says Thebes. 'You tell me about you and Detective Inspector Kallas, and I will tell you about Friday evening.'

'I ask you questions, and you answer them. That's the deal.'

He stares blankly across the table.

'Friday evening, seven to midnight.'

Those cold, blue eyes. What movie was it, d'you suppose, where Newman's eyes were the coldest and the bluest and the deadliest? He must have played deadly at some point. I don't really know Paul Newman movies. Nor, for the matter, his salad dressing.

Focus!

'I did not go out. I spoke to no one. I worked until eight. I set down my tools, arranged the workshop area appropriately, then I cooked a tuna steak and made a light salad. Green leaves and sugar snap peas, tossed in a little oil and lemon juice. Some sesame seeds. Tuna steak grilled on a high heat, one minute each side, still red and succulent in the middle. I sat at the table while I ate. I read Murakami's *Killing Commendatore*, and I drank two glasses of Chablis. A William Fevre. Sits well with the tuna. You know Murakami's work, Sergeant?'

'When did you go to bed?'

'I enjoy the flights of fantastical thinking, though I find latterly he tends to overwrite. Three-hundred-page novels stretched to six hundred. Or, in the case of *1Q84*, thirteen hundred. And he does sometimes appear pre-occupied with the breasts of teenage girls, which seems unnecessary. I think perhaps that's a cultural difference. I'm not terribly familiar with Japan. Are you familiar with Japan, Sergeant?'

'When did you go to bed?'

'I washed the dishes, and then I sat and listened to music for a while. I enjoy the Sinatra albums from the 1950s. Some say he invented the concept album with *In The Wee Small Hours Of The Morning*. I'm no expert. The slow albums, the break-up albums, are a suitable soundtrack to our times. To all times perhaps. Life, after all, is full sadnesses. Moments of joy are fleeting, the ones that last are perilous, shot with danger. Sadness, however… sadness lingers. Sadness can last a lifetime.' He pauses, and I need to ask the question, repeat the question, ask another question, but he wraps the room in his words, and I know that he's only paused, not stopped, and so I let myself believe it's good that he keeps talking, as the more he talks, the more chance there is he says something he'll regret. Even though I know there's absolutely no chance he'll say something he'll regret.

'And you know all about sadness, Sergeant. My God, your eyes. How do you even look in the mirror?'

'When did you go to bed?'

'But this isn't the sadness of your unrequited love for Detective Inspector Kallas, though, is it? This is older. This is the lifelong sadness of the true sufferer. What happened to you, Sergeant?'

'When did you go to bed?'

'Eleven-thirty. There's a camera in the foyer of the building, there are another two outside, there's one in the small car park beneath the building. You will be able to note that I neither came nor went all evening. As you will be able to do with Monday evening, when, if one is to accept what has been written in the newspapers, Julia was killed.'

'The cameras were deactivated all weekend. There is no record.'

Another pause, another one of those silences.

'Well, look at that,' he says. 'I can't tell whether you're lying.'

He smiles guardedly, adds a small nod. A moment, his eyes drift to Kallas, and then he looks back to me, he holds that, and then he turns to the mirror. Impossible, of course, but somehow I know he'll be looking right at Eurydice. Going round the houses of the police squad on the investigation.

And finally he's back.

'The cameras are meaningless, nonetheless. As you will

surmise, I could steal down the outside of the building from my apartment, I could throw on a hat and a fake moustache and walk past the cameras, and perhaps I did do that, and now you will have to go through all the rubbish from the building to see if you can find a fake moustache and a discarded hat. Unless the cameras were really deactivated, in which case I obviously wouldn't have needed the fake moustache.'

'OK with the fake moustache…'

'You're a drinker, currently on the wagon,' he says. 'But it's a struggle, isn't it, Sergeant?'

'Tell me about Monday, start to finish. What did you do on Monday?'

'Your eyes are a book, a world of tales and experience and painful retrospection. I hope this case doesn't push you back over the edge. Sometimes it can take so little. How is it with you, Sergeant?'

'Monday,' says Kallas, the word delivered in the familiar monotone.

Dr Thebes does not take his eyes off me. Focussed and searching, burrowing inside my head.

'Not so unrequited after all,' he says.

17

He's right. I'd love a drink. Intense cases push me over the edge. For sobriety I need calm and order. One day blending dully into the next. Nothing happening. That's who I am.

Perhaps there are others in my position who need stimulus. They need things to be happening to keep their mind off it, to get their buzz by some other means. Not me, though. I need the repetition of familiarity. I need zero stress.

I wonder if I would drink if I had Thebes' life. An activity to do every day. Simple, yet absorbing. No outside pressure. The jigsaw, while being in a different league to his model making perfection, is at least mentally of a similar construct. The absorption, the detachment from stress and reality.

Perhaps that's who the Jigsaw Man is. A recovering alcoholic, hiding in a corner of a small café in the centre of Glasgow.

Of course, I'm projecting no outside pressure on Thebes, because he looks like the type of fellow who is completely in control. He will be given a commission. He will estimate how long it will take, more or less to the hour. That is how long it will take him. He will dispatch the finished article. He will be paid. The notion that someone could be calling him up, hassling him, shouting, demanding, is inconceivable.

Could that be my life? A mundane but delicate task. Day after day. Listening to melancholic music in the evening? I know those Sinatra albums, but only because Dylan mimicked them. *Shadows In The Night*. An album of gloomy fifties Sinatra songs. Has melancholy coming out its arse. Right up my street. Tried listening to the Sinatra originals and hated them. Lush and syrupy. I thought Bob did them better because his voice is so rough. Can't sing for biscuits. If you're a Sinatra fan, Bob's versions probably make you want to flamethrow the CD player.

No. The life of Thebes could not be mine. The best part of the narrative description of his Friday evening was the two glasses of Chablis. *That* I could imagine.

'You will go to a meeting this evening,' says Kallas.

I don't reply. I don't want to go to a meeting this evening. I want to wallow. I want to let him win. I want to let him under my skin. Fuck, man, the guy's already under my skin. Let it roll.

'You must.'

*

We're on a field trip. Dispatched by Eurydice to the provinces to speak to witnesses.

'That was good questioning, Sergeant,' Eurydice said. 'He is so naturally and effortlessly guarded it barely seems he's trying. But slowly he reveals himself. It's good.'

She recognises the danger in him, however, and so rather than having Kallas and me sitting in there, being batted around the room, she's sent us to speak to Marc Johnson and Daisy Johnson, Benjamin Wright, and the session clerk at Julia Wright's church, John Abercrombie.

Eurydice has talked to them all, of course. We read the reports, we know what they said. We're not necessarily looking to pick holes in their testimony. They're not suspects, as such, any more than anyone else is a suspect at this point, and considerably less than Dr Thebes is a suspect. But it would appear that Daisy Johnson was as close to having a friend as Jennifer Talbot allowed herself; what Benjamin Wright knows about his wife that we don't will be limitless; and church officers know things. They hear things. Everything official that happens at a church will pass through them, and everything unofficial, the stories on the margins, will find them just the same.

*

Standing at a window in a large sitting room, looking out on a long stretch of garden down to Gare Loch, where it joins the Firth of Clyde. Rhu Marina to the right, the cold, grey sea before us, where the submarines pass on their way out into the world. At the end of the garden, on the left, the boathouse where Jennifer Talbot lived for the last three years.

An elegant sitting room, speaking of travel and wealth. Maps on the walls, a standing globe in the corner. Bookshelves on two walls. Two elegant sofas, a high-backed armchair, a coffee table of dark wood in the middle of the room, on a richly detailed rug, that one imagines, because of the surroundings, must have come from a market in old Damascus, long before the fall of Syria. But who knows? Maybe they got it in the Barras. Or IKEA.

Mrs Johnson is making tea. I would have said no, but Kallas accepted the offer, and so tea it is. We drove down here mostly in silence. We are so shit at this.

'It is interesting that the British government placed a nuclear arms facility so near to a major population centre,' says Kallas, suddenly.

There are no submarines currently in sight – after all, it's not as though there are a hundred of them or anything – but it's not an unreasonable thing to think about down here.

'We got here in forty-five minutes from Glasgow. That seems close. An independent Scotland will not want such weapons on their territory, no?'

'That's the plan,' I say. 'Nevertheless, the road to independence will be paved with quid pro quos.'

'Time will tell,' she says.

The door opens behind us, and Daisy Johnson enters carrying a tray. Three mugs, a plate of chocolate brownies. That's good. Starving. I will feast upon those brownies.

We settle down in triangle formation, me in the armchair, the ladies on separate sofas, mugs of tea. I take a small plate and a large brownie, Kallas, inevitably, does not.

Daisy Johnson looks tired and sad. So often we interview people in these little crime dramas of ours – and what of them are ever so grand and so magnificent that they will be passed down through the generations – and the people are guarded and wary, they do not give of themselves, so secretive and cautious, it is as though they barely cared. And maybe they don't. Maybe most people are so wrapped up in introspection, they care mostly for themselves.

Daisy Johnson, on the other hand, looks as though someone she cared about just died.

She does not take a brownie either. Nevertheless, I will eat my brownie, and I will not be bullied into brownie guilt by the society of chocolate baked confection deniers.

'Have you discovered who killed Jenny yet?' she asks.

Rightly, there will be no introductory small talk. We do need to get on, after all. Accordingly, with speed in mind, I take half the brownie in one bite.

'No,' says Kallas. 'As you will understand, the investigation is in its early stages.'

'The news said you had someone in custody?'

'We have a person of interest, but this person has not yet been charged.'

'Was it someone who knew her?'

'Did Jennifer ever mention to you that she was seeing someone?'

There's the question, there's the look. The shadow across the eyes. What did *that* mean?

'How d'you mean?'

'Did she mention that she was in a sexual relationship?'

She lifts the tea but is obviously not used to drinking it when it's so hot, as she flinches at the touch of the mug on her lips. Meanwhile, the hungry detective sergeant pops the rest of the brownie and eyes the plate, wondering how he can help himself to more without breaking the delicate atmosphere that has arisen out of nowhere after one question. Probably best to accept that I can't.

'No.'

'You were close friends?'

Again, no immediate answer. This woman has was-having-sex-with-the-victim-unknown-to-her-husband written all over her, which of course throws her into the suspect ring.

'She was... yes, we were friends. I don't think Jennifer was capable of being too close to anyone, however. She'd spent so much of her life alone. She was very self-sufficient.'

'You were not upset that your husband offered the property to his ex-wife?'

She laughs ruefully, shakes her head. She's answered this already with Eurydice, but she obviously doesn't mind. She *wants* to talk about Jennifer Talbot.

'I was so pissed off. I mean, can you imagine? Marc can be such an unthinking idiot sometimes. He has an idea, it seems practical and logical, and he never, *never*, brings any kind of sensibility to it.'

'And how did you handle that?'

She laughs again, smiles, lowers her head, stares at the IKEA rug.

'Well, I was determined to be angry. I was so determined. I thought, I will get close to her, I will make her life

---

106

uncomfortable, she will not get to enjoy her stay, she will not get to insidiously insinuate her way back into Marc's life. It was my imagination, running wild, it was running wild. I had all kind of movie situations playing in my head.' She laughs, laughing sadly at herself. 'And then, I don't know, we'd spent fifteen minutes together and... I was in awe. She was extraordinary. The things she'd done. But still, I thought, don't let her win you over, that'll all be part of the plan. But you know, I doubt she and Marc have spoken more than a handful of times these last three years. Even if she joined us for lunch, which didn't happen often, they were completely disinterested in each other.'

'Perhaps the disinterest was faked,' says Kallas. 'Part of the plan.'

'To have an affair behind my back? Really? Marc wouldn't give a shit. He'd bang his PA where you're sitting right now, while I drank tea. He's spent six years ignoring my feelings. I don't know why he would've thought any different of relations with Jenny.'

'Did Jennifer ever talk about the rowing club?'

Daisy Johnson stares vacantly across the room, not reading anything into the change of subject.

'I know she went. She enjoyed it, getting out on the water. It kept her fit. But she never spoke about the people. I never got the impression she really talked to anyone there.' The stare across the room is still the stare out to sea, settling on nothing, focussed only on the woman who's no longer here. 'That was Jenny. All those stories, the tales of the sea, the scents of faraway lands carried on the wind... they were never about people. It was like she met no one. It was all about wind and waves, and sea creatures, and rocky cliffs appearing out of the mist, and deserted sun-kissed sandy beaches lined with palm trees.'

'Did she ever mention a Dr Crispin Thebes?'

Brought back from her faraway, sun-kissed beach, she stares at Kallas, thinking about the name, perhaps plucking it out the air because she wasn't fully paying attention when the question was asked.

'Who's that?'

'Did Jennifer ever mention that name?'

'Really? No. I think I'd remember.'

'Why d'you think Jennifer was taking so long to go back to sea?' I ask, first time I've spoken, tossing the question into the mix from the side-lines.

The careful thought, the question she will have been considering long before Jennifer was murdered.

'It takes time to repair a yacht. It had seen a lot, after all.'

Such a basic and obvious lie. It at least points to everything else she's been saying as being the truth.

'Might it have been because of you?' asks Kallas.

'Why?'

Suddenly, injected with a need for plain-speaking, so we can get on with this business, I say, 'Because you were in a relationship, Mrs Johnson.'

She looks at me, looks at Kallas, back to me. Faced with two brilliant officers so obviously on top of the situation who know more than she can understand us knowing, she has no lie to retreat to. She nods, her head lowers.

Kallas and I share a quick glance. Well, Dr Thebes was on the money. Daisy Johnson may not have known about him, but he knew what he was talking about in relation to her.

I don't know if he's guilty, although I have to agree with Eurydice that it all points in his direction, but even if he's not, it feels like the path to the killer still goes through him.

'Do you think she was too scared to return to the sea?' I ask.

'What?'

'That she was burned out, that the years alone on the ocean, weeks on end out of sight of land, had taken their toll?'

She does not really know what to do with this either, and although she does not immediately jump to deny it, it's also clearly not a thought she's ever had before.

'Where are you getting this stuff?' she asks, her voice small, confused.

The door opens, and she positively jumps out of her skin, gasping lightly, putting her hand to her chest. Marc Johnson glances at her with just the right amount of contempt, then looks at Kallas and I.

'What'd I miss?' he says.

18

The drink oozes out of Benjamin Wright. I can tell we won't be here long. Kallas won't have it. She'll know what I'm thinking, she'll know I'm sitting here breathing in the fumes, the smell of the cheap vodka stupidly intoxicating. I mean, the guy smells like he's spent the days since his wife got murdered getting absolutely fucked out of his face. Let's not get carried away about how great that smells. Yankee Candle ain't going to be adding it to their repertoire, that's for sure. But for me? Running around on the three-wheeled wagon, waiting for it to topple over at any moment? The slightest suggestion of drink is the siren's call.

'I don't know,' he says, his voice with a solid hint of persecution, the tone of someone who thinks everyone's against them. *Why me?* he cries to the night. *Why me?* 'She always worked hard, always did far too much. For years I'd be like, really, you're going out again? But it was what she did. And then the virus arrived, and the church closed down, and for a while... ha! For a while, I thought, maybe we'll actually get something of a life together. It can be what it was like back in the day. I mean, before that first commission, before the church took over. But no, it turned out she gave herself even more work to do. So many people suffering, so many people lonely. *I will be there for them all*, that's what she said. *I will be there for them all*. I don't know how many of them regularly attended on a Sunday morning before all this shit started, but last time I asked, which was last summer some time, they had five hundred and seventeen members. That's an awful lot of people.' Head shake, a look around the room – with the eyes of a man looking for his next drink – another head shake, possibly at the fact he doesn't spot any alcohol. His previous consumption has, at least, loosened his tongue.

On the drive here Kallas said she appreciated the blunt questioning. It had worked well. Do it again.

Here goes.

'Was it always work that kept her out in the evening?'

He lifts a quick finger, wags it above the table.

'Oh no, you're not going there. I've had that for four days now. Four days. There was no one else. That was not – *was not* – who Julia was. She was a good wife. She cared about people. She would never… she would never have done anything like that.'

'Do you know the name Dr Crispin Thebes?' I ask.

Sometimes one might be reticent about throwing names around, even though the question needs to be asked. People can go online and look folk up, they can ask around, they can start digging, it has potential, at least, to be a little uncomfortable. This does not apply to Dr Thebes. No online presence, no friends. He also wouldn't care. There would be no agitated phone call from Dr Thebes saying, *I can't believe you've done that*.

'Who's that?'

'You never heard that name?'

'Would I be asking who it was if I had?'

The liar will often ask such a question, so yes, you would. Kallas and I stare across the table. The drink-soaked widower stares back. On this occasion, in relation to Dr Thebes at least, I do not think he's lying. Nevertheless, even the genius detective such as myself can be wrong sometimes, so I must persevere.

'Dr Thebes states that he was having an affair with your wife.'

He stares at me, that curious look of the dumbfounded. When it's not genuine, it can take a bit of acting. I don't sense that in him.

'Fuck off,' he says. Not aggressive, more incredulous. A you're-kidding-me kind of a fuck off.

'Dr Thebes states he was having an affair with your wife,' says Kallas, more or less word for word repeating me, and he switches his look from me to her.

'Really? What? I mean, who even is this guy?'

'There was a gift given to a retiring church elder, Mr McDonald. He was a yacht hobbyist. John Abercrombie arranged for a replica model of his yacht to be made.'

'I remember.'

'Dr Thebes made the model.'

He still looks incredulous. He's playing a blinder. This is Paul Rudd convincingly pulling off an ant-sized superhero level of acting. If it's acting.

'Wait, what? I remember the boat. I remember... I mean, I remember Julia saying they'd got some guy to make it. But, I mean, what? They were having a... wait, what? You can't say shit like that just because she *knew* him. I mean, really? Are you going to say she was having an affair with the guy who did maintenance on the church's sound system?'

Kallas and I answer in joint silence.

'I mean, what?' says the confused widower.

*

'People are heinous.' John Abercrombie. Banking executive; church officer at St Andrews; bit of a dick. 'They are malicious, and they are gossipy, and they are small-minded. You know, I would sit in that church every Sunday, listening to Julia, listening to the words of the Lord, and I would think, is anybody, *anybody*, listening to this? And you know what? I very much doubt that they were.'

He looks between Kallas and I. We're sitting in his office, all three of us wearing mouth and nose coverings. We're at that stage with the masks where some expect it, some demand it, some don't care. We, the police, vaccinated all round, have to go with the flow. Come prepared, for when interviewees insist.

Don't get me wrong, I don't judge. I mean, obviously *I judge*, but not about masks.

It does, however, make it easier to lie, so there's that.

'And my God, the session meetings we'd have. And once they started happening over Zoom, good grief. They made those viral parish council meetings that everyone talks about, seem like a stoned-out orgy in Haight-Ashbury in the summer of '67.'

He used the same Haight-Ashbury line when talking to Eurydice. He must think we don't speak to each other, that we don't write reports.

'You think all the talk of Julia's promiscuity was malicious?'

'Yes! Good grief, yes! Oh, my goodness, these people, they were... they *are* outrageous. There are many things in life to test one's faith, but nothing quite like the people who supposedly share your beliefs. They never cease to stagger me.'

'You are familiar with Dr Crispin Thebes?' I ask.

Not so blunt and out of the blue as my first questions to the others, as it was Abercrombie who mentioned his name in the first place.

'The model maker. Exceptional man. At least, a man with an exceptional talent, even if it is rather a trivial one. You've spoken to him?'

'Yes, we have. He informed us he'd been having an affair with Julia.'

His brow furrows, his pompous windbaggery appears to have been punctured. He leans forward slowly, settling on his elbows. His hand, now with a bit of a shake to it, removes his mask.

Oh, that reminds me of something. I know. Hitler, when he removes his glasses in that *Downfall* clip everyone spoofs. I haven't seen the movie, just several hundred send-ups of that scene. Maybe I'll watch the actual film one day. Somebody I slept with once said it was good. Can't remember who.

'That's not...' he begins, but doesn't appear to have anywhere to go with that. 'He said... em, I don't think... you know that, you know, Julia was a minister. She had made, you know, we all make vows, all of us who are married, but she had made... *she was a minister*. Don't tell me things like that. At least, not and expect me to believe it.'

'You think Dr Thebes is fabricating an affair with Julia?'

'Yes!' he bursts forth. 'Yes, I do! Obviously, he's fabricating it. Julia hardly knew him. I mean, she met him once. Once! I barely met him, and I was the one dealing with him. It's absurd.'

'Why would he make something like that up?' I ask. 'It involves him in her life, it implicates him. Why make the police suspicious of your actions when you have nothing to hide?'

The pompous windbag is back. He laughs, he smirks, he shakes his head, he pulls his mask back on far more deliberately than the affected way in which he took it off.

'You will have to ask him,' he says, 'because I'm sure I don't know.' He looks from me to Kallas, back again. 'Like I said, people are... malicious.' A pause. 'People are small-minded.'

19

It is after six o'clock by the time we get back to Dalmarnock. No further progress has been made in our absence. Eurydice attempted to speak to Dr Thebes, once again he refused. There have been no further murders with a similar m.o., nothing further to implicate anyone other than Dr Thebes in the murders, nor to implicate Dr Thebes himself.

Eurydice does not see the point in speaking any more to him this evening and wants to resume in the morning. She's still talking to the lawyers. I can see she has an air of defeat. She does not think she's going to be able to hold on to him. Not that anyone believes he's going anywhere when he's released. He's going back to his apartment, and if we don't return the tools to him straight away – which we won't – the likelihood is that he'll order more of them, listening to Sinatra while he waits for them to arrive.

We ought, at least, to make sure the press don't get hold of his name. They haven't yet, and given the stink of these two murders, they're feverishly trying to find out. They won't give a fuck if he's guilty, they'll be out for blood, in their all-too-familiar way. Eurydice runs a tight ship, however. There are not many people in on the current incarceration of Dr Thebes, for exactly this reason.

And so, DI Kallas and I are back in Cambuslang, looking over any on-going business we might have wanted to take care of. We needn't have done, it not being expected of us since we're fully seconded to the double murder investigation. Kallas, however, is just that type of person. Me? I'm just here because it feels too early to go home. I don't know what to do with evenings that start at six p.m.

Kallas sits in the seat opposite, the one that was, when we returned, occupied by DC Ritter. DC Ritter has now gone off for the evening, however, as she is due back in tomorrow morning at eight.

'How are things?' asks Kallas.

'Things are quiet,' I say.

'You did not need to come back.'

'Neither did you.'

We hold the familiar gaze across the desk, and then she looks at the clock.

'Your meeting starts in twenty minutes. You do not want to be late.'

'Yeah, I'm just heading. I'll be off shortly.'

'You are lying. I will accompany you to make sure you go. You are doing well, but we all know the temptation that grabs you and pulls you down, particularly during an intense investigation such as this one.'

You'd think when you listened to people lie every day as part of your job, you'd know how to do it properly yourself. But apparently not.

'I'll be fine.'

'I have watched you all day. I will accompany you.'

'Eileen is…' and I look around the office.

'I spoke to Eileen. She is in Stirling on a work-related matter.'

'Stirling. That's only like –'

'She will not be back here until after nine o'clock. I will accompany you to the meeting. We can talk about the case. You will go to the meeting. I will take you home. You will have an early start tomorrow, and you cannot afford to start drinking, Tom. Do not let Dr Thebes get to you.'

We do our thing. The stare across the desk thing. There must be some historical or literary reference for this. Some great, doomed lovers of old I can compare us to. All I've got is Fred and Daphne in Scooby Doo, and that's probably not appropriate.

'I can go on my own,' I say. 'It's fine, you don't have to worry about me.'

'I will come.'

'What about Anders? He'll be expecting you back. You need to see your children.'

'DCI Hamilton informed me I could take tomorrow off. I do not think she has given you that luxury. I will have all tomorrow to spend with Anders and the children. I do not think… I do not think that Anders will care. The children might, although I believe we all, in society, overestimate how much time children over the age of four want to spend with their parents.'

She pauses. Time moving on, as it does, slowly, quickly, whateverly.

'I will be fine. My family will be fine. I am not so sure about you, so I will spend this evening making sure, as much as I can, that you will be fine.'

'I will be.'

'Dr Thebes is a particular man. Gifted, in many ways.'

Another pause. There's something else she wants to say, and she hesitates. This is not just natural Estonian hesitation.

She swallows. She looks at the clock.

'We should go. There might be traffic.'

'Say it,' I say boldly.

We know each other well enough that she knows what I mean. She knows that I recognise she's not saying everything that's just come to mind.

'We should go.'

'After you've said the thing.'

'Very well.' A beat. 'Dr Thebes sees through us. I do not know if other people see through us so easily. Perhaps they do. But Dr Thebes says the uncomfortable out loud, and now I have said it out loud, and these are the things that lead to alcohol. I will accompany you this evening and will make sure you do not drink.'

He sees through us.

He certainly does. And he does it a lot better than I do.

20

Saturday morning. Awake at five-thirty. Stare at the ceiling, and the grey light of dawn. Lift my phone and scroll through social media, anything to occupy my mind. It all seems bland and uninteresting. I lay down the phone, resume staring at the ceiling.

I get up at twelve minutes past six. Cold water on face, brush teeth, into the shower, get dressed, into the kitchen. Drink a long glass of cold water, get the kettle going, put two spoonfuls of coffee in the cafetiere. Look in the cupboard. The only cereal is Shredded Wheat.

I was talking to Rebecca. My twenty-four-year-old daughter who buys me jigsaws. She made me list my five favourite breakfast cereals. I don't have five favourite breakfast cereals. I said Shredded Wheat, she lambasted me for even including it as a food substance, and so I, in the light-hearted spirit of the conversation, moved it to number one on the list. The next day she sent me a box of Shredded Wheat by DHL.

It was funny, it was almost worth the cost of DHL for the gag, but it's sat unopened in the cupboard ever since. So, now I open it. I have no idea what one does with Shredded Wheat, but fortunately there's a picture on the back of the box with two Shredded Wheat in a bowl with some milk and the words *serving suggestion* beneath. I mean, thank God, right? If it hadn't been for that I'd likely have deep-fried them or eaten them with curry sauce.

I eat Shredded Wheat and drink coffee, and stare out of the window at a cold, bright morning in April, and at some point I remember I'm going to have to walk into work, as I left my car there yesterday when Kallas drove me to the meeting before bringing me home, and that has me thinking about her *he sees through us* line, which makes me think I'm in the middle of an old-fashioned melancholic episode of doomed love, which at least takes my mind off the Shredded Wheat.

Third cup of coffee of the day, me and Eurydice in the canteen. The place is relatively quiet, we're sitting by a window, looking down on the river. About to go back in with Thebes, although there's a curious feeling around it, like an awareness of its pointlessness. Ostensibly we're here to talk before I go in, but she's been silent and distracted since we sat down, and only slowly have I realised that if we're to talk, I need to rescue her from whatever ruminations have taken hold. Usually in a work situation, I'm happy with any silence. Particularly when it's accompanied by a view over a river and a cup of coffee.

'How are you getting on with Dr Thebes' backstory?'

A moment, she seems to become aware that I spoke, she searches the last five seconds for the remembrance of what I said, then nods at her return to the table, takes a drink of coffee, and says, 'Bits, here and there. I mean, it's fair enough. There are plenty of people who will make absolutely sure there's nothing of themselves on the Internet. Why wouldn't you, it's a shitshow out there?'

'Yeah. And I can imagine he's built a pretty good reputation for himself. Word'll have got around.'

'That's about the size of it. So, far as we know, he went to Gordonstoun School at the age of fourteen. He doesn't appear to have existed before the age of fourteen. Then St Andrews for his degree, Oxford for his master's and PhD, then he ran a small art dealership in London for twenty years, and then he retired up here about five years ago. And this art dealership may have been small, but you can imagine the kind of mark-ups for the dealers that come with selling art.'

'And now he makes models…'

She takes another drink of coffee, nodding as she does so.

'Well, as you reported,' she says, 'he's currently making a model of the Andrea Doria for close on thirty thousand pounds, so let's not trivialise it as an occupation. He's getting paid a damn sight more per hour than you or I.'

She takes another drink. She's mainlining that coffee since she started drinking it. I guess it's nearly time to get on.

'We must give model making the respect it deserves, I guess,' I say.

'Nevertheless, although it would seem to suit one part of his personality, such as it presents itself – meaning the calm demeanour, the attention to detail, the exactness of everything he says and does – there are huge chunks of how he comes across that don't fit the mould of whatever one imagines a maker of models to be.'

'I don't know, maybe it's just private school assholery,' I say, bringing all my top psychological profiling to the table.

She smiles, shakes her head slowly.

'Private school assholery, eh?'

'I mean, you don't meet many of them around here, but it's that Conservative government minister thing, isn't it? Rees-Mogg and Johnson and whoever. Always act like you know you're right, never apologise, work off the basic assumption that you're better than everyone else. And while I grant you that our man doesn't exactly come across as a Tory government minister, maybe this is just how his natural air of superiority manifests itself.'

'As a psychopath?'

'Yeah.'

Coffee.

She gives this some thought, staring vaguely off to the side, nodding as she goes.

'I like that,' she says. 'There's no question there's an assuredness about him. An innate confidence that stems from that kind of education.' Her eyes return, she engages me across the table. 'I mean, I'd know.'

We share the look. Well, of course someone called Eurydice went to private school.

'Private school assholery isn't a patch on middle-aged white man assholery,' I say drily, and she laughs. 'It's when you combine the two that you get a perfect storm.'

Another laugh, and this time she stands, finishing her coffee as she does so, placing the cup on the table.

'Right then, Mr middle-aged white man asshole, let's go, you've got work to do.'

I finish my coffee, place the cup on the table, get to my feet. Find a little bit of Dr Crispin Thebes rubbing off on me, as I neatly push the chair beneath the table. I can see her still hanging on the end of the joke as we walk away, while I stare at the ground and start to get myself into the right place. Dealing with the well-organised, entirely functional, might-be psychopath.

Standing in the elevator to go down one floor, I stare

straight ahead at the door. The kind-of flirtatious conversation with Eurydice, the smiles and the jokes, the way she wears those white blouses, the outline of her white bra beneath, the curve of her breasts. *Fuck me.* Are there no unattractive women anymore, or is it just that I find all women attractive?

Perhaps I'm not a very reliable narrator.

'Head in the game?' says Eurydice.

I nod silently. The door to the elevator opens.

21

We're staring at each other across the desk. Dr Thebes and me. Locked into our parts. The investigator, tasked with breaking through the impenetrable barrier; the murder suspect, utterly implacable, apparently with nothing to hide.

Dr Thebes is the kind of guy you want on your side when you're going into battle. There's an air of the Bond about him. And I mean, the old Bond, the Connery Bond, the character who just knows he's untouchable. Always in control, always the central character in any situation, always coming out on top. Except, there's no such character in real life. The untouchable protagonist is a thing of fiction.

And so, perhaps, this is the perfect place for Dr Thebes. He's not a spy, he's not a soldier, he's not getting into Tom Cruise action hero shit, where he could actually be harmed. All he does is sit at a desk making models. There's your action hero, people. All this, all this bullshit: the command performance, the sneer without a sneer, the disdain without disdain, the all-knowing, all-seeing air of dominion, it's just an act.

So, he understands people? So, he worked out I fell for the attractive detective inspector? So, he knows I'm an alcoholic? The man is well-educated, classically trained. He's been out in the world; he knows how it works. Big fucking deal. Let's see how he gets on acting like this in the middle of a pub fight on the Gallowgate on a Saturday night.

I'm convincing no one. This guy would boss a pub fight on the Gallowgate on a Saturday night. And yet, and yet, he's a model maker, that's all.

'Do you know if either Julia or Jennifer talked to anyone else about your relationships?'

The question greeted with the regulation period of silence. The silence that is wrestled over, as he asserts his dominance.

'I feel we may have covered this already.'

'You know how this goes,' I say. 'We ask the same questions repeatedly over three days, waiting for the moment you answer inconsistently. The inconsistency is the crack in the wall, at which we start hammering.'

His eyes acknowledge the blunt honesty.

'I like you, Sergeant.'

'Fuck off. Do you know if either Julia or Jennifer talked to anyone else about your relationships?'

'Jennifer may, I suppose, have talked to Daisy Johnson. As I said, you would have to ask her, which I presume you've done by now. In fact, I presume you yourself may have done it yesterday. So, you will know better than I whether or not Jennifer talked to Mrs Johnson.' A moment, he is considering the situation we're in, he's considering me as a person and an interviewer, then he decides to go a little further. 'Jennifer had gone a long time without male companionship. She got that from me without fear of complication. Julia, of course, was a completely different circumstance. A different person, a different situation. She was married, she was having sex with her husband. I was, therefore, an extra.'

'Why?'

'I don't know. I never really stopped to wonder why.'

'Perhaps you could do it now.'

He holds my gaze across the table for a moment. For a moment? The gaze never leaves. Perhaps he's genuinely considering Julia Wright's motivation, perhaps he's just deciding what to tell us. Perhaps those calculations have all been made lying alone in a cell at night, staring into the dark.

I believe that he doesn't care whether he's charged with murder. I believe he wouldn't care if he went on trial, either way, guilty or not guilty. He will do whatever needs to be done when he gets up in the morning. He is bigger than this.

'She told me she and her husband had been unable to have children. This was him, rather than her. She'd wanted children when they got married, and she'd had to give up that particular dream. While she was not sleeping with me in the hope of getting pregnant, perhaps there was something inside her, something that blamed her husband, a deep psychology that said her husband was inadequate. She said they continued to have sex, but she may have been lying. People lie, after all. What's the cause of *your* trauma, Sergeant, I'd really like to know? Perhaps I can help you.'

'You have a degree in art history,' I say, allowing myself to be drawn into the sudden change of subject.

'And you will judge me on it?'

'Do you think Julia was having sex with anyone else?'

'You mean, me and her husband and a third man?' Another one of those small, knowing smiles. 'A third man, what a wonderful concept, isn't it? So evocative. Are you familiar with Plato's Third Man Argument?'

'You're fucking hilarious,' I say, immediately annoyed at allowing myself to get annoyed. Got to rein it in.

'I do not know if there was a third man,' he says prosaically.

'From what you know of Julia, do you think it possible?'

'This is interesting. Are you searching for another motive for why I might have wanted to kill her, or are you searching for another suspect? Am I in position to be able to say, well, I think she might have been sleeping with Mr X, and off you'll scurry to see what you can dig up? This trauma of yours, deep-seated, I think. Old. It has plagued you for some –'

'We're not trying to lead anyone anywhere; we're not trying to invent suspects. We just need to know the truth about you, and about the women with whom you were involved, and who are now dead. Do you think Julia was the type of person to have been having sex with someone else?'

'Of course,' he answers, this time without hesitation.

'Of course?'

'Yes. Extra marital affairs are like… guns.'

I look deadpan across the desk. He smiles.

'They say there are more guns in the United States than there used to be, but they're in the hands of a smaller percentage of the population. If someone owns a gun, they're more likely to get another gun than the guy next door is to get his first gun. It's the same with affairs. There are the types of people who would have an affair, and the types who wouldn't. If you're the former, when you've done it once, you're far more likely to do it again than the person who hasn't done it yet. This is how the world works.'

There he goes, reaching into my head, spreading the contents around on the desk.

'Ever been married, Sergeant?' he asks.

*

Saturday passes, a long tiring day, me and Thebes looking across the desk at each other. I know we're going to get to nine-fifteen and we're going to have to release him. It is all but guaranteed. I get the feeling that if it was entirely up to her, Eurydice would issue charges, and hold him until the trial. She's not messing around, and she's convinced. The lawyers, however, have not seen enough. And we know they've not seen enough.

We spent, Dr Thebes and I, some time talking about the third woman. His third woman. He is completely in control, and if there's the slightest hint of a breakthrough, it's because he wants there to be. Which means it's no breakthrough at all. And on the matter of the third woman, we ultimately get nothing.

We like each other, Thebes and I, even though he's a double murder suspect. Nevertheless, I don't care either way. Fact is, if we didn't like each other, I wouldn't be here. If we didn't like each other, he wouldn't even be speaking to me, and would have blessed some other detective with his favours.

Ultimately, however, there's nowhere for this to go. He controls this narrative the way Rupert Murdoch controls the minds of fifty percent of the planet.

Seven-fifteen, coffee break. I've come through to the room on the other side of the mirror, while Dr Thebes remains in place, sitting at the table, staring straight ahead. Aware, from the clock high on the wall, that we have two hours left before we will release him.

He doesn't do the thing of turning occasionally and looking at the mirror. Looking through it, into the heart of the operation behind: the small room, the monitors, the laptops, the low hum of air conditioning, the smell of coffee.

I just came in, now standing by the door, hands in pockets, looking at Eurydice and Blumenthal. Thought there might have been others in here, but I guess everyone has better things to do on a Saturday evening. We're at the stage where it's hardly worth keeping a troupe in here at this time of the weekend. If there's anything that requires further analysing, it's all being recorded in any case.

'You're doing a decent job in a hopeless task, Sergeant,' she says.

I'm tired, had enough for the day. We all know there will be no last-minute victory. No goal in the fifth minute of injury time, no flurry of wickets, no holed bunker shot on the 18th at Augusta.

'We have a little headway on Dr Thebes' work connections,

at least. You may as well take this in with you for the final run.'

'Who came through?'

'HMRC. Someone higher up must have called someone else higher up, paths were smoothed over. Not sure how that happened so quickly, and a little surprised to be honest, but we do not need to reason or wonder why.'

She hands me a sheet with a list of payments, alongside the business, individual or organisation from whom it came. There have been twenty-three such transactions in the past five years.

'Go with that, see where it gets you. Either way we'll start speaking to these people tomorrow and Monday. It's a wide net, but this has been a wide net operation so far, so why change now?'

I finish looking through the list with little enthusiasm. At least it's something else to talk to him about. And really, this man gets paid an amazing amount of money for making model boats.

'You have no optimism about this,' says Blumenthal.

'Not really, though I agree it needs to be done.'

Look up, take the two of them in with a look, get another waft of coffee. How many cups have I had today? Eight maybe? Perhaps I'll sleep tonight. Perhaps I won't. I have to call Eileen when this is over and she's going to insert herself in my Saturday evening, whether I like it or not.

They don't do this every weekend, Eileen and DI Kallas, but it's like they have a different operating manual for me when there's a major murder investigation taking place. And, after all, it's not like I usually *fall* off the wagon in these circumstances; I dive heard first off the wagon.

So, Eileen knows when the doctor will be getting ejected from the building, she knows when I'm likely to be free, and she's going to make sure I don't drink.

As a result, unusually, I'm not even really thinking about it. I mean, I'd love it 'n' all, the thought of going home and cracking open a bottle of wine, sitting at my wee table looking down on my wee patch of the world, is so glorious that it fills me with warmth just thinking about it. But it ain't happening, so this evening I'm not tormenting myself. Trying not to torment myself. Eileen is never shaken off, so she'll come back to mine, maybe we'll sit and eat dinner together, we'll talk about God knows what, then she'll make a judgement on whether she thinks I can be trusted not to head out as soon as she's gone.

After this day, sitting in there with that guy, I'm just exhausted. All I really want is bed.

'You thinking the same thing about Jennifer Talbot that I'm thinking?' says Eurydice.

'I found out about her entirely by chance,' I answer, like she's testing me to see if I've correctly established the flaw in this new plan. 'I could have spoken to the rowing club chairman rather than the captain, and maybe he'd have had no idea that Thebes and Talbot spoke to one another. So, it's going to be the same wherever we go, whoever we speak to. So, Thebes had a commission from such and such a museum? We maybe identify someone he developed an intimate relationship with, but the odds are slim. Ultimately, we're going to have to throw a fuck-tonne of resource at every one of these places, and we're not going to be able to do that in…,' check the clock, 'the next two hours.'

I realise I'm being overly negative, and I dispatch the negativity with a casual wave.

'Granted,' she says, nodding, 'but it's all we've got for now. Cup of coffee?'

'Love one, thanks,' I say, and Blumenthal automatically fills the assigned roll of a senior detective sergeant by getting up off his seat to make me one.

'There's also the possibility,' I continue, clinging on to the negativity for a little bit longer, 'that he's lying about the third woman. Or, of course, that he's lying about sleeping with the first two.'

She lets out a long sigh, nodding her way through it as she does so.

'He's a piece of work, I'll give him that.'

'Will you put a car on his building from tonight?'

'Already got it set up,' she says. 'And we'll have someone across the river keeping an eye out. It's hardly completely covered, and he could do all sorts of things to elude us if that's what he wants to do, but we'll cover him best we can, while trying to keep it low key.'

'He'll know.'

'I don't doubt it.'

Blumenthal hands me a mug of coffee. As ever with this guy the coffee has exactly the right amount of milk. I lift my eyebrows at Eurydice to ask if there are any further instructions, she shakes her head and gestures towards our suspect, then, as

I'm about to leave the room and head back, Thebes finally turns and looks directly through the mirror. Like he knows. Like he can sense the disturbance in the Force.

Cold, blue eyes, slowly sweeping the room, every now and again falling on one of the three of us.

'Jesus,' I say. 'Let's get this over with.'

And off I go.

22

Gone eleven. Eileen and I, sitting at my small table, eating Asian takeaway. We got a meal for two, which saved thinking about what to order. Coke Zero all round.

I'm knackered, and Dr Thebes is back out in the wild. Just because my chances of success were incredibly low, does not mean that I don't feel the weight of the failure.

'You look terrible,' she says.

Here we are, settled in with our food, Dylan's *Rough And Rowdy Ways* playing quietly in the background, Lady Agnew of Lochnaw peeping at us from beneath a couple of place mats.

'Thanks, Sergeant, I do what I can. You're looking pretty tired yourself.'

'All happening in Cambuslang,' she says.

Rice, sauce, chicken onto the fork, nod, try to focus on the conversation.

'What'd I miss?'

'I've got an enthralling embezzlement case. Three sons arguing with each other, two of them arguing with their mother, the other one turns out to be having an affair with the mother, though under further review at least it was revealed she was his stepmother rather than biological, and it all kicked off after the dad died of Covid last year, something one of the sons is getting the blame for.'

'There's a lot to unpack there.'

'As they say, nowatimes.'

She eats beef in a dark sauce.

'Did you just say nowatimes?'

'I did.' She continues eating.

'Is that a thing people say now, or...'

'Slip of the tongue.'

'Right.'

'It's a shitshow. And, you won't be surprised to hear, none of them are nice people. None of them. But crime has, no doubt, been committed, and someone has to look into that crime, even

---

127

if the victims are as unpleasant as the accused. I'll tell you what though, it ain't making anyone's crime novel plotline.'

'Wait until someone gets murdered.'

'No one's getting murdered. It's not that kind of story. It's just sad and seedy and depressing. But hey, that's the job description, right?'

'Boo-yah!'

We clink glasses. Nothing says *booyah* like toasting with a zero-calorie soft drink.

'You didn't have to come, you know,' I say. 'I'm good for nothing except collapsing into bed this evening.'

'I like the unwinding,' she says. 'And anyway, I'd have Kadri to answer to if I didn't look after you. I don't want your girlfriend shouting at me.'

She uses the girlfriend line sometimes. As ever I give her the rueful smile, she replies with the cheeky smile, and on we go with the meal. The scoop of slop, the crunch of prawn cracker, the emptiness of any meal eaten without alcohol.

'You can crash here if you like,' I say. 'I can sleep on the sofa.'

She nods along.

'Thanks. But I'll sleep on the sofa. Hundred percent. If you suggest otherwise, I'll tell Kadri we anally banged all night.'

Can't help laughing at that.

'Jesus, you're funny. Fine, you have the sofa.'

And she laughs with me, and so the evening goes.

*

When I wake in the morning, the alarm on my phone noisily interrupting the deepest of sleeps, I see that Eileen climbed into bed with me at some point. She stirs, back turned, we sort of acknowledge each other like an old married couple, and another day begins.

23

Thebes held firm right to the end, like we knew he would. His control never wavered. A professional.

Once he saw we were in possession of a list of his commissions, he was quite happy to talk about each one. The models, at least. He refused entirely to talk about the people. And naturally, he refused to reveal whether this third woman he claims to exist was someone he met as a result of one of these commissions.

So, that filled the better part of the last couple of hours, which, if nothing else, made a change. Gave us something to talk about. A model of the Waverley for the city's Riverside Museum, price twenty-five thousand pounds. Two models of the Titanic for the maritime museum in Falmouth, something about which he seemed dismissive – how mundane! – but a commission he accepted, nonetheless. One of the ship in its brief pomp, one of it as it now rests at the bottom of the ocean. Maybe he needed the money, maybe he owed someone a favour. Although that would be some favour, where they pay you ninety-one thousand pounds for you to do it for them. The Santa Maria, an eighteenth-century Portuguese packet ship out of Lisbon, and the HMS Agincourt, a WWI dreadnought, for the Imperial War Museum in London, and on and on. The man has contacts, and he has a reputation.

Just how many contacts, and exactly just what reputation, we are about to find out.

*

I get to Dalmarnock. Eight-twenty-eight. Contemplate getting the first coffee of the day from the canteen, decide instead to head straight to the ops room, see the lay of the land, get my instructions for the day.

I noted that Thebes had made a model of a WWII minesweeper for the maritime museum in the Finnish city of

Turku. Now I'm an educated chap, I like to think, but I have to admit, I ain't ever heard of no Turku. Turns out to be Finland's second city. Their football team must be one of those ones that gets knocked out of the Europa League in the first qualifying round in the middle of June, by some mob from Albania called Weetabix Tirana 1967.

When one thinks of it, I probably couldn't name anywhere in Finland other than Helsinki. Nevertheless, I think now might be the time for DI Kallas and me to travel out to Turku to investigate. Could be a valuable clue we miss if we don't.

The Sunday morning, hard core team is already here when I enter the room. Eurydice, in her familiar white blouse, sleeves rolled up, Blumenthal in his familiar blue shirt, and DI Kallas, looking as put together as ever. There are also three others present, faces I recognise, names I've forgotten or never learned.

I nod hellos all round, get a few in response. There's an air about the room, although I don't think it's particularly aimed at me. I have, after all, walked into a tonne of rooms in which everyone present thinks I'm a moron, and this isn't that.

'What'd I miss?'

I'd intended heading straight for the coffee machine but note upon entering that no one else has coffee. Not even Eurydice, who drinks more of it than I do.

'Fuck it,' she says, words not directed at me, instead at any nameless object on the desk she's standing beside.

I lift my eyebrows to the rest of the room. They were deferring to her, what with her being the boss, while she looks too angry to speak.

'Dr Thebes went home last night from the station,' says DI Kallas. 'We made sure he arrived, we stayed outside to make sure we would know when he left. He left the building at six a.m. this morning.'

She leaves it at that. She is Estonian, after all, and the rest of it tells itself.

'Ah.'

'Jesus fucking Christ,' says Eurydice. 'How can you lose a fucking guy at six o'clock in the morning in a deserted city? Fuck me, I'd be pissed off, but at least I'd understand, if it was rush hour, or lunchtime, or Saturday afternoon shopping, or Old Firm weekend or, I don't know, the fucking souk in Marrakesh. But Glasgow at six a-fucking-m on a Sunday?'

'They missed him leaving?'

'No. I mean, if the stupid fucker had fallen asleep, at least it'd be understandable. But, no, he was wide awake. Followed the doctor into town. The guy was carrying a shoulder bag. Big clue there. Somewhere between Central and Buchanan Street we lost him. Fucker could be anywhere...'

She lifts a mug and hurls it angrily at the floor. The mug noisily smashes, splinters flying.

Holy shit. This is some woman. The passion! She must be absolutely sensational in bed.

Not appropriate, huh?

'I'll get the coffee,' I say, flippantly. I mean, I'm not going to cower at her temper, am I? Who does that? 'Anyone else?'

Five hands go up. I have no idea how three of these people take their coffee.

'Fine,' says Eurydice, 'coffee's fine. But while we're drinking it, we need to get on with this shit. We need to get out there, and we need to find this third woman. We don't even know who it is, but she's in danger. And you know what, she's not even going to know.' A moment, then, 'I'll have a cappuccino, please.'

*

Half an hour later comes the big bang. Not the discovery of a third body, it being much too soon for that. This is an unexpected big bang. This is the big bang you don't see coming, *at all*. And really, when you're investigating murder, you're kind of ready for all sorts of shit. All sorts. The additional murder no one was expecting, the killing of a suspect, the sudden intervention of a completely unseen character. And while real life may not match the absurd caricatures of fiction, and more often than not we know right from the off who's guilty – it being more a matter of compiling a case – there's also far more likely to be a *deus ex machina*, a completely unanticipated turn outside the regular confines of the narrative. Because real life is like that. It doesn't have to meet the expectations of the reader.

But this? It's not even that. This borders on the bizarre, and yet, *and yet*, somehow not in the least surprising. In fact, it helps things make sense.

We're divvying up the day, going through the list of people with whom Thebes has done business, such as we have it. Most of them will require phone calls at this stage. Indeed, given that half of them are overseas, there will be no more than that, though we do need to get into whether or not Thebes will have travelled to any of these places. Outside possibility of needing to get Interpol involved. That won't be for the likes of me.

There are, however, six locations in Central Scotland, although again, each of these will inevitably start with a phone call. That small maritime museum in Edinburgh won't have been open in several months, never mind on a Sunday morning in April.

And, of course, we cannot put everything into chasing a possibly mythical third woman, when we are nowhere near finished investigating the lives of the first two. And let us recall that the principal suspect has gone on the lam. Accordingly, Eurydice has put the call out, and fifteen poor bastards who were still in bed, thinking their Sunday was going to be a heady mix of pancakes, bacon, maple syrup, fun, sport, social media, sex and booze, have had their day utterly laid waste.

She's splitting us up, which means I don't get to drive around with Kallas. Probably for the best. I mean, it feels like this thing between us is coming to some sort of a head, that at some point one of us has to take a knife to it, but it ain't going to end well. It can't. There is no good end. And so, let us postpone the torture a little longer.

A phone rings, Blumenthal answers, the meeting continues without him. Looks like I'm getting put on the trail of a replica whaling vessel at the Museum of Transport in Dundee, and one of HMS Erebus, lost seeking the northwest passage in the 1840s, that Thebes made for the National Maritime Museum in London.

'I need to go,' says Blumenthal, slipping the phone into his pocket. 'Be back in a minute.'

When he returns two minutes later, he is not alone. The meeting, winding down as it is with work to be done, grinds to a halt as we all look expectantly at the newcomer. Blumenthal does not look like he's much the wiser for having spent those two minutes in her company, and he gives Eurydice a small shrug.

'Can I help you?'

'Elizabeth Bishop,' she says. 'NCA. We need to talk.'

Nice, the National Crime Agency. The Feds are in town.

Eurydice holds the gaze for a moment, looks around the room, makes the call on whether she will talk with everyone present – thinking wrongly it's her call to make – then says, 'I'm all ears.'

'Alone,' says Elizabeth Bishop. Then she takes a moment, looking around the room. 'They say there was someone else doing the bulk of the interviewing the last two days.'

'Sergeant Hutton,' says Eurydice, nodding in my direction.

'You can stay, everyone else,' and she makes a small head movement in the direction of the door.

Naturally, no one moves. Eurydice, however, is not one to be drawn into any pointless, willy-waving alpha bullshit, and she makes a gesture towards the door, accompanied by a *you heard the woman* shrug.

This is impressive authority with which Elizabeth Bishop has walked in here. She ain't taking anyone's shit.

It's one of the things that always amazes me about politics. How come we end up with the bullshitting, disingenuous wankers that we do, when you get serious people like this working in government? If this woman stood at a lectern and told you to stay the fuck at home for six months, you'd stay the fuck at home.

The room clears, Kallas and I exchanging one of those glances as she goes, and then the door is shut and it's just me and the two power women. It's wrong in a situation like this to think of them both being hot – I mean, I *know* it is – but they're both really hot, by the way.

Look, at least I don't immediately start imagining them having lesbian sex, so there's that. I feel I'm growing as a human.

'What do you have for us, Ms Bishop?' asks Eurydice.

'This time yesterday you were holding Dr Crispin Thebes on suspicion of a double murder, and then you released him at just after twenty-one hundred hours last night.'

'I'm aware,' says Eurydice.

'You shouldn't have done that.'

Eurydice, who, of course, had not wanted to release him in the first place, gives her the appropriate look.

'Thanks for that. Perhaps you could tell me what I should have done, given that the procurator's office told me I didn't have enough grounds on which to charge him. Gut instinct aside, I know they were right. And while we'd all love gut instinct to be taken into consideration…'

'We should have communicated better, I admit,' says Bishop.

'You *should* have communicated better? You didn't communicate at all.'

'We arranged for HMRC to supply you with information that could further your investigation.'

'Seriously? Two hours before he was due to be released! Am I supposed to thank you for that?'

'That's a reasonable point. We played our hand badly.'

'And what hand is that exactly?' I say, thinking I may as well contribute, rather than sitting here, basking in the raw sexuality of two strong women who are kind of annoyed, but not actually angry with each other. Yet.

Bishop holds my gaze for a moment, lifts her head a little, looks as though she's just recognised the smell of coffee, then she looks around the room, identifies the machine, and says, 'D'you mind?'

'Fill your boots,' says Eurydice.

Bishop lays the small, zipped folder she's carrying on the desk, and then walks over to the machine.

'Everyone else all right?'

'Sure,' I say. Eurydice answers with a nod to the woman's back.

'So, here's where we are,' says Bishop, as she takes a quick squirt of hand sanitizer, rubs her hands together, then lifts a Styrofoam cup, places it beneath the small pipe, takes a moment to consider her options, then presses the button.

She then stands and watches the coffee fill up, like a child awaiting an ice cream, or a stranger from the backwoods who's never seen a coffee machine before. Eurydice and I share a glance as we wait, the knowing look of the put-upon minion, which is interesting, as for all we know Ms Bishop here could be a Detective Constable. The machine, fortunately, doesn't hang around, and we're not all stuck in this picture, like characters in a Hopper painting, staring at a point in time, waiting for something to happen.

She lifts the cup, takes a sip, and then returns to the desk, sitting down in the seat where she left the folder.

'Apologies for the tediousness of this, but it needs to be said. This doesn't leave the room. If you think you need to impart any of this to anyone else in the investigation, I'd like you to run it by me first.'

'Are you now part of this investigation?'

'No, not unless you'd like me to be.'

———

134

They hold the stare across the desk, then Eurydice, who's playing this pretty cool, says, 'Let's wait and see where it goes.'

'Sure,' says Bishop. 'So –'

'And why's the sergeant here?'

'You're thinking it's above his pay grade?'

They're talking about me like I'm not in the room. This is what men have to go through when dealing with women in authority. They barely know we exist.

I glance at the camera. The camera tells me to fuck off.

'I have no idea,' says Eurydice. 'Sure, he's interviewed Dr Thebes, but at various times, so have DI Kallas and Sgt Blumenthal.'

'Reasonable. But let's imagine that Dr Thebes is the One Ring.'

A moment, she leaves that comment hovering just above the desk, but neither Eurydice nor I decide to grab hold of it.

'In this analogy, Sgt Hutton would be Frodo, while DI Kallas and Sgt Blumenthal would be Sam.'

'Frodo gets to go to the Grey Havens, Sam gets to go home and have chips,' says Eurydice.

She's funny.

'Exactly. I'm glad we cleared that up.' Bishop takes a sip of coffee. 'This is where we are. Dr Thebes' father was the eleventh Earl of Fife. Thebes was an only child, which should make him the twelfth earl, but we'll cut to that part and say that he rejected his claim to the title. He grew up with his father not around much and his mother an alcoholic.' Sip of coffee, this time a small nod to herself appreciating the taste. 'His mother died in a house fire when the boy was eight. There was some suspicion among the police at the time that the boy might have been the one who set the fire.'

She looks between the two of us.

'Not an accident?' I say.

'You've met Dr Thebes, you can imagine. It was never proven; the father did not want to accept that possibility in any case. The father married again. Then, with a younger wife, and feeling some responsibility, he started spending more time at home. It is not entirely clear how he and his son conducted relations with each other. We may surmise it did not go well, from the fact that the father, and his second wife, died in a car accident when Thebes was fourteen.'

At this, Eurydice says fourteen at the same time, seeing that connection coming, and Bishop nods her appreciation.

'Again, some suspicion that the boy was involved, but nothing anyone could prove. Indeed, he had a very carefully worked alibi. But that brake fluid had been let out by *someone*. Now we have the future twelfth Earl of Fife orphaned, there were no grandparents who wanted anything to do with him – it really was a very dysfunctional family – and so the State moved in. And when I say the State, I don't mean social services. The *powers that be*,' she says, giving the phrase the appropriate tone, which is interesting, as she sure as fuck is coming across as a *power that is* at the moment. 'From here you will know some of the biography. Gordonstoun, St Andrews, Oxford. The next bit, the bit where he was running a small art dealership in central London, that was his cover.'

'Fuck,' says Eurydice. 'Fuck, I knew it.'

'Yes,' says Bishop. 'He was a man of certain talents, and while being potentially guilty of parricide may mark someone down as undesirable to most people, it had certain departments within the broad church of government fighting for his services. MI6 won.'

'Fuck,' again from Eurydice. 'He's not still there, is he?'

'With the exception of glibly stating that one never really leaves, no, he's not. He left five years ago, when his cover at the art dealership ended. He retired. He moved to Glasgow, and he settled down into this life of the... well, the model maker. Such as it is. We have no idea how long he intends leading this quiet existence, although he does actually seem to have been quiet all this time.'

'You've been keeping tabs on him?' I ask.

'Of course.'

'Are you MI6?'

'No. As I said, NCA.'

No one now believes this woman is NCA.

Eurydice leans forward, elbow on the table, running her hand across the chin. Processing this, putting it into the perspective of where we are with the investigation.

'You know where he is now?' she asks.

'Nope.'

'So, he retired in, what, his late forties?' I ask. 'Seems early.'

'Yes.'

'What'd he do?'

She closes her mouth, although at least she doesn't do the zip thing along her lips. Instead, a small shake of the head.

'Would it be more accurate to say that he *was* retired?'

'We shall say that it was in everyone's interests.'

'These murders we're investigating,' says Eurydice, 'you're familiar with the details?'

'Of course.'

'Are they consistent with anything Dr Thebes has done in the past?'

'I just told you he may well have killed his mother when he was eight. Someone who is capable of that at that age…'

'I meant the meticulousness and the precision.'

'Yes, that was interesting, wasn't it? Very particular. No, one cannot say that he has previously, in the name of the British government, carried out a murder in such a specific and precise manner. He has, nevertheless, committed certain officially sanctioned acts that would not meet universal public approval.'

Ha!

'Would you have any idea where he's gone?' asks Eurydice.

'Nope.'

'He didn't have, I don't know, like a contact within the service, or a bolthole of some sort when he was on the run?'

'That's not who Dr Thebes is. One doesn't like to throw around the phrase *lone wolf*, if for no other reason that it is rather clichéd, but it does apply here.'

'He did his own thing when he was in MI6?' I pitch in. 'He must've answered to *someone*? He must've received instructions from *someone*?'

'Yes, of course. Those lives are not fiction. Yet, he had a particular skill-set, and the number of people who knew that he worked for the Service was very limited.' A pause, and then the slightly theatrical, '*Very* limited.'

'This woman he talks about,' says Eurydice. 'The third woman. Do you suppose she will now be within his sights? That this is him disappearing, she will be dealt with, and then,' snap of the fingers, 'he's never seen again?'

'There's a lot going on in that question,' says Bishop. 'Does the third woman even exist? Who knows? I should say that you cannot, of course, trust anything Dr Thebes says. He will say what needs to be said at the time, he will say it with complete conviction, and it does not matter one bit whether or not it's true. If you don't already know the truth of the matter, speaking to Dr Thebes will enlighten you no further. If she exists, our third woman, then whether she is now in more or less danger is entirely dependent on whether Thebes is guilty. If he is, then the woman is as good as dead. If not, then we can assume that someone is coming after Thebes by targeting people with whom he is intimate, and so it just depends on whether or not he gets to her in time.'

'I thought perhaps the notion of someone killing the others to set him up might be too far-fetched,' says Eurydice.

'I see that,' says Bishop, nodding. 'Nevertheless, what we're talking about here would not necessarily be someone trying to set up Dr Thebes. It could be revenge, perhaps even revenge with a touch of mockery. It could be, in the world in which Dr Thebes previously operated, a number of reasons. It would appear, at this stage, that we do not have enough information to even speculate, so there seems little point.'

'How do we find him?' I ask.

'You won't find Dr Thebes. You might, if you're lucky, stumble across this third woman, if she exists. In that case, by that means, you may find Dr Thebes. It's possible, of course, that he may choose to find you.'

Eurydice looks at me, as this last comment was directed my way.

'I'm not really getting why I'm so special,' I say. I mean, I'm not playing it cool. I really don't. Sounds like this guy was doing some serious Jason Bourne type shit. He lived the life. He really is a man apart from society. No idea why he'd be interested in me.

'I read your file,' says Bishop. Oh, great. Another one. 'Thebes likes damaged. He's drawn to damaged. He likely recognised a fellow sufferer.'

'What was *he* damaged by? He was the one who murdered his parents.'

'There's a theory he was abused by his father. It was the late sixties, the seventies, no one wanted to talk about it. His mother couldn't protect him, so she drank, and he hated her for it. Hated her weakness in the face of the dad's barbarity. So, he killed the mum. Maybe he tried to kill the dad previously, we don't know. Don't know why it took him so long. Then he finally did it.

'But, as I say, all theory, all speculation. Maybe there was

138

no abuse, maybe there was no murder.'

She waves an airy hand, looks between Eurydice and me, and then smiles, albeit humourlessly.

'I'm starving. I'm going to go and grab some breakfast in your canteen. They say the food is adequate. You can talk about me, and you can discuss everything I've just imparted, then we can see how we progress this. We need not, of course, work in tandem if you'd rather not. It would be wise, however, to at least coordinate.'

She drains the coffee, sets the cup down on the table, then gets to her feet.

'I get that you might need some confirmation. Far as you know, I'm just a random stranger in off the street.' She takes a card from her pocket and lays it on the desk, nods to us both, and then walks from the room, closing the door behind her.

Together we stare at the closed door, as though waiting for something further to occur in its vicinity – I guess opening again is pretty much the only thing likely to occur – and when nothing does, we turn to each other.

'Well, that just happened,' says Eurydice.

'It did.'

'I didn't see it coming,' she says, 'and yet, it makes perfect sense.'

She picks up the card, takes a quick look, shows it to me – it's a London phone number and nothing else – slips it into her trouser pocket and shakes her head.

'I fucking hate these people.'

I don't say anything to that, just sit and stare at the desk, really no idea how this is going to play from here on in. We still, however, have our jobs to do.

'You don't?' she says.

'I don't hate them?'

'Yeah.'

'No, not really. I grew up watching Bond, I read every Ian Fleming fifteen times. I love that shit. That desire to go abroad and get in adventures in the first place, even though when I did, it was as a photojournalist, came from those books.'

'So, you're still a little boy and you're in awe?'

I smile.

'More or less.'

She taps her fingers on the table. She holds my gaze. She's thinking something, obviously isn't quite ready to say it yet. It's as though there's a thought-formulation graphic being projected onto her face.

'What?' I finally venture.

'Thinking,' she says.

'You consider this woman the opposition?'

'Well, I'm not an MI6-fanboy like some people, so yes, I do.'

I smile at that too. She's funny.

'She said she was NCA.'

'She's lying.'

'All right. Tell me what you're thinking. You're looking at me like I'm a crash test dummy.'

She keeps looking at me like I'm a crash test dummy for a while, then she nods, taps her fingers a little more.

'That video of you,' she says. 'Having sex in the garden.'

'We're talking about that?'

'Yes, we are.'

I make the appropriate *all-right-then-what-about-it?* gesture, feeling an unexpected squirm of embarrassment.

'It states in your file that it came about because your DCI asked you to sleep with the woman to try to get information.'

I nod. That was pretty much what happened. Free, green-lit, on-the-job sex. I couldn't get around to her house quickly enough. Of course, it turned out that the man controlling her, had instructed her to get me into bed, and I unthinkingly walked into the trap, all the blood having gone from my brain to my penis.

'So, you know, you have history of this kind of thing.'

Stupidly I struggle for a moment to see where this is going, then the penny drops.

Really?

'You want me to sleep with Elizabeth Bishop?'

She holds my gaze for a moment then smiles.

'Why, on all the earth, would she want to do that?' I ask.

She lifts her eyebrows.

'She's seen your file. You think anyone looks at your file and doesn't watch that video?'

I've got nothing to say to that.

'So, who knows? She's watched you; she knows what you'll do. She's, you know, all right, this is just dropping her into some sort of fictional stereotype, but *she's a spy*. These people literally lie for a living. Can any of them be trusted by their partners? These people do what they have to do. They lie, they kill, they fuck, they do whatever. So, you know, she may well come looking for you. It's a solid start that she even wanted you in the room.'

Well, DCI Eurydice Hamilton is a pragmatic woman after all. She asked Kallas to sit in with Thebes just to see how he'd react to the presence of beauty. That one didn't seem to particularly reap any reward, so why not try this? She makes a judgement, then makes the call. Kallas didn't mind getting asked that, and I won't mind getting asked this.

And I don't.

I look at the door, the last place I saw Elizabeth Bishop, as though that might help me picture her. And picturing her doesn't really make a lot of difference either way, attractive though she is. 'I think I'm good,' I say, looking back at Eurydice.

She looks curiously at me. She's read my file after all, and in that file it will say that I have sex addiction issues, and that I invariably end up sleeping with the wrong person. Yet here we are.

Obviously I've still got guilt from four days ago. Look at that.

'Fair enough, Sergeant,' she says. 'I hope you didn't mind me raising the prospect.'

'I appreciate you thought of me,' I say. 'Perhaps you could try to interest Sgt Blumenthal instead,' I add, and she bursts out laughing.

24

There goes the day, any old Sunday in April. Some time spent on the lives of Julia Wright and Jennifer Talbot, some time spent on the search for the third woman, where all we've got to go on is Thebes' previous work contacts. Phone calls to museums and clubhouses, where we can make them, given that some of them are closed. Vague questions about contacts he made there, rapidly coming round, in the face of very little information being divulged, to the blunter, *has he kept in touch with anyone?* fully aware that there is little chance the question will get anywhere. The man knew how to keep a secret, and he knew how to pick a woman who could keep a secret.

Plenty more calls to make tomorrow, when hopefully more offices will be manned, and all we can do is hope it's not too late.

Eurydice goes off to speak to a woman who had dealings with Thebes on his work on the Waverley, the meeting based on hope, rather than expectation. There's nothing to expect from any of these people. All we've got is, find a woman, any woman, ask her questions, hope we see the sign of the lie, the flinch, the unnatural reserve, the prevarication, the evasion. Hard to pick up on any of that over the phone.

Just after three in the afternoon. A long day looking at computer screens, waiting for phones to be answered, talking around the subject of Dr Thebes. Getting nowhere. Desperate to get out there, find someone worth talking to, but the only person who was a remotely plausible candidate was in Dundee, and we've been told to take all out-of-town trip options to Eurydice, and this one wasn't a strong case. We called someone in Dundee and asked them to do it. They did, they had nothing of significance to report back. The problem with farming out the work, when much of it will be reliant on a good nose and intuition, is that you have no idea whether you can trust the person who's doing your bidding.

Grabbed a Coke Zero and a chicken wrap in the canteen,

passed Kallas on her way in, as I was walking out, asked her if she wanted to join me for some fresh air. Now, here we are, standing on the bridge by the police HQ, looking north-west, as it is at this point, looking down at the water, and at the bare trees lining the banks of the Clyde.

The chicken wrap is tasteless, the Coke at least ice cold and refreshing in the light of a mild and uninteresting afternoon. Behind us cars pass by in ones and twos, Sunday afternoon roads with little to say for themselves. Up above, low grey cloud, no threat of rain. A nothing day. A grey day.

'You have a good day yesterday?' I ask.

First thing either of us has said in five minutes. Would be nice to think we'd been standing here in companionable silence, but companionable silence is still some way off for us.

'Yes, thank you,' she says. 'The girls and I went for a walk around the small lake at Drumpellier.'

'I investigated a murder there once,' I say, as it's the first thing that comes into my head. 'Well, wasn't much of an investigation. There was a body in the woods, round from the other side of the car park. Guy got chibbed. He'd been in a couple of pubs with two other blokes the previous night, they were spotted arguing outside one of them. We spoke to the two guys, they cracked like that.' Those guys really were morons.

'We had ice cream, and the girls played in the park,' she says, a mundane response to my mundane tale of a guy getting his head put in with a half-brick. These are the stories we tell each other.

'Eurydice asked me to sleep with Elizabeth Bishop,' I say. The thought, the words, everything about that sentence just appeared out of nowhere, as if my subconscious suddenly decided to take over. *Here you are, you're looking at the river, talking to the reason you're not entertaining the idea of sleeping with Elizabeth Bishop, so just get it out there.*

She gives me a slightly curious glance, then turns back to the water.

'That does not seem very professional.'

'I think she kind of had a point. I didn't mind.' *Here's the kicker!* 'But I said no.'

'Who is this Elizabeth Bishop?'

There's the thing. I've already said too much. Like Michael Stipe, that time he was in the corner.

I shake my head, instantly hate myself for being so weak as

143

to have raised the subject in the first place.

'You cannot say,' she says. 'That is fine, of course. There are not too many options, particularly when someone arrives from London to interfere in an investigation, and given Dr Thebes demeanour and his talents, particular as they are, one can at least imagine who she might be. We should not talk of that.'

Yep. As ever, DI Kallas nails it. Doesn't say much, but when she does, etcetera.

We watch the ducks, we eat, and we drink. She also has a chicken wrap.

'She is an attractive woman,' says Kallas. A pause, then, 'Elizabeth Bishop.'

Give her a glance, look back at the ducks. The ducks, by the way, aren't doing anything remotely interesting. No way either of these little bastards are making an episode of David Attenborough.

I think of the video of me having sex in the garden, Eurydice's line about how anyone who looked at my file is going to have looked at that video.

'Eurydice thought it possible Elizabeth Bishop would approach *me*,' I say.

I can hear her calculating whether it sounds rude to bluntly ask why, as she would already have done having this conversation back home in Estonia, and then she bluntly asks, 'Why?'

The Coke Zero is certainly loosening my tongue.

'Both ladies have stated that they've looked at my online police file. That video of me in the garden from a couple of years ago is still there. Would be nice if it had been removed by now, but there it is. On the record. Perhaps to remind people, in case anyone ever thinks of promoting me to Inspector.' A moment, then I feel obliged to add, 'That was a joke. I know no one's ever going to promote me to inspector.'

'I know you were joking.'

'OK, cool. So, Eurydice observed that Elizabeth Bishop, having looked at my file, might decide for her own ends, whatever they may be, to sleep with me. And that this was something I might, I don't know, exploit in some way.'

We're standing a yard apart on the bridge. She turns to look at me, an unfamiliar look of amusement on her face.

'Has she made an approach yet?'

'Weirdly, no, but I'll be ready for her when she does,' I say,

---

smiling in reaction to her amusement.

'Would you like me to take up a case of sexual harassment for you?' she asks. 'We are laughing about it, but it would be quite a different matter if these were two senior male officers.'

'Let's say Eurydice knows her audience and has made a correct judgement of what's acceptable. I get that the optics aren't great, but it's not like I'm telling anyone other than you.'

'And Sgt Harrison.'

'That may happen. I think my secrets are safe within this triangle. Or, in this case, Eurydice's secret.'

We're looking at each other as that little spurt of conversation comes to an end, we hold the gaze for a moment – how nice it would be to be lying in bed, post sex, staring silently into those eyes with no need to speak or go anywhere – and then we turn away and look back at the river and the bare trees.

The question comes into my head. Since we're here, and we're alone, and we've been talking about my online file, and that video. And I know I'm going to ask it, and I hate that I am, because it's so fucking needy.

I don't want to be needy. No one *wants* to be needy. Maybe a tonne of needy people don't really think they are. In this instance, being aware of my own neediness, doesn't really mean anything. Not if I blindly forge ahead, neediness on full display.

'You've looked at my file?' I ask.

Fuck me. Just stop.

'Yes,' she says. 'I did not when we started working together. I thought your past of no significance. I was only interested in the work that we did. I have looked at your file since then, however.'

I allow myself the small glance towards her. She looks a little red in the face. I should shut the fuck up. All the way. Shut all the way up.

'Did you look at the video?'

See? This is what happens? This is the same kind of stupid impulse that says drink when you know you shouldn't drink, and do the thing, when you know you shouldn't do the thing.

She's silent, staring impassively at the river.

'Did you look at my file just so you could look at the video?'

Fuck me. Will you, in the name of all fuck, shut your fucking mouth?

It's time to go. I need to just apologise and say we need to get on.

'We should go back,' she says, taking a last look at the river, her eyes travelling past me with a quick glance, and then turning back towards the road.

Dammit. Goddammit.

'Sorry,' I say.

That's all I can think of.

We stand at the edge of the pavement, wait on a white Audi, a red Nissan to pass, and then cross the road, and get out our IDs as we approach the gate.

'Sorry,' I say again. 'Didn't mean to sound... you know, like that.'

'That is OK.'

And we're there, and we're speaking to the guy on security, and so the afternoon goes.

25

And there goes the day.

There aren't supposed to be days like this in the middle of a major murder investigation. Sure, MI6 pitched up and dropped a fifteen-tonne nuclear warhead into the middle of the whole thing, but other than paint a broader picture of the mysterious Dr Thebes, what did it do for us? Other than *don't bother looking for him because you'll never find him*, what did it tell us? Other than illustrating the extent of the iceberg that remains beneath the surface, what did it show us?

In terms of taking the investigation forward, there was nothing. Positively, there have been no other murders, so there's that. But no hint of who the third woman might be, if she even exists, no further confirmation of whether or not Dr Thebes was telling the truth about his relationships with the two victims, no clues to his whereabouts, no further revelations about either of the victims, and nothing to point to anyone else being involved in the murders.

The off-licence is still open when I pass it on my way home. In there, there are thirteen different types of vodka. I've had them all. I don't have a favourite. I've never counted the types of white wine. They call to me as I pass, the thirteen vodkas and the innumerable varieties of white wine.

I accelerate.

Park the car, up the stairs, fifth floor, as usual when I jog up, kind of out of breath by the time I get there, the next hour mapped out in food and sugar-free nothingness. Into the house, into the sitting room, light on, jacket off.

I stop in my tracks. There's been a visitor.

Take the temperature of the room, look around to see if there's any sign of him. Swallow, then try not to breathe. Ears strained. Listen to the house. Try to get the sense of whether there's anyone else here.

Don't get it. The house feels empty. Quick check.

Into the kitchen, then through to the bedroom, the en suite, back out into the hall, quick look in the second bedroom, which is little more than a box room without a bed, where I stick the detritus of life, finally the toilet off the hallway, and then stop at the front door. Open it, make a careful check of the lock outside. Nothing to suggest that it has been tampered with. Whoever broke in, knew exactly what they were doing. Just as I know exactly who it was who broke in.

I can get the crew round to take prints, but there will be none other than mine.

Close the door, back into the sitting room, then go and stand by the table. Such a small thing. Such insignificance. And yet, in the way of the master, it is laced with threat, or amused omnipotence, or casual, dismissive boredom, or playfulness, or menace. Take your pick. But there it is, the jigsaw of Gertrude, Lady Agnew of Lochnaw, over which I've laboured the past couple of months, completed while I was out of the house all day.

I do not need to wonder who will have done it. And in the seamlessness of the break-in, further proof of the man's abilities, as reported by Elizabeth Bishop.

Despite the premise it displays, that he can break in to my apartment, he can have the run of it, he is comfortable enough that he can take the time to sit and finish off a jigsaw – although we all know he'll have done it in a tenth of the time it would've taken me – I really don't feel any threat. Perhaps he might even say he was just amusing himself while he waited for my return.

Nevertheless, I go back into the hall and put the chain across the door. How flimsy it feels in the face of someone with action movie hero abilities. I don't suppose he'll be coming back in any case.

Into the kitchen, crack open a can of Coke, then sit down at the table.

Heavy sigh, shoulders slumped.

'What d'you say, Gertrude? How was it being with another man?'

Gertrude stays quiet, although she has a look about her. I think she might have enjoyed her time with him.

'Keeping schtum, eh? Well, maybe you appreciated it, but I'm a bit pissed off. I mean, you look nice 'n' all, with your dress complete and everything, but I was quite enjoying it. The slow process. Now this fucker comes in and there it goes.'

Gertrude maintains her own counsel.

'Maybe I could disassemble you, but I'd always know you'd had someone else.' I smile, Gertrude remains enigmatic.

Shake my head, elbow on the table, forehead into the palm of my hand.

I ought to call it in. Of course, I should call it in. If this was a movie, you'd be watching, saying, why the fuck aren't you calling this in, you eejit? And you'd pause the movie, and you'd say to the person you're watching it with, that's such a shite plot development, he would absolutely call that in in real life. Just like in real life the teenage girl wouldn't walk up the stairs in the horror movie, and the young couple who fancy each other would just talk about it in the first five minutes, rather than go through ninety-four minutes of romcom situation before arriving at the inevitable.

But the decision is made without even thinking about it, without even, really, making any decision. I'm tired, and I don't want the conversation with Eurydice. I don't want the team coming round, I don't want the next three hours of Sunday to be taken up with this. I'm going to be in bed long before this would finish playing out. It sounds lazy and poor, reeking of work avoidance. But it's not work avoidance, that's just the added bonus.

The main reason is Thebes himself. He wanted me in the interview room, and now this is him speaking directly to me. He doesn't want this conversation to be shared, and he's expecting me not to share it. This is the opening salvo. There's more to come.

'Not a word,' I say to Gertrude. 'Tell no one.'

Gertrude looks back, amused at the very idea. We stare in silence at each other for a while, and then I go into the kitchen, pick a pizza from the freezer, and try not to think about how much better pizza tastes when it is served with wine.

*

So, if it's not Thebes who killed these two women, then who did? And how does it relate to Thebes, because if he was having an affair with them both, and now they're both dead, then surely their murder relates to him? Unless he's lying, toying with us, inventing affairs just for his own amusement. Sure, he knew both of the women, but it's possible to know women and not sleep with them. That's a thing apparently.

———

There's always the outlier, the person we've not thought of before, or come across before. Always the possibility that these two victims are as random as we wondered they might be before Thebes appeared on the scene. A killer stalks the streets, indiscriminately picking off women. And yet, this psychopath just happened to use the implements of the model maker? This psychopath just happened to murder people who'd come into contact with the model maker? And having killed two people in three days, this psychopath just happened to not kill anyone else while the model maker was in custody?

This leaves it either being Thebes, or someone who wants us to think it was Thebes, and my starting point is that it's not Thebes.

We have, so far, four up-front favourites. The yachtswoman's lesbian lover, her ex-husband, the minister's widower, the church session clerk. Of course, it could be some complete outlier, but there was a reason Eurydice sent Kallas and I to speak to these four in the first place, and our work there is by no means done.

I should go and speak to them all again tomorrow, and I fall asleep, unusually for me, thinking about work, and how I'm going to be able to pull off inserting myself positively into the investigation like this, rather than waiting for directions from the top.

26

Elizabeth Bishop talks a lot, which is surprising.

I went in this morning and made my pitch on why I thought Thebes wasn't our guy, and why I needed to re-interview the four horsepeople of the apocalypse, and Eurydice, while not being at all convinced, at least set me on my path, as there was nothing else she thought a better use of my time. And then Bishop asked that she join me, and now here we are, sitting in the car, stuck in traffic, on the way to Partick – a ten-minute drive, turning into half an hour – and it seems that she's not as cagey as one would anticipate a spy to be.

'So, just so you know, Sergeant… hmm, Sergeant… doesn't sound right. You all right if I call you Tom?'

'Sure.'

'Just so you know, Tom, I'm absolutely in the background here, OK? I'm completely leaving you to it.'

'Probably best.'

'I mean,' and she smiles, in her way, 'I'm likely to stick my nose in after we leave. I'll be like, why didn't you ask such and such?'

'We'll play it as it lays,' I say.

Where did that line come from? A book somewhere. It's the title of a book. *How do I know that?*

'Great.' A beat, but already with the vibe that it won't be a long one. 'Detective Inspector Kallas seems pretty switched on.'

'Yeah, she's good.'

Can feel her looking at me.

'You sleeping with her?' she says out of the blue. I mean, I say out of the blue, but these people ask any old shit, don't they? Not slow in coming forward.

'Nope.'

'Right. One of those things, eh? She's married?'

'She is,' I say. 'Let's not talk about DI Kallas. She's good at her job, that's all we need to know.'

She pats me on the leg. I mean, what the fuck?

'You're a good man,' she says, then with barely a breath between thoughts, 'you know who I'd like to get alone in a room?'

'Can't wait to hear.'

'Bezos. You know, the Amazon guy.'

I glance at her, though not for long, as the traffic is stopping and starting, and there's too much chance of ramming the car in front.

'Good looking guy,' I say.

I always say that line.

'I don't want to sleep with him,' she says. 'I want to ask him something.'

'Go on.'

Finally make it to the light, squeezing through at the arse end of a departing amber.

'He's spending money on space. I mean, all these people spend money on space, right? It's like, what am I going to do with all this money I don't need and make sure I don't have to pay in taxes? I know, I'll be Hugo Drax. And yet, Bezos, the amount of money he has at his disposal, rather than dreaming of going to a far-off barren planet, how about helping to save the one we're on? Well, first of all, how about actually paying the people who work for him? Then how about cleaning plastic from the oceans? How about spending money to reforest the actual Amazon? How about investing in the forest plantation across Africa, to prevent the desertification of the entire continent? How about reversing all those palm oil plantations in Indonesia and Borneo?' She pauses for breath, or possibly just pauses to consider the work of George Gilbert Scott, such as it was, as we pass along University Avenue. 'Nice. I mean, rainforest regrows at a prodigious rate. It would easily regrow *in his lifetime*. It's not like rewilding, I don't know, the Highlands or something, which could take centuries to do naturally. Rainforest grows more or less as you look at it. Sure, I get it. Space is sexy. Logistically, space is easy. You build a facility, you get scientists in, you throw money at it.' She snaps her fingers. 'I'm not saying the science bit is easy, but it's easy to throw money at. But reforestation? Shit, there are people involved, there's politics, you have to provide all those farmers with other employment, you have to make sure they don't deforest elsewhere as soon as you've bought their farmland. In Africa, you've got Boko Haram, you've got ISIS, you've got Christians

---

152

and Muslims burning each other first chance they get, you've got civil wars, and no end of shitshow. It's difficult. It's way more difficult than going into space. Way more complicated. But every clown's going into space. Musk and Branson, the Chinese, the Russians, NASA, the Indians, the ESA, every single clown in the clown parade is heading to space. So, Bezos has this choice. He could replant the forests and see marked difference in his lifetime. He could literally be the man who saved the earth. Or he could be just another guy who put a rocket in space. And he wants to be the rocket guy.' She stops, she looks around. 'Why have we stopped?'

'We're here.'

She notices the church, across the road to our left

'Cool.'

I turn off the engine, get out, close the door. Look up at the sky – a classic, west of Scotland nothing day – wait for her to come round the car, and then the two of us walk up the path to the manse.

*

'Get to fuck!'

Well, this isn't going well.

He's hammered, and he's angry. That'll be the Glasgow version of hangry, I suppose. Yeah, all right, not just Glasgow. There are drunk, angry assholes all over the world.

Today I'm not so taken in by the intoxicating aroma of fresh alcohol. Today is about not arguing with the stupid prick. I mean, I get it; his wife was murdered, and quite possibly murdered because she was having an affair. That's shit all round for any bloke. He doesn't *have* to be a giant cock about it, but it's easier behaviour to accept under the circumstances.

'I mean,' he says, then pauses for the glug at the bottle of rosé. Yep, he's drinking rosé from the bottle, *in April*. That's how low he's fallen. 'I know what you're doing. You insist my Julia was having an affair, so hey, naturally I'd've wanted to kill her. I mean, it's obvious. I have absolutely no idea why you think I'd've wanted to kill this other woman, but screw that, eh? You're the police.' He stares harshly at us both, leans across the broad desk towards us, and says, 'You don't need a reason, do you?'

When we arrived, he said he was working, even though he

hadn't mentioned that when I called to make sure we'd find him in. Works from home, which is entirely believable of course, as plenty of people have been working from home in the past year. Now says he has a Zoom in five minutes. Works at a small marketing agency, they have a contract for a double-glazing firm.

No idea whether or not he's making that shit up. It sounds plausible, but also a boringly predictable lie. And if he really does have a meeting to attend online, I'd kind of like to stay and watch, because this guy is going to be an absolute car crash.

'Did you and Julia ever talk about her having an affair with Dr Crispin Thebes?'

Slams his arms down onto the desk, the open palm of his hand slapping hard. The sharp pain of that flashes across his face, the grimace comes and goes, teeth pressed hard together, words spat out from between them.

'No! I fucking… said… no!'

More wine, bottle attached to that ugly sneer. In one dark, grim corner of my mind I am reminded of the way I treated Eileen last year. I really was this much of a dick.

'Did you ever talk about her having an affair with anyone?'

'Jesus Christ.'

He angrily flips open the top of the laptop which he earlier pushed to the side. Waits a moment, points at it, and says, 'I'm going to be doing this in a minute. You two can show yourselves out.' He looks at Bishop, a vicious, sneery, *why are you even here?* look.

'Bear in mind, Mr Wright,' I continue, 'we now have access to all Julia's communications. If anything was ever written down between you, or if she ever wrote anything to anyone else, we *will* know about it.' I let those words fester for a few moments. 'Factor that into your calculations. You may think you can keep your mouth shut, and Julia won't be talking, but she's still got plenty to say.' The bottle goes to his lips. 'If you acknowledge knowing about her having an affair, it hardly points the finger at you. If you deny all such knowledge, and then we find out that you *did* know… *that* points the finger at you.'

He holds my gaze for a moment, then looks at Bishop, with the same misogynistic loathing as before, then looks back. Red cheeks, crazy eyes, demented and deranged and drunk and dilapidated, this guy is going to be the greatest walk-on funeral shitshow disaster ever, when the day comes. Albeit, that day is still some way off. Perhaps he'll have drunk himself to death by then.

'Get out,' he says, teeth still clenched together, spittle and wine and seething fury spurting from his moist lips as he talks. 'Get out of my *fucking* house.'

Whatever app he's using on his laptop starts ringing. A last look of loathing, a dismissive, 'Go,' a head twitch or two, a slug of wine, the near-empty bottle then placed behind the laptop, and he opens the call.

'George,' he says, without much enthusiasm.

And we're up and we're out the door, his, 'No, no, it's fine, really,' delivered in the voice of the drunk, the last thing we hear before we close the door behind us.

27

'That was good,' says Bishop.

The short drive to Abercrombie's house now, as he's also working from home. Not sure what to say to that, so I remain silent. I can feel her looking at me. I look at the road, the traffic, the red light a hundred yards up ahead.

Elizabeth Bishop. Mid-fifties. Hair still dyed blonde, cut short. Regulation fifty-year-old women's hair. As a studier and judger of fifty-year-old women, I approve.

Judge not, and ye shall not be judged. The Bible, verse something, chapter something-else, some book or other. Might be Old Testament, might be New. Sounds like the kind of thing Jesus would say, though, right? After all, all those Old Testament bastards were as judgemental as fuck. They did not give two shits before casting judgement.

I like to think I largely keep my judgements to myself, but of course I share them with Eileen, as she too is a judger of women, and since I think them, and often enough talk to myself – or, at least, talk to Gertrude these days – those thoughts are generally out there in the Universe. They exist, the Universe knows they exist, and so I will in turn be judged for my opinions.

So be it, Universe.

Bishop has an attractive look of authority about her. I don't know what one is to think of MI6. If she is MI6. I don't even know about the terminology of spies and assets and agents. I know that anyone working for them would, in tabloid terms, be called a spy, but do they themselves think of someone who sits in Vauxhall processing paperwork a spy? Or do you actually have to go out into the field and gather intelligence, while killing and shagging for the Queen, to be considered a spy? No idea. And, presumably, most people who pitch up at Vauxhall every day to work just look like regular folk pitching up at an office.

Bishop has such an air about her that one can imagine her putting a bullet in someone's back or sleeping with a contact just to get a piece of information, or just because that was what she felt like doing on that day. Maybe she has a husband and three kids. I mean, spies must have kids too, right? What do I know? But I like the look of her. Intelligent, composed, an air of authority, and nice hair.

Of course, maybe she's not lying, and she works for boring old NCA after all, and she's just one of us. However, I tend towards Eurydice's interpretation of events. The woman has, in our estimation at least, MI6 written all over her.

'You're an interesting fellow,' she says.

I don't say anything to that either. Slow to a stop at the lights. Check the street signs to make sure I've got my bearings. Turn to her. She's staring at me, that knowing look on her face. I'm being appraised by a woman. Again. Well, I'll take it. Better than being ignored by them, I suppose, though there are plenty of days when I wouldn't care.

'Still a sergeant after all these years.'

'Yeah,' I say, turning back to the road. 'You've looked at my file.'

'We need to know who we're dealing with. Curious to know what Dr Thebes saw in you. I see it now, of course.'

'Being familiar with my file, you will understand that the surprise is not that I'm still a sergeant, but that I'm still in the force.'

'You've had the right people on your side.'

The lights change, into gear, head off along the road. Wish I'd stuck Dylan on when I got in the car. That I didn't was me showing her undue deference. I have *Fallen Angels* in the CD player. That'll keep most people quiet.

'That itself says something about you. That the people you work directly to want to hang on to you. They appreciate you. DI Kallas has written some very blunt things, but one finds that often enough with the Estonians. They have a refreshing and brutal frankness.'

I stop myself asking what she said, although for just about the first time in my life, it makes me want to look at my own file.

'A good woman to have on your team, all the same.'

It feels like she's trying to lead me somewhere. Maybe just teasing me. Whatever she's doing, she's not finished. I kind of preferred it when she was talking about Bezos. Although, with the talk of the file, the mention of my participation in a porn video can't be too far off, and that's the point of the conversation, right? This is her living up to Eurydice's prediction. This is the bit where she says, I like the look of you in that porn video, and she leaves that hanging there, and my desire kicks in, and I get the weird feeling in the back of my throat, and I start wanting her, and there's nothing getting in the way of that, because why should there be?

'You have some back story. I mean, let's not get carried away, I know people with way more shit in their lives than you.' I give her a quick glance, she's staring at the dashboard, I get the flash of introspection she's feeling, the self-acknowledgement that she's one of those people, then she's back. 'But, of course, it's not a competition. It's not zero sum. And you have some serious shit. Your trouble, if I can just diagnose…'

'Oh, go right ahead.'

She smiles.

'You've got that old-fashioned copper vibe, probably even before you were a copper. You dealt with your issues in the pub, and by getting into bed with whoever you could find.'

'Thanks, Freud,' I say, 'but I've made that self-diagnosis many times in the past. Identifying the problem is not, in this case, the first step to solving it.'

'Oh, you know, it definitely is. The issue is that the first step itself doesn't mean anything unless you take the second.'

'I go to meetings,' I say, immediately cursing myself for the defensiveness of it.

'I know,' she says, her tone softening further in the face of my edginess, 'I've seen the file. Tom, I'm sorry, I'll shut up. You obviously don't want to talk about you, which is fair enough. No one likes talking about themselves.'

'Tell me about you,' I say, just to make sure the subject gets changed.

'What would you like to know?'

The tone lightens out of nothing other than the joint force of will, and we're almost at Abercrombie's house in any case, and I feel I can relax a little. Jesus, how quickly I tense up when I'm the topic of discussion.

'So, you actually work for MI6, right?'

She laughs, shakes her head.

'Sure.'

'Cool. So, tell me some basic spy shit. How many people have you killed and how many, on average, do you have sex with every year?'

'Nice. Should I ask you how many murders you investigate down at the amateur dramatics club?'

'People get murdered all the time in amateur dramatics clubs,' I say. 'Shakespeare, for example, will definitely be getting murdered, as we speak, somewhere in the world.'

She laughs again.

'You're funny. Well, I'm afraid you've been watching too many films. I've never killed anyone in the line of duty. To be honest, despite genuinely working for the NCA, I have served overseas a couple of times, but they were both brief spells. I spend most of my time at a desk in London. And I've been married for twenty-nine years now, thank you, and that's all the detail of my sex life you need to know.'

Pull up outside Abercrombie's, park, turn off the engine. Look at Elizabeth Bishop from two feet. She smiles, a kind of, *glad we cleared that up, mind on the job* smile.

What about my sex video? What about the offer of sex? What about that turned on feeling I was starting to get in the back of my throat?

Guess I was misinformed. Everybody needs to calm the fuck down.

'Thunderbirds are go,' she says.

And out the car she goes.

*

I'm aware that I'm looking for signs of Thebes everywhere. Now that he's been in my home – and really, why on earth would the man know where I live? – I expect him to anticipate all my movements. Everywhere I go, regardless of whether or not I'm accompanied by Elizabeth Bishop, I expect him to have a left a sign. *The model maker was here. I know what you're doing. I know where you're going. I know everything.*

There's my limited imagination. Perhaps Dr Thebes will be much grander in his statements. More ominous. More threatening. Maybe a clue to his next victim.

Nothing leaps out at me. No billboards, no small signs left at the side of the road, nothing so surreptitious that only I would notice. Unless, well, *unless the obvious*, that my police skills are not up to the basic level with which Dr Thebes invests them.

Now Bishop and I are in with John Abercrombie. Just

walked into the room, having been shown in by Mrs Abercrombie, who left us immediately without the regulation offer of a cup of tea. She had the nervous look of someone who does not want the police in her house. Not a look with which we're unfamiliar, of course, but it does immediately arouse suspicion, particularly during a murder investigation.

And what reason would Mrs Abercrombie have for being wary of the police in this matter? She knows her husband killed the minister? Or, she thought her husband was having an affair with the minister, and so she herself killed the minister. She's the *deus ex machina*, the suspect from out of left field. The minister's lover's wife, who somehow got to hear of the existence of Dr Thebes, and his other lover, and who went out of her way to frame him.

Abercrombie himself is yet to look at us. This time he's not wearing a mask, and so neither Bishop nor I have put one on. Guess he was toying with us the other day. Because he's an asshole. Now, back turned, he's painting. Your classic middle-aged man's activity, up there with writing a book, running a marathon, having an affair with a younger woman and buying a red 1964 MG Midget.

This guy can paint though, I'll give him that. Not sure what it is your average middle-aged bloke does when he turns to art. Landscapes, probably. Rolling hills, fields of wildflowers, maybe a cliff face and a not-very-good crashing sea. I mean, shit, I'm slagging those people off, but I'd struggle to do a jigsaw of the sea, never mind paint it, so I really ought to not be such a disdainful twat about it.

This guy ain't painting the sea, though. He's gone for what is perhaps an even more middle-aged thing, the female nude. God knows who it's supposed to be, but a completely naked woman is holding a bloody sword in one hand, and a man's decapitated head in the other. Abercrombie is currently painting the decapitated head.

Bishop and I exchange a glance, and I assume she's thinking the same thing I'm thinking, then she says, 'Judith and Holofernes?' which, if I'm honest, elevates the conversation way above my level. So, no, she's not thinking what I'm thinking, given that I'm now thinking, who the fuck was Judith? And do you have her phone number?

'Yes, of course,' he says, then he turns, ignores me, and looks at Bishop.

'And who might you be?'

'Detective Inspector Bishop,' says Bishop, smoothly lying in the way of her kind. I'll bet she'll have the requisite ID on her in case anyone asks.

He regards her gruffly, then looks at me.

'What happened to the other detective who you came with two days ago? What happened to this, what's her name, the Eurydice woman who's leading the investigation? How many detectives do you have on this case anyway?'

'Beyond counting,' I say. Might as well crack on. 'We'd like another word.'

'Fine,' he says brusquely, and he turns, lays down the brush, picks up a rag, considers it, considers wiping the brush or wiping his hands or wiping something, hard to tell, and instead he just tosses the rag back down, and then turns and sits on the stool next to him.

His head is now positioned right next to Judith's breasts. And I'll tell you what, the guy can paint a pair of tits, I'll give him that. Wow.

Hmm, I wonder if John Singer Sargent did one of Gertrude naked. Man, I bet I'd get that jigsaw completed a lot more quickly.

He snaps his fingers in front of the breasts – yep, I've been caught staring – and says, 'Lovely that you appreciate the art so much, Detective Sergeant. Really, although there is evidence to the contrary, I have work to do. You interrupt my half-hour break.'

'You don't need to justify yourself,' I say, and he looks as though he's about to start objecting, then he gives me a half-hearted nod of acceptance, and offers a hand, to say, *very well, then, peasant, ask away*.

'Tell us about you and Julia Wright.'

His eyes widen a little, his shoulders straighten, he looks at Bishop, and then he turns, picks up the rag he'd discarded, and starts wiping his hands.

'Maybe I'll have to get back to work sooner than I anticipated.'

'There's nothing leading about the question,' I say. 'It's nothing more than it is. You are the senior, I don't know what you call it in church circles, you're the senior civilian.' He barks out a laugh. 'You run shit. You make decisions. Julia would have worked more closely with you than anyone else.'

'Well, I cannot argue *that*, I suppose.'

'So, what kind of relationship did you have? How often did you see each other?'

'Really, I went over this already with Eurydice in her original visit, and you and I talked of this two days ago. I'm not entirely clear why it is we're talking about it again.'

He holds my gaze for a moment, then switches to Bishop.

'Is this for your benefit?'

Bishop doesn't answer. She's introduced herself, said her piece, and from now on she's going to be cold. He rolls his eyes at her silence, turns back to me.

'What d'you want from me, Sergeant? This really is tiresome.'

'This is a regular murder investigation, Mr Abercrombie. This is what it's always like for us. We go over and over the same questions, and some people understand that's the process, and some people are assholes about it.'

'Good to know I'm not alone, then,' he says. 'Are we done?'

'No, we're not done.' Note the way I left the word *fucking* out of that sentence. It was borderline.

'Look, I get it, I really do,' he says, trying to be less of a dick, and failing, 'you need to ask and ask and ask, waiting to pounce on the deviation, the mistake, the slightly changing storyline. Well, how about we accept that I am a senior executive at *the Royal Bank of Fucking Scotland*, and my story is not going to change. Not one bit. And you know why, because I don't even have a story. There is no story. Julia and I were colleagues at the church. We worked together. As a result, we spent time together. Sometimes we were alone together. I don't know about you, Sergeant Hutton, but I am quite capable of being alone with a woman without, God, I don't know, without... fucking her.'

He says that *fucking* in a completely different way from the previous one, as though he's being a bit naughty. As though that's the one he shouldn't have said. Using the word as an intensifier, totally legitimate. But as a verb? Out of line.

'I don't believe you,' I say.

'What?'

'We have heard a lot of talk of Julia Wright's infidelity. You can be as bumptious as you like in the face of these allegations, but in general, it's what people believed. No one was willing to put a name to it, but it makes the most sense that it was you.'

He's still rubbing his hands in that rag. Perfect symbolism there for him trying to rub the smell of Julia Wright's pussy off his fingers.

Too much? Yeah, all right, I'll cut it from my official memoir.

'Get out,' he says, cold fury in his voice.

I really don't find the cold fury at all convincing.

'Tell us about you and Julia.'

'You know everything you need to know. Now, and I hope I don't have to say this again, get out. You can always choose not to, of course, but I am done talking.'

He sneers, he looks angrily at Bishop, he turns his back on us, back to his painting. Judith and the head of, God, I forget, some guy, some time, somewhere. Got what he deserved, more than likely.

Bishop and I look at each other. I really didn't handle that terribly well. I consider a throwaway comment to the great artist about how we'll be back, but decide not to bother, and then we leave, out into the hallway, closing the door behind us.

The hallway is not grand, but nevertheless would be big enough for cat swinging. If it was an apartment in London, the hallway itself would cost three-quarters of a million. Not that that's saying much. You'll find a parking spot in London for three quarters of a million.

'Where to now?' she says, heading to the front door.

'We're not leaving yet.'

She raises her eyebrows, and with it comes a clatter from the kitchen, a low, muttered curse, the sound of something being placed in a drawer.

'Come on, we're not going to have long,' I say.

I go to the front door, open it, wait a couple of seconds, loudly close it, then indicate for Bishop to follow. I feel I don't need to put a finger to my lips or anything. She's a spy, she should know this shit, and this is pretty low-level chicanery, the pretence of leaving aimed at the man of the house.

There's a dining room between the study, where Abercrombie is painting his decapitated head, and the kitchen, so hopefully we'll be able to talk for a little while without him realising.

Into the kitchen, and Mrs Abercrombie stops unhappily in

her tracks as we enter. We get the harsh look, quickly followed, as the thought processes play out on her face, by resignation. She knew we'd likely come looking for her. She knew instinctively we'd faked leaving the house.

A hesitation, then she goes about her business. Doing something in the kitchen, though it's hard to see what that is. Moving implements from one place to the next, possibly preparing to do something in particular, possibly just a distraction. She was distracting herself in here before we entered.

'Can we ask you about Julia Wright?'

'I did that already,' she says, lifting a dish towel, picking up the closest thing to hand to wipe down.

People have big, fuck-off kitchens, don't they? When this house was built in the Victorian age, who knows what this room would have been for, but now, it's an immaculate, big, fuck-off kitchen. Someone's labour of love, some time. Or, more likely, the banking executive throwing forty-grand at the bespoke kitchen design company.

Rarely ever seem to go into shitty little kitchens anymore. Maybe I just don't notice them, because one expects to see shitty little kitchens. I have a shitty little kitchen. Then again, I have a fridge, and the fridge is big enough for bottles of wine and tonic, so what else does a kitchen actually need?

'You did what?'

'I spoke to a woman a few days ago. I told her everything I knew about Julia. I told her… I told her about, I mean, Julia and I didn't have an awful lot to do with each other. I helped out at things, I'm in the Guild, I saw her often enough, but… we didn't have a particular relationship. I left that to John.'

'And what kind of relationship did John have with Julia?'

She pauses her mindless act of wiping the thing that doesn't really need wiped. Lips set hard in a hard face. This woman is a million miles from Julia Wright. She can only be perhaps ten years older than the minister, but she looks as though she's from a different generation. This woman is maybe in her early fifties, and she already looks like someone's gran. Julia Wright was young at heart, had a carefree look about her – at least, she does in the pictures and videos we've seen – and a woman you could imagine throwing caution to the wind, deciding life was for living.

All right, I'm not saying that just because you're someone's gran you can't think life's for living, but there's an inevitable caution that comes with parenting and then grandparenting, and that caution is written on Isobel Abercrombie's face. Or maybe it's nothing to do with kids, and it's just who she is. Some people never grow up – no names, no names! – and some people hit their twenties with their arsehole so tightly wound their entire existence is controlled by set rules of appropriate behaviour.

'They worked together. Show me a session clerk and a minister who don't, and I'll show you a dysfunctional church. I dare say there are a few of those around Scotland.'

'Were they having an affair?'

The audience wouldn't have thought it possible, but her lips tighten even more. Her sphincter must be an impenetrable barrier by now.

Jesus, trust you to bring penetrating her sphincter into this. Concentrate!

She turns her back, lays the thing, whatever it is, down on the kitchen top, lifts something else. It would appear my knowledge of kitchen equipment is insufficient to carry on an entirely reliable narrative. I don't think it's particularly pertinent though.

'They worked together; they were supposed to work together. They were supposed to talk, they were supposed to have meetings.'

'How often did they have meetings? Just the two of them, having a meeting?'

She turns back, manages the words, 'Twice a week, maybe.'

There's the confirmation. The tone. The pain of it. The look on her face that says, *twice a week? That seems quite a lot, now that I say it out loud. Most ministers and session clerks won't meet twice a week.*

I hold the stare. I don't think she's going to crack though. Repeating her husband's cover out loud may be giving her pause, but it's not like she hasn't known it all along. She just hasn't wanted to think about it. And she's not keen to start thinking about it now.

'Are you uncomfortable talking to us with your husband in the house?' I ask.

She doesn't answer. The look on her face does not break.

I dig a card out of my pocket and place it on the kitchen counter beside me.

'Here's my number. Give me a call when you can. It may be that we officially ask you into the station for questioning in any case. In the –'

'Why?'

'You husband was having an affair. His lover is dead.'

I leave it at that. She swallows, loudly, eyes widening.

'Call me when it's suitable. We'll arrange to talk somewhere neutral, or tomorrow morning maybe, if John is back at work.'

Holding my gaze, she reaches over, lifts the card, doesn't look at it, quickly places it in a drawer next to the sink.

When she turns back to me, I get the look. She won't call. People like Mrs Abercrombie never call.

Shit.

We're done, I think. So the theories start to stack up. Now we need to discover some link between John Abercrombie and Jennifer Talbot, even if it's just finding out how he knew she was sleeping with Dr Thebes.

'We'll see ourselves out,' I say.

I nod, her face expressionless, and then Bishop and I turn away from her and head towards the kitchen door.

I know he's going to be standing there even before we get into the hall. He's by the front door, like a two-bit horror movie character, blocking the exit.

I spoke quietly, it's a big house, I'm not particularly worried he will have overheard. He and Isobel can have an argument about it once we've gone, although I suspect they'll be the quiet rage type. Hating each other for the rest of their lives in silence.

'I thought you left,' he says.

'My colleague needed to use the bathroom,' I say, enjoying the obviousness of the lie. 'We're just going.'

He doesn't move. Shit. I'm not going to get into some bullshit, testosterone war, so I make my power play. I look at him as if he's five, like he's being a naughty boy. It works. With a sharp grimace, he stands to the side.

My phone pings. I could wait until we're outside to read the message but decide to do it right here. This prick has been lying to us, and his time is coming. I don't really think he's our killer – albeit, if it's not Thebes, it has to be *someone* – but the lying sticks in the throat.

The text is from Kallas, and here's the proof.

We found e-mails between Rev Wright and JA. They were sleeping together. References to husband's knowledge of affair. No mention of, nor messages to, Thebes.

Type a quick *thank you* in reply, phone back in pocket, look at Abercrombie. Well, there we are, you lying piece of shit. Same goes for the husband. We're all shocked.

Unlike my balls-out decision of the other day, I decide to regroup at HQ with Eurydice before ploughing ahead. I think we have enough to get these two clowns into the station, but I'll let her make the call.

Maybe it's just because I'm not out here on my own.

Time to go, to end the stupid game. As we pass, Abercrombie's eyes go over my shoulder, and I guess Isobel has appeared in the doorway, and the two of them can now share a long, lingering look of loathing.

Outside, fresh air, the door is slammed shut behind us.

Take in the day for a moment, the sky and the clouds and the clean air, then head down the short flight of steps to the front gate.

'All coming together,' I say to no one in particular, albeit obviously within Bishop's hearing.

'You think our killer is to be found under that roof?'

'Way too early,' I say, as I open the car door. 'But that faint buzz you feel in the back of your brain, that's progress. That's all.'

28

Back in HQ, having eschewed immediately going down the Clyde to see Mr and Mrs Johnson. That will come. I thought it was worthwhile coming back to see Eurydice, but I'm also hoping Bishop decides she has better things to do than traipse around with the detective sergeant. Especially now that it turns out she doesn't want to sleep with me. I mean, hasn't she read the blurb on the back of the packet?

We're in the canteen. Eurydice, Kallas and I. Bishop took her leave, said she had calls to make. I get the impression she won't be coming back out, but difficult to read these people.

'So, why does he run?' asks Eurydice. 'If we're seriously thinking that perhaps Thebes isn't the killer, why run? Why, in fact, implicate himself in the first place? When you turned up at his house, why didn't he just palm you off and then make himself scarce? He would have had time to go anywhere, do anything, before we'd have been onto him. Yet he more or less invited us in.'

'He did not know the murders had been carried out with model maker implements,' says Kallas, 'and therefore need not have anticipated such a quick reaction from the police, despite his acknowledgement of the affairs.'

'It helps, certainly,' says Eurydice, 'that we had this extra hook on which to hang our suspicion, but holy shit, the double affair was enough on its own. And he's so calculating. This running thing really sticks in my throat. The guy could be anywhere. It's not the action of an innocent man.'

I take a drink of coffee. This would be an appropriate time to mention that he's been in my apartment. A very good time. Just as a phone call last night, or in the office first thing this morning would also have been a good time.

'The man may have no end of secrets,' I say. 'His reasons for running could be completely unrelated to our murders. Or perhaps he thinks he's being set up, and he just wants to take himself out of the way until the dust settles.'

'That feels like driving faster so you get through the speed trap area more quickly.'

'Not if he sends us a postcard from Belize, the same day someone gets murdered in Bellahouston.'

'Well, he may think that proves his innocence, but I think I'd find that even more suspicious,' she says.

'Wherever he is, whatever he's playing at, I'd like to leave that to others for the moment,' I say. 'There's a potential tangled web of sex secrets here, particularly if Thebes is being honest about his affairs. People get caught up in tangled webs, and who knows what comes out the other end. From the inspector's work, we know Abercrombie and Julia Wright were sleeping together, and we know Mr Wright and Mrs Abercrombie knew about it. We know Jennifer Talbot and Daisy Johnson were sleeping together. Let's find out who else knew what. I'd like to go and see Daisy Johnson again, and we need to schedule another chat with Abercrombie.'

'I'm going to go and speak to him now,' says Eurydice. 'I was careless in our first conversation. I had him down as just another boring church person, with his own political games to play. You did a good job, the pair of you.'

'I merely looked at e-mails,' says Kallas, 'which a desk clerk could have done. Sergeant Hutton did a good job.'

I give her a glance, first time I've looked at her since we sat down.

'Either way, you are working well as a team, I appreciate it. Perhaps you could go down to Helensburgh together, see what else you can dig up. I will work this end, there are others on the matter of Dr Thebes, and we can reconvene later in the afternoon.'

She looks between the two of us. We both nod, then in unison we lift our coffee cups to our lips. The conversation is wrapped up, the coffee finished, or not, and then we're heading down the stairs and on our way.

*

'You are convinced Dr Thebes is not the killer we are looking for?'

We're heading along Great Western Road, as the M8 looked like the roads out of Los Angeles in a disaster movie. Or, possibly, the roads out of Los Angeles literally every day. Fuck do I know? Never been to LA, can safely say I'll die never having been to LA.

There was something of the Obi Wan quote in Kallas's line there, and coming from someone else, I'd likely think that was the intention. But with DI Kallas, not so much. She's not the dropping Star Wars references randomly into conversation type.

'Convinced is too strong a word. I have a feeling it's not Dr Thebes.'

'He has run.'

He's not gone very far.

I don't say it. I also can't mention his past. Curious that Eurydice would send us off together like this, but then, perhaps it makes sense. The dual perspective. One person looking at everything from front on, one through the lens of all that spy shit. Except, that didn't seem to apply when I spoke to Wright and Abercrombie. Guess Eurydice is making decisions on the hoof, based on the information gathered in the previous thirty minutes. Just like the rest of us.

'He seems like a complex man,' I say. 'Maybe that's why I like him. He's challenging, he's on top of his game. He could sit in that room for a year, interrogated every day, and he wouldn't change. You get the feeling that even if he's not guilty, he'd be quite happy to spend some time in prison. He is where he is in any given moment in time. Living in that moment. His life is in his head, his surroundings are incidental.'

'You are suggesting he exists on some higher plane.'

I sit comfortably at thirty-three miles per hour, the traffic steady, catching a run of green lights.

'I guess I am, though I'm not thinking in such lofty terms. And I'm not saying that's how *he* sees it. There's just something abnormal about him. Something elevated. Or, at least, something that elevates him above the rest of us.'

'Perhaps the abnormal thing is that he had a dispute with his two lovers, and then killed them both. As we speak, he is plotting the third murder. And then he will disappear.'

'Possibly. Look, I'm not sucking the guy's dick here. I just think…'

The vulgarity of that analogy catches up with me three words into the next sentence, and I stop talking. Give her a quick glance. Her face is, of course, expressionless. I used to say stuff like that all the time to Taylor, and I'd say that to Eileen, and it would just be something I said, and no one would care either way.

'Sorry, that was a little unnecessary,' I say.

'It is an appropriate phrase. You and Dr Thebes have seemed to hit it off so well, one can imagine you might suck his dick.'

I look at her. She's staring forward, now with a small smile on her face.

'Funny.'

'It is not something I will imagine, however,' she says.

'Good to know. Let's move on.' I quickly try to think of something else to say, a change of subject urgently required. 'Was that a Star Wars reference you made earlier?'

'Yes, of course.'

Well, look at that.

'Didn't think you'd like Star Wars.'

'Why?'

'I don't know. Thought maybe you'd spend your time watching bleak and serious films about Estonia during the Soviet occupation.'

Now she looks at me, we share a quick glance, then I turn back to the road. Here we are, having a normal conversation, so let's try to hang on to it.

'Are you familiar with such films?'

Finally get caught at a red light, but we're well clear of the city by now, and the drive down the Clyde is not going to take too long. Good call on avoiding the motorway.

'I watched *The Fencer* a while back.'

'You watched *The Fencer*?'

Modern film, set in a bleak, early-50s Estonia. Depressing as fuck. At least, I thought so. I don't usually watch such movies. Real life is shit enough as it is, I don't know why anyone would want to be depressed by someone else's existence. For me, movies have to be either funny, or rampant escapism. I suppose early-50s Estonia is another world and lifetime away, but definitely not for me, nevertheless.

'Yes.'

'You didn't say.'

No, I didn't. I mean I watched it entirely so we'd have something to talk about, and I was drinking while watching, and by the end I despised myself for being this sad, miserable wretch, watching a movie I hated, just so Kallas would know I was interested in her country's history, and by extension her, which was particularly needy of me given she's someone else's wife, and someone I can never have.

Such feelings are always slow to leave. I never mentioned the movie the next day, and thereafter this small Estonian film about an ex-soldier who'd fought in Estonia against the Soviets, on the side of the Germans, became unavoidably linked in my head with self-loathing.

And lo! (as those cunts would've written in the Bible), that has not changed, and I feel the darkness descend.

'No,' is all I say.

'It is a good film. Did you enjoy it?'

'A little bleak for me.'

'Oh. I did not think of it as bleak.' A pause, and then she adds, 'There are much bleaker Estonian films.'

I bet there are. I nod, but that's that for idle chitter-chatter. It has run its course, stumbling inevitably into familiar, forlorn territory.

And on we drive, the road to Helensburgh mercifully clear.

29

First time interviewing Marc Johnson on his own. We didn't get much out of him the other day when he blundered pompously into the conversation with his wife. Eurydice has also spoken to him already and got very little from him. Time has passed however, information emerges slowly from the woods, people are prised open, inch by bitter inch.

He's sitting behind a large, teak desk. A plush office, grandfather clock in one corner, shelves of books, rich carpet, a painting of an old United States battleship on the wall behind him; through the window behind and to his left, a gorgeous view out over the firth to the hills on the other side. Greenock looks so much better from this distance.

'How long have you been in Scotland?' asks Kallas.

'So, what are you?' he asks. 'Swedish? Norwegian?'

He's an old white American twat who thinks he should be in charge of any conversation. Certainly, has no intention of deferring to a woman twenty years his junior. Poured himself a glass of whisky before he sat down. Eleven-thirty-seven. One recognises the symptoms, though he is the kind of wealthy business guy who will think drinking whisky before lunch is perfectly acceptable. Fortunately, it's one of the few drinks I have no problem turning down. Two-fingers worth will have me puking up within minutes. Humphrey Bogart would think I was a pussy.

'It is not important,' says Kallas. 'We need to know about you.'

'Like, what I said to you before, what I said to the female officer who was here a few days ago, wasn't enough?' He smiles, he tries to include me in it, he turns back to Kallas. 'Came here when Obama first became president. Didn't want to stick around while the country went to hell in hand cart. Spent four years during the Trump presidency intending to go home, and before you know it, missed my chance, and now we've got that crazy old loon in charge. I'll go back one day. Maybe the country'll see sense and we'll get Donald back.'

Well, this guy wears his asshole on his sleeve, doesn't he?

'Tell us about your relationship with Jennifer Talbot.'

'Boy, this really is a rerun. Whatever, I can give you twenty minutes of my time.'

What a prick.

'I'd read about her. I mean, it wasn't like she was famous or anything, but I'd read about this woman who'd sailed around the world a couple of times and was planning to do it again. What an interesting person, I thought. I mean, when you find a woman like that. I arranged a meeting, we kind of hit it off. She had stories to tell. She was a little weird, you know, interactionally, but we ended up in bed, and my God, she was sensational. My divorce with Linda had just come through, and I thought, well, why not? Linda just had no idea, and I mean, no idea how to orgasm. Hell, maybe it was me, but you know what, I think we all know it was her. So, I'd found great sex, and I thought, why not marry it? It was never going to last, me and Jenny, but you might as well enjoy yourself, right? I knew I'd end up paying her some money, but she wasn't greedy, like most women. She needed enough to get the boat done, and off she headed. Divorce came through some time when she was off the coast of Cape Verde. I remember the photo she sent.'

'Then you married Daisy?'

He seems to have to think about it, then he shakes his head. 'Next was Caitlin, then it would've been Sandra. Sandra was probably a mistake. Daisy seemed nice enough at the time, but, you know, things haven't worked out so well. Still, it's been a few years now. She keeps on keeping on, as Dylan would say.'

You get Bob's words out your mouth, you right-wing, American fuck.

'Why is that? You seem to have had no trouble divorcing women in the past?'

He smiles, takes his whisky, swallows loudly, eyes on Kallas the entire time.

'I did some business with her daddy. The business continues. It would not currently be politic for the marriage to end, but it's of no concern. We more or less lead separate lives.'

'Tell us about Jennifer Talbot moving back into your boathouse.'

He regards Kallas appreciatively, gives me a similar, if slightly less sexual look, then nods to himself.

'I like you two, you've got something about you. That woman who came here the other day, I don't know. Kind of got my back up. Didn't much feel like talking to her.'

'It would be best if you just answer all our questions honestly and fully, regardless of who is asking them,' says Kallas, as straightforward as ever.

'Sure thing,' says the arse. 'Jenny got in touch, I never saw any reason to say no. I think Daisy was a bit worried about it at first, but seems they got on well enough.'

There it is, in the tone. He knows about his wife and his ex-wife.

'Did you sleep with your ex-wife after she got back?'

'Shit, of course I did. Just a couple of times, though. I don't know, wasn't quite the same, you know. Guess we'd both moved on. Maybe it was just her. There was certainly something about her, something had changed.' He takes a drink; a feigned wistfulness comes over him. 'Now, we'd barely spoken these last couple of years.'

'Do you know why anyone would have wanted to kill her?'

'Are you kidding me? No one would've wanted to kill Jenny.'

'Someone killed her,' says Kallas prosaically.

'Sure, but it couldn't have been someone who knew her. Must've been some random kind of a thing.'

'How did you feel about Jennifer Talbot and your wife having an affair?'

Nice from Kallas. Don't think the big fella was expecting that. The eyes widen for a moment, then he gets his face under control. He takes a drink, lowers the glass, glances between the two of us. The measured, I'm still dominating this conversation, look.

'Some men might find it emasculating,' she says.

'Would they?'

'That their wife needed to find sexual satisfaction in the arms of a woman, rather than their husband.'

Terrific from Kallas. The guy really doesn't like it.

'And I murdered her for that, is that the implication?'

'We are just trying to understand the situation, Mr Johnson. The dynamic.'

'Well, the dynamic is that it turns out my wife's a dyke, but I can't divorce her for business reasons. We live separate lives. She's my sixth wife in all, and really it's been doing me no harm to have to wait for the seventh.'

'Very romantic,' says Kallas drily.

'Whatever, honey.' *Honey?* Seriously? 'Even if this was my reason for killing Jennifer, wouldn't I have had more reason to kill Daisy? Daisy, in case you hadn't noticed, is still alive. And what about this other woman, this minister? I never met her, I don't know anything about her, I've never been near her church. Hell, I don't even know what religion that Church of Scotland is.'

'Tell us about Dr Crispin Thebes?' I say, as Kallas leaves a small gap, which I – completely in tune with my partner – take as an invitation.

Johnson looks at me, brow furrowing. Tough to tell whether or not it's feigned, that old, rubber American face giving nothing away.

'Well, you're going to have to tell me who that is, Sergeant.'

'Someone with whom Jennifer was also having a relationship.'

He holds my look for a moment, and then bursts out laughing.

'Well, holy shit,' he says, 'would you look at that. Good on her. Does Daisy know?' He looks between the two of us. 'No? Can I tell her?'

He laughs again.

Well, I suspect that Kallas was about to ask the same question, but there I go, one intervention from me, and I completely trashed the atmosphere. Turns out there are many, *many* reasons I remain a sergeant after all these years.

*

The conversation with Daisy Johnson is proving fruitless. She remains genuinely upset. Genuinely, in the judgement of this senior detective. And by senior detective, let's just clarify that I mean by age, rather than rank.

'I don't believe it,' she says.

'Jennifer never mentioned Dr Thebes?' I ask, Kallas leaving the questioning to me this time.

'No. I mean, Jennifer never mentioned anyone.'

'Is it possible your husband knew about Dr Thebes?'

She looks as though she's about to object to the question,

perhaps just the basic negative or the *why would he have done*? but the words stall on her lips as she gives it consideration.

'I don't know. Marc knows people. Who is this guy anyway?'

'Is it possible your husband knew that Dr Thebes and Jennifer were involved?'

'Really? Marc hasn't the faintest idea about my life, why would he know anything about his ex-wife? I mean, do you *know* how many wives he's had?'

'You're number six,' I say, just as a place marker to the fact that we've spoken to the guy and we're not completely ignorant.

'A fair measure of the man,' she says. 'I doubt he knew anything about any of them.'

'He knows you and Jennifer were having an affair.'

'No, he doesn't.'

'DI Kallas said to him we were trying to understand the dynamic between the three of you, and he said, and I quote,' and really, I hate it when people say *and I quote*, but there it is, I've just done it without thinking, '*the dynamic is that it turns out my wife's a dyke, but I can't divorce her for business reasons.*'

She stares across the kitchen table. She swallows, she lifts her cup of tea, takes a long, loud drink, places the cup back down.

'Marc said that?'

'You two really don't talk to each other, do you?'

'Never,' she says. 'I mean, obviously we talk sometimes, but really…'

'You have separate rooms?'

'Yes,' quickly followed by, 'Wait, what? What's that got to do with it?'

'So, it's quite possible there was something between Jennifer and Marc and you wouldn't have known anything about it?'

Wide eyes, another swallow, and no answer. You never know, really, what's in someone's head, but she's showing all the signs of being brutally trampled upon. Keep going Hutton, you vicious bastard, this is a murder investigation, and she's a suspect, and you have a job to do.

'Did you and Jennifer ever talk about Marc?'

Small head shake.

'Did you know they'd slept together when she first moved into the boathouse?'

177

'That's not true.'

I leave it there, the question, hovering over the kitchen table.

'Did he tell you that?' she asks.

'Yes.'

'Oh my God…'

Eyes drop, head shakes.

'Do you believe it, now that we're telling you he said it?'

'Did he really say it?'

'Yes.'

A moment, and then the nod. The small, barely perceptible nod.

'Then, yes. I don't know why he would have said it otherwise.'

'You think he could've known about Dr Thebes?'

'Marc is a well-connected man,' she says, her tone having been dragged into the depths. 'He knows everyone. So, he quite possibly knew this Dr Thebes in any case, and if he didn't, then sure, why not, perhaps Jennifer told him.'

'Is it possible Marc knew anyone at the church in Partick?'

She looks a little confused at that, so I let it process for a while, then she says, 'Wait, you mean, did he know the minister who was killed?'

'Is it possible? Her, or anyone she might have known.'

'I… I really don't know. Was it attached to the university? The church, I mean.'

'It's not attached to it, but it's in its proximity. It's certainly possible that there were people common to both the university and the church.'

'Well Marc does some work up there. I'm not sure what exactly, it might just be funding for one of the research departments. I mean, it's stupid, given we've been married six years, but I have literally no idea what he does all day. Wait…' Another pause. She's got her use of the modern day *wait* down to a T. 'Are you implying that maybe Marc killed the minister? That he killed Jennifer?'

'I'm not implying anything, Mrs Johnson. We're still at the rooting around stage of the investigation.'

'It's been a week!'

'Sure, and Jack the Ripper's been a hundred and thirty-three years, and people still haven't worked it out. Sometimes it takes time. We're still trying to write the narrative of this, so really, anything you've got to say…'

'Look, Marc and I don't have a lot of time for each other, as you'll have worked out, but to be honest, I've said quite enough about him now. Quite enough.'

Kallas's phone pings, Daisy and I look at her, as though we know this is something of significance, Kallas takes a second, types a quick reply, then slips the phone back into her pocket.

She gives me a glance, one to assume temporary control of the interview, and then she turns to Daisy and asks, 'Does the name Finola Stephens mean anything to you?'

Again, Daisy does something of the rabbit in the headlights look, ending with a small head shake.

'She's in Cardross,' adds Kallas.

Another headshake.

'We need to go,' says Kallas abruptly, turning to me, rising as she speaks.

The third woman. Got to be. This is interesting. Feel like there's some momentum picking up, coming on the back of most people knowing about everybody having sex with everybody else, and Marc Johnson being involved with the university, which at least puts him in the proximity of Rev Wright's church.

'Thank you, Mrs Johnson,' I say, as I get to my feet.

She stares back across the table, utterly defeated. Lover dead, thinking her husband might be a murder suspect, realising that he was far more aware of her infidelity than she'd known, the woman faces a long afternoon into evening, staring into the depths of the emotional abyss.

She does not see us out of the house.

30

'Just, fuck off.'

Splendid. More naked aggression. Eurydice found this woman, the curator of a small naval transport museum on the River Leven. They bought a model of the 1930s turbine steamer Duchess of Montrose from Thebes last year. The order was placed in the middle of the first lockdown, when nothing was open, and no one was doing anything. The museum had time and money to kill.

We spoke to Eurydice in the car. 'I got the impression,' she said. 'Going with my gut. She definitely knows him, but of course, let's not get carried away. Nevertheless, she was defensive, straight from the off, so let's see what we can get.'

Finola Stephens' defensiveness continues.

We're standing in a field at the back of her house, where she's brushing down a horse. Nice enough day now, high clouds, a slight feeling of warmth in the breeze, the birdsong speaking of spring.

I'm standing in front of the horse, some couple of yards away. It's looking at me. It sees me. The horse knows which one of the two of us is the alpha.

I hate horses. Kick you in the face, soon as look at you.

'We need to know whether or not you continued to have contact with Dr Thebes after you arranged for and received the model ship commission last year,' says Kallas.

The basic questions to kick-off the interview, try to establish some ground. Get the conversation going. However, in the face of refusal to talk, Kallas will give it no more than two or three, and then she'll bluntly cut to it.

Stephens' back is turned to us. She does not answer. Her brushstrokes down the side of the horse are becoming more brutal. Given we've already established that the horse is a bastard, it's getting no sympathy.

'We're investigating the murder of two women, Mrs Stephens. When two seemingly unconnected women are murdered, it is not unreasonable to worry that there may be a third and a fourth murder.'

Another angry stroke down the side of the horse, and another, and then she finally stops. She stays in position for a moment, so that the camera of life can zoom in on her face to see how irritated she is by this interruption to her day, and then she straightens up and turns.

'And what exactly is it about these two unconnected women and Dr Thebes that brings you here?'

'He was sleeping with both of them,' says Kallas bluntly. 'So not so unconnected after all.'

Boom.

Blood drains from face in real time. Like a special effect. She swallows. Poor Mrs Stephens, she must have thought she was the only one. That, at least, appears to be written all over her.

Well, look at Eurydice, she called this from one phone conversation.

'That's,' she begins, and then the sentence fades away. Her brow furrows a little, she looks like she's struggling to understand the concept of her lover having someone else.

'Were you also in a relationship with Dr Thebes?'

'There must be some mistake,' she says quickly, mundanely.

'Obviously we cannot ask the women in question, but Dr Thebes stated it to be the case.'

'Crispin told you that?'

Crispin… It's just wrong. Sometimes I feel like this guy ought to be referred to solely as The Abominable Dr Thebes, even by the women he slept with.

'Yes.'

'He's not in custody?'

'Have you spoken to him in the last twenty-four hours?'

And here come the brakes to the conversation. She does not answer.

'Have you spoken to him in the last twenty-four hours?' repeats Kallas.

Oh, Stephens is torn. On the one hand she naturally wants to protect her lover. On the other, turns out he was a bit of a love rat, not to mention that two of those other lovers have been murdered and so, slowly the wheels turn, she has to accept the not outlandish possibility she might be next in line.

'Mrs Stephens, I do not need to lay out the implications here,' says Kallas, as she can see those implications playing out across her face. 'Have you spoken to Dr Thebes in the last twenty-four hours?'

'Why don't you ask him? You've obviously already spoken to him.'

There she goes. We had her there for a moment, needed to see which way she'd turn. Inevitably, she turns in Thebes' favour.

'He was in custody for a while. We released him. He has now... gone into hiding.'

Gone into hiding.

'And you're looking for him? And you thought I might tell you where he is?'

And here comes the tone. Kallas, however, is not dicking around.

'Does your husband know Dr Thebes?'

Bit of a sphincter-tightener there for Finola.

'What's Eric got to do with it?'

'Does he know Dr Thebes?'

'No, why would he?'

'Does he know that you are having an affair with Dr Thebes?'

Oh, that's gorgeous by the way. Nice line of questioning, up against solid evasion tactics. An interviewer and obfuscating interviewee, both at the top of their games. Like the first Ali-Frazier fight in Madison Square Garden, in '71.

Wait, I should probably have a women's sporting analogy for this, right?

I look at the horse. The horse reads me like a book. *You sexist bastard*, thinks the horse. Must be a girl horse. There's probably a name for a girl horse.

Focus!

'We need to find Dr Thebes, and we need to find everyone who might have been in any kind of intimate relationship with him, and there is no time to mess around,' says Kallas. 'You need to talk to us, and I will be blunt. If you do not, then I will feel we need to talk to your husband. You can make the choice.'

Oh, Chris Evert and Martina Navratilova, how's that? Anyway, Chris Evert just got her arse handed to her. The *let's go inside, and talk* is no more than one sentence away.

She nods, she stares at the ground for a moment, she turns

to the horse, runs a final brush down her side, mutters a farewell word in the horse's ear as though they might never see each other again, and then she turns back to us and starts leading the way towards the kitchen, where she can kill time by making a cup of coffee, while giving herself something to hide behind at the table.

31

Finola Stephens talked easily enough in the end, it seemed, but ultimately, did she tell us anything?

Thebes called her last night. Told her she might be getting a visit from the police, but that there was nothing for her to worry about. Said she should be as open or as closed as she chose, there was nothing she could say that would do him any harm. He did not say why the police might call, nor did he mention either Wright or Talbot. He did not say where he was calling from, though there was nothing to suggest it had not been his house.

They'd been in the habit of seeing each other once every couple of weeks, so not seeing him in the past week had not been unexpected. Equally, it was not uncommon for him to be slow in returning calls. Their affair – so low-key, she said, it was barely worth the name – had been going on for just over six months. Her husband had no idea. Neither would he care, she said, though there may have been some wishful thinking or projection going on. The only way to know would be to speak to the husband.

It wouldn't be the most outrageous of possibilities for the husband to be guilty of the first two murders, committing them as cover, saving his wife for last. Except, here we are, the police already speaking to his wife, and it would have been stupid in all kinds of ways. And that's not to mention the improbability of the husband having known about the other two women.

We will speak to him, but for the time being we've put it in her hands. She can choose to tell him on her terms if she likes, but he's going to find out in the next day or two either way.

Of significance was Kallas asking if Thebes had mentioned the likelihood of her being in any danger. She did not answer, but in her silence, answer enough. If his other lovers have been murdered, there should be plenty of reasons to worry about her. Unless, of course, he knows for sure she's in no danger, and there's really only one reason that would be the case.

Back up to town, a slow drive, stuck in traffic, Kallas

untalkative, a not unusual state, and I don't force anything. To begin with she calls Eurydice with the update, conversation briefly fills the car as she puts the call on speaker, but I have nothing to add. Eurydice perhaps does not even realise I'm included in the conversation. They arrange to get eyes on the Stephens' residence with immediate effect, anything further to await discussion back at the office.

Thereafter the trip passes largely in silence, little further conjecture to be had on the matter of the investigation. We are where we are.

In the silence I decide that, confronted by another woman's infidelity, coupled with the obvious guilt on show, Kallas is internalising her own guilt at her feelings for me. She will reject those feelings, and make sure nothing of any consequence ever passes between us. This is who she shall be from now on, a woman committed to her husband, deserving of her commitment or not though he may be.

I drive, and I slide into melancholy. And not one of those good melancholies. A shitty melancholy, bleak and grim and grey and heart-breaking. I'm desperate to talk myself out of it, to talk my way through it, and utterly clueless what to say. Although, of course, if she is really thinking along the lines of my dark assumptions, then there is nothing I could say in any case.

We return to the office, we are back in with Eurydice, the afternoon continues into early evening. More talk, more examination of the known facts, more attempts to find pieces of the jigsaw that fit together, although too many of them don't even belong in the same picture. And so the day goes.

*

Get a call from Eileen at seven-thirteen. Notice the time on the large, ugly digital clock above the door in the office as I take the call. This will be my evening, mid-case, *just checking you're not headed to the off-licence* call.

Every day is a toss-up. God, it's exhausting. A day without rain would be so nice. A day when I don't have to fight the fight, when I don't have to embrace the denial. The good days are the days when I give in to it and manage to couple that with not feeling guilty. The days of thinking, *well, fuck this, to the off-licence, men!* The guilt, the self-loathing will come the next day, but just for an afternoon I can look forward to the taste and the feeling and the sheer relief and joy of giving in, and I can get the hour, maybe the hour and a half, before it starts to taste bitter, and the feeling goes, and it's replaced by need and greed and there's nowhere to go other than deeper and deeper into the depths of the Dead Marshes.

And, of course, those days, the days when I don't feel guilty about drinking, and I know well in advance that I'm going to give in to it, are already shitty days. Days of melancholy and doubt, days of holding the metaphorical gun to the head. There is, of course, no actual gun. The drink is the gun. Some metaphor. And that's about the size of it. The shittiest days are the good days, because at least I don't have to feel bad about drinking at the end of it.

And what makes today so bad? That see-saw – for it is little more than that – is very delicately balanced, and clearly it is far too dependent on the minute shifts of DI Kallas's slender weight

'How's it going?' asks Eileen

'We're good.'

I know there's no point in trying to hide the tone. Some days I try to hide the tone, and I don't so much fail in my quest for opacity, as she annihilates that quest with extreme prejudice.

'Getting anywhere?'

'It's a process,' I say. 'We found someone else our man was involved with, another woman, and so, I guess, another potential victim, but we'll see. We've got the place covered. However, still no sign of our guy, which is the main thing. Until we get him…' I shrug down the phone. 'How about you?'

'Brawl at a house party in Drumsagard this morning. We got called out at four a.m. Seventeen arrests, three people hospitalised, two of them still there.'

'We can hope at least that they die, and that'll be two less of them to trouble us in the future.'

I can see her look down the phone.

'You sound shit,' she says.

'Yeah, I guess.'

'I'll come over this evening.'

I don't want her to, but I don't even try.

'When are you leaving?' she asks.

Another look at the clock. Still seven-thirteen. Like it's stuck there, like we're all stuck at seven-thirteen.

'Eight-thirty.'

A pause, then she says, 'Eight-thirty?'

'Jesus, Eileen, I don't know. I've got a few more things to do, then I'm going to leave. If you think you need to come over, come at eight-thirty.'

'I'll be there earlier.'

Fuck me.

She's right. She's the best friend I could have. She can come over and I can even talk to her about this stupid infatuation with the married detective inspector. But sometimes, *sometimes*, you just want to go home on your own, and *drink a bottle of fucking vodka*.

'Thank you,' I say, forcing the civility from my lips.

'OK, chum. Well, hang in there. I'll see you shortly.'

I nod down the phone, we say goodbye, I hang up.

And not for a second do I think I won't be drinking tonight. It's on!

Phone in pocket, last look at the laptop, close it, stand up, look around the open-plan. Not sure where Kallas is, Eurydice and Blumenthal talking in the ops room, the door open. Elizabeth Bishop in there too, not engaged in their conversation, scrolling through her phone. Plenty of others still in the office.

Time to go. This wagon won't fall off itself. I'll take my telling off when Eileen arrives.

*

Park opposite my house. Have vodka, have tonic, have two bottles of white wine. Probably won't drink them all this evening. I really just want the vodka. However, while neat vodka performs one aspect of its mission statement – the need for alcohol! – it fails the taste test. You really do need the tonic to enjoy it. The wine is here so I've got something to drink for the minute it will take me to make the vodka mixer.

Maybe I'll take a little longer over the wine. We'll see how that first glass goes down. But Eileen will be here soon enough, and that vodka needs started upon.

Into the entrance hall, don't check my mailbox, there's never anything other than bills anyway, then up the stairs. That fifth floor seems a long way up sometimes.

Into the house, hands shaking already. I did well not to take a slug of the wine while I was in the car. The edge slightly gone from the anticipation thanks to the imminent arrival of Sergeant

Harrison, a long evening's descent does not await me, but I can start. I can leap off and see how far I can fall.

Into the sitting room, in my expectant rush, no sense that there's anyone else in the house, and then, there he is, sitting at the window, sitting by Gertrude in the half-light of early evening, waiting for me.

'Detective Sgt Hutton,' says Dr Thebes. 'You disappoint me.'

32

I'm sitting in the guest seat at the table. The seat that Eileen sits in when she comes over. My daughter, on occasion. There are no other guests.

Thebes is in the kitchen, pouring two bottles of wine, the bottle of vodka and, for good measure, the tonic, down the sink. I can't watch. I can't breathe in the smell of it.

When he comes back into this room, he will sit in my seat at the table at the window. Were David Attenborough narrating this scene, he would comment on the arrival of the new alpha male, the submissiveness of the previous incumbent of the position. Perhaps he might conjecture that I am biding my time, waiting to choose my moment to pounce.

He would be wrong.

The basis of this, of course, apart from my general sudden capitulation to events, is that I think him guilty of nothing other than being set up. Hopefully the submissive beta will be able to rouse himself to action should Thebes be here to confess.

He re-enters the room, takes a moment as he sees that I've sat down opposite where he was, then takes a seat.

'I'll take the empty bottles with me, there's no use you having them around the house.'

I hold his eyes for a moment, then when I lower them, I'm looking at Gertrude, upside down.

'A beautiful portrait,' he says.

We stare at it together, surrounded by a warm silence. The evening is not playing out as expected.

'Why did you finish it?'

'I needed to see whether you would report it, or whether you would positively anticipate further contact.'

'That's not what I meant.'

We share a quick look, and then he turns back to Gertrude, nodding.

'You were enjoying it. The gradual appearance of the woman, her slow emergence from the confusion of parts. I see that this could have been disappointing for you. I apologise.'

I shake my head, even though he's not looking at me.

'Sgt Harrison is coming here shortly,' I say. 'So, this is either you handing yourself in, or you'd better go. I do have some quest –'

'She will be late.'

'What did you do?'

'Sgt Harrison has been detained. She will be here soon enough.'

'*What did you do?*'

'I didn't do anything. Things come up in your line of work, it's what happens.'

'How d'you know then? I mean, that Eileen will be late?'

He doesn't answer. He's never going to answer that kind of question.

'You spoke to Finola,' he says.

'Jesus.' I mean, is there any point in even talking to this guy? 'We did. Did you listen?'

'I'm not omniscient.'

'Good to know, you kind of give that impression at times.'

'I like to know as much as possible,' he says. 'But in that, at least, I am not alone.'

'So, tell me, Dr Thebes, if it wasn't you who killed Julia and Jennifer, how can you be so sure that Finola is safe?'

I get the low glare, his hands clasped lightly together, elbows on the table, chin hovering just above, but not on, his hands.

'Someone is setting me up, that is clear. I do not know who. As to why, there could be innumerable reasons. Now, the relationship I had with Julia was different from those I shared with the others. We talked more. Julia knew about Jennifer Talbot. I do not know if either woman told anyone about me, but I did not tell Jennifer about Julia. I told neither about Finola.'

'The relationships with married women were kept secret, the relationship with Jennifer Talbot, who would not have suffered from the news being revealed, was not.'

'Exactly, although, as I say, I told Julia. I did not tell anyone else.'

'Why even tell her?'

'A reasonable question. Julia was also involved with John Abercrombie, the session clerk at her church. You will have spoken to him. Indeed, you are likely already aware of this. She was troubled by this. I told her of my other relationship to indicate to her that she need not be troubled on my account. That the concept of multiple sexual partners is neither exceptional nor remarkable.'

'Fine words for a minister to live by,' I say drily, and he smiles.

'As I say, I do not know with whom, if anyone, Jennifer, Finola or Julia shared details of our relationships. However, should they have been talkative, only Julia could have shared information outside of her own relationship with me. Therefore, when looking for the genesis of this, how it started and why it might have happened, Julia talking to someone would be a good place to start. Indeed, I can think of no other. In which case, Finola would be in no danger.'

'Had Julia said she was worried about anyone?'

'No.'

'Were her extra-marital relationships limited to you and John Abercrombie?'

'As far as I know, but she was a woman of a certain quality.'

'What does that mean?'

'She could be insatiable.'

Sometimes they're the best type, although, to be honest, you likely wouldn't want to be married to one of them.

'She, naturally, felt a certain degree of guilt as a result.'

'So, what of her husband? Do you think he might have taken his revenge on her, having killed Jennifer Talbot as part of his set-up plan?'

'You have met her husband?' Enough of an answer there, to be honest. 'He is a hopeless drunk. One can make mistakes in life by underestimating people, Sergeant, but I do not think we would be making a mistake in this instance. The man is incapable.'

'Do you know him?'

'We have not met. I heard enough from Julia. Few people know a man's qualities quite like his wife.'

'Then you think this could be the work of John Abercrombie?'

The calm stare across the table, the considered response.

'Certainly, a more capable candidate. However, clearly Julia knew a lot of people, and we all know that the politics of any organisation, religious or otherwise, are small and petty and vindictive and can lead who knows where.'

'What about you?'

'What does that mean?'

'You had a life before you came to Glasgow and started making models, didn't you?'

A slight narrowing of the eyes. A tension in the shoulders that wasn't there before.

'And what do you know of that life?'

My turn not to answer.

I get the look then, the deep stare, the stare that really isn't about me, isn't a stare deep into my head, but through me, beyond me, the calculating stare.

'We are two of a kind, Sergeant, forever trapped in the space between truth and lies, unsure which way to turn.'

'There are plenty of times when we know which way to turn,' I say.

A further slight movement of the body, the change of position. He's about to leave. Fuck, I really haven't handled this well.

'Did you kill Julia Wright and Jennifer Talbot?' I ask.

'To the point, Sergeant, I suppose,' he says. 'You imagine that in this more natural setting, you will be able to judge the veracity of my answer. Your police instinct, the thing that has managed to keep you in a job when most people would anticipate you to have fallen, will see you through.'

And so he continues, seeing the investigating officer coming before every bend in the road.

'That's exactly it, Dr Thebes.'

He stands quickly, he goes into the kitchen, the clank of bottles shows his intentions in going there, and then he is back into the sitting room.

'I will leave,' he says. 'I have explained to you why I believe Finola is in no danger.' He looks as though he's about to add to that, then he shakes his head at his own thought, gives me a nod and turns towards the door.

'And you will not answer the basic question at the heart of the case.'

He stops, turns.

'I killed neither Julia nor Jennifer,' he says simply, eye contact, no elaboration.

'You don't seem upset by either death.'

'Nor am I,' he says bluntly. 'Life happens to us all, in stops and starts, in shades of grey. We all live, we all die. The conventions of the day, as you previously observed, would suggest that I am on a spectrum. Perhaps I am. But I feel nothing, Sergeant, that is all.' A pause, more words to come, then he says, 'Now I must go.'

'I'd like to be able to get in touch with you.'

'You will likely not see me again.'

He does not speak. He turns, the bottles tapping against each other.

'What does the name Elizabeth Bishop mean to you?'

Another hesitation. The question, the words, linger in the air, the echo of them, waiting to be picked up, waiting to be run with, but I can feel that he's not going to turn. A moment, a tick of the clock from one second to the next, and then he is quickly out of the door and gone.

I sit there, as impotent as when he arrived, staring after him, at the space where he'd been. I cannot hear the clank of the bottles on the stairs outside, however, though one might expect the sharp sound to travel. He must be holding the bag close to his chest.

For the first time in ten minutes, I think of the alcohol. The drink I was so desperate for. The wine I intended to guzzle quickly, the vodka I would relish. Gone.

I walk into the kitchen and look down into the sink. I heard him run the tap, he knows the drinker will often enough attempt to retrieve the dregs from around the plughole, grotesque though it may be, so there is nothing here, not even the aroma as a parting glass.

Into the fridge, lift out a can of Coke Zero, back through to the sitting room, sit down by the table. Gertrude stares back at me. We hold the stare.

'You know what, Gertrude?' Nothing. She gives me nothing. 'I don't even want it. At the moment, at least. That's what ten minutes with a psychopath does for me. I should get that fucker to move in.'

I look at the door, as though he might be standing there. Take a drink, tap my fingers on the table, on Gertrude's pale, violet dress.

'And I just let him walk out the door…'

Gertrude has nothing to say. The silence between us grows, as though she knows it was not me who put this version of her together.

33

Twelve minutes after eight, Tuesday morning. Kallas and I having coffee in the canteen. I want to tell her that I saw Thebes last night. That I choose not to is nothing to do with it getting back to Eurydice. If I gave reasons for Kallas not to speak of it, I'm sure she wouldn't. But then she'd be in the same boat as me, and I don't want her in the same boat. Not this one, at least. It's bad enough for her career needing to navigate having me as her sidekick, but at least she's never guilty of the same abuses of office as I am. But this would be one such abuse. This would be complicity in the concealment of a murder suspect. Very career limiting.

Happy to limit my own career, but I can't be dragging Kallas down with me.

We drink coffee. Sitting across a four-seat table, doing that thing where we try not to look at each other too often, too directly. There's a light aroma of jasmine in the air, coming from Kallas's neck, I dare say. I try to neither look at, nor think of DI Kallas's neck.

A currently grey morning, though one of those days where the weather will change every fifteen minutes. A four-seasons-in-one-hour kind of a spring day.

'Eileen came to see you last night,' she says, looking down on the river.

'She brought Chinese food. Lemon chicken for me, beef in black bean sauce for her. We talked about taking a holiday to Switzerland together when all the coronavirus madness is over.' A pause, then I throw in, 'We're going to book something for summer 2032.'

'She said you surprised her.'

'Wait, you spoke to her after we had dinner?'

'She texted later to let me know you were all right.'

'You really don't have to...' I start, unusual annoyance creeping into my voice, then I stop myself. Well, obviously I get annoyed all the time, at all sorts of people, just unusual for it to be at Kallas. 'Thank you,' I say, 'but you know, I'm, you know, I'm fifty-four. I can look after myself, or not, and if I don't…'

'I do not like the sound of *if you don't*,' she says. 'That is all.'

What can I say? I have two attractive women taking it in turns to check up on me most nights. All right, one's married with three kids and one's a lesbian, but it's better than being massaged through the evening by a bottle of vodka.

'What happened last night?' she asks, turning to look at me.

'What d'you mean?'

She considers her phrasing, I guess, then says, 'You seemed off at work. We have both seen you like this. You drink, that is how you deal with it. She said she found you quite relaxed. What happened in between times?'

'I just… do I have to report every movement? I mean, I appreciate –'

'It is not that. Whatever you did in that short time was obviously of great benefit to you. It is perhaps something you could consider doing again. At least… if it is appropriate. Is it something you could consider doing again?'

Got a weird feeling in my chest. I think it might be the truth waiting to burst out. Yep, that's it. I can't lie to this woman.

Jesus. Just lie. Just do it. I mean, seriously mate, history is awash with instances of you lying to women you care about.

'It is a hard switch to flick,' she says, talking through my silence.

'I bought alcohol on the way home,' I say. 'Two bottles of wine, and a bottle of vodka. I got the wine, so that I'd have something cold to drink straight away, while I made the first mixer.'

'You were going to drink two bottles of wine while you made your first vodka and tonic?'

'One was back-up.'

'What happened.'

I poured them down the sink. Just say it, say the lie. *I poured them down the sink.*

She smiles curiously.

'You do not want to tell me.'

'It's not that.'

She asks the next question with raised eyebrows, eyes slightly widened. Reeling me in. Those eyes, that smell of jasmine.

It's not about confessing! It's not about telling the truth! It's about protecting her. So, in the name of fuck, just shut up.

'Thebes was in my apartment.'

In an inversion of the conventions of cinema, the entire audience side-eyes the screen.

You absolute moron. Words in my mouth, the way they sometimes are, coming out of nowhere, the way they sometimes do.

Her brow furrows, the Estonian equivalent of completely losing her shit.

'He was waiting for you?'

I stare dumbly across the table. Still grappling with whatever moronic half of me it was who was stupid enough to speak. The unconscious half. Must think it knows better, the stupid bastard.

'Tom?'

Dammit.

'When I got home from work on Sunday evening, the jigsaw had been completed. As of Sunday morning, I'd barely done half of it.'

'You knew it was Thebes?'

'It wasn't going to have been anyone else. He was testing me, to see if I reported it. I don't know his methods, how he knew that I then didn't report it. Perhaps he just waited to see if I had a team of SOCOs turn up at the apartment. However he thinks or however that worked out for him, he felt safe enough to come to my place last night. He was waiting for me when I got in.'

'And what happened?'

Another pause. She doesn't need to push it though; she knows I'll get there. I take a drink of coffee, can't take my eyes off her.

'We talked about the case. He is obviously…' Hesitate again, try to find the right framing. 'If we suppose he is innocent, which I do, he is obviously working his own angle to identify the killer. He explained why he thought Finola Stephens to be in no danger. He denied, naturally… he denied killing Julia Wright and Jennifer Talbot.' A pause, and then, 'Then he left.'

'There's nothing there that can help us.'

'No.'

'You've been over everything he said? Thought it through?'

'Repeatedly.'

'And there's nothing?'

'Nothing.'

'I feel you are not being completely honest.'

Reads me like a kipper, every time. However, blurting out tales that involve me is one thing. Dishing up on me raising the issue of his former life, and him being cagey, coupled with the hesitation when I mentioned the name of Elizabeth Bishop, is something else.

If he's so all-seeing, given how much he seems to know about our investigation, wouldn't he already have known about Bishop?

Perhaps not. Perhaps much of what he seems to know is just him using logic.

'No,' I say. 'I'm sorry, I'm uncomfortable with the whole thing, that's all. I shouldn't have told you. It puts you in a bad position. You either have to report it to Eurydice, or you become complicit along with me. I shouldn't have done that.'

'I will not report it. I will become, if it is the word you choose to use, complicit.'

'Sorry. I really shouldn't have said.'

'Why did you?'

Another one of those long looks across a narrow table.

'You have the whip,' I say.

'What whip?'

'Like Wonder Woman.'

'Wonder Woman's Lasso of Truth?'

'Yes, that.'

She takes a drink of coffee. This is a perfectly normal conversation for two adults to have. I was thinking that she'd likely have no idea what I was talking about, but then, she has three daughters. What mother with three daughters won't have watched Wonder Woman? Even though that last one was an absolute stinker, by the way.

'You are incapable of lying to me?'

'Yes.'

'Then tell me what other conclusions you came to after speaking to Dr Thebes.'

Very matter of fact. No questioning why I might consider her to be holding Wonder Woman's magical lasso, when she obviously isn't. Just straightforward, this is the case, it is what it is, let's see where it gets us.

I take a drink of coffee.

Really, I've told her the Thebes thing, which is way more damaging than the MI6 thing. She's not going to tell anyone; she's not going to give a shit. Why not just get it out there?

Our phones ping simultaneously, breaking the spell. The lasso's spell.

Simultaneously pinging phones are not good. We open them with synchronicity. The message is from Eurydice.

Ops Room.

That's it.

A look across the table, take a last glug of coffee, and we're on our way. And here, crime fans, is where it all… falls… down…

34

Practically a queue getting into the ops room. That message went out to everyone involved. Into the room, look around, already about twenty people in here, decide to not bother taking a seat, standing instead at the side, hands in my pockets. Eurydice and Blumenthal at the front.

Got one of those bad feelings about this. Not sure what it's related to, and it's hardly the weirdest thing on earth for us all to get called in, but nevertheless… My guts have decided, through no consultation with my brain, that however this plays out, I'm about to get rogered.

Eurydice looks up, indicates for the woman nearest the door to close it, waits for the click, and then gets to it.

'The third woman in the Thebes case is missing. Her husband, Eric Stephens, reported that she told him last night she'd been having an affair. They did not argue, as such, he claims – although, there's the likelihood he's just saying that because he doesn't want to implicate himself in her disappearance. He slept in their normal bed; she went to the spare room. When he checked on her this morning, she was gone. However, wherever and however she left, she did not take anything with her. No purse or wallet, no coat, no bag. On the face of it, this does not sound like a woman leaving home. Always the possibility, of course, that she's just gone out for a walk, or had gone to spend time with her horses. But then…'

She indicates to Blumenthal, and he presses a couple of keys on his laptop, and a photograph projects onto the wall.

'Here we go,' mutters someone at the back, (and the voice in my head). There are another few murmurs around the room.

'We got the news half an hour ago,' says Eurydice. 'We ran the photographic check through the city's CCTV system, and we just got this back.' The pause for us all to study the photograph, although we're all already studying the photograph, such as it needs to be studied. Dr Thebes at the wheel of a car, middle of the night, no one else sitting in the car. At least, no one else in sight. The contents of the boot or the rear seat footwells are obviously not on display.

'This was taken at traffic lights less than a five minute-drive from Mrs Stephens' home. There are coincidences, there is happenstance, and this is neither. Finola Stephens has disappeared, Dr Thebes was in the vicinity, the two are inexorably linked.'

Is there a difference between coincidence and happenstance? She's just making a point, I suppose, that I, more than anyone in the room, know is right to be made.

She starts talking again, but I have to interrupt her. The points and counterpoints race in an instant through my head: whether I should say anything at all, whether I should take counsel with Kallas, whether I should tell a half-truth, add a lie that I tried to detain him, should I let the room clear then speak to Eurydice, should I just balls-out get it over with in front of the crowd, who are all going to be as incredulous as the DCI? Options, options, and after the supercomputer has run the gamut in five seconds, I lift my hand. Like I'm in class. Seems marginally preferable to just interrupting her flow.

I don't look at Kallas.

Eurydice stops, looks at me with ill-masked annoyance, I get half a shoulder raise from her, and a blunt, 'What, Sergeant?'

This is going to go well.

'Dr Thebes came to my apartment last night.' I leave a gap, but it's fair to say the gap is really just filled with a stunned hush, so since I've started, I may as well, in the blessed name of Magnus Magnusson, finish. 'He was waiting for me when I got home. We talked for a few minutes. He stated his reasons why he thought Finola Stephens was in no danger. I believed him. He insisted he hadn't killed either of the others. He left.'

That's it. After all, that's all there is to say.

Silence.

You could hear a pin being stuck in someone's eyeball.

Wait, that doesn't work.

Shut up!

'He left?'

'Yes.'

'Did you try to stop him?'

'No.'

She's too shocked to even bother with the expected profanity. Her angry, incredulous gaze turns to DI Kallas.

'Did you know about this?'

'I'd just informed Inspector Kallas in the canteen, she stated that I had to tell you, I was about to come downstairs when we got your message. Now I'm telling you.'

'Now you're telling me. Bully the fuck for you, Sergeant.'

Hands on hips now, the look at the floor, the look around the room, the shake of the head.

'Sergeant,' she says to Blumenthal, 'start divvying up, you know what to do. You,' she says to me, 'come with me.' A moment, then she starts to stride quickly towards the door, the word, 'Fuck!' bellowed loudly into the air.

I don't look at Kallas as I follow Eurydice from the room.

35

'I really don't know where to start, Sergeant.'

DCI Hawkins looks at me from across the desk. Here I am, back in the familiar haunt, the familiar saddle, getting my arse handed to me.

Eurydice didn't hand me much of my arse. She's not an arse-hander, even though she comes across like she'd be pretty good at it. She just wanted to know all the details of the conversation. I included everything, starting with the alcohol down the sink. I don't know if I said that in order to give a total picture, or if I thought it might make her back off a little. I thought I didn't care if she went at it full bore, but who knows? My subconscious and I have an uneasy relationship. Same as every bastard and their subconscious, I suppose.

'What did you want me to do?' I say, deciding I might as well defend myself. I do, after all, have some sort of defence.

'Sorry?'

'I'm not sure what anyone wanted me to do. We released him. We weren't about to take him back into custody. We had no grounds to do that. Yes, I get it, we wanted to keep track of him, and perhaps I ought to have trailed him as he left my apartment...'

'Yes!'

'But I didn't. I chose to trust him. Unlike DCI Hamilton, I don't for a moment think he's guilty.'

'Based on gut instinct?'

'Yes!'

'Jesus. You fucking detectives. And I presume DCI Hamilton's gut instinct is that he is guilty?'

'Yes.'

'Well, look at that. I don't know, two people disagree on something, one of them's in charge, and one of them's there to be told what *the fuck* to do, which one gets to make the decision?' She makes an exaggerated *what-to-do* gesture, then says, 'In this case, that would be DCI Hamilton. Because she's in charge.'

'I'm a detective sergeant, I have to make decisions on the spot. That was a decision I made on the spot. And she's pissed off, and she's kicked me off the case, so there we are.'

'It's pretty fucking simple, eh?'

'Can I go back to work now?'

'No! No, you cannot go back to work. You've excelled yourself this time, Sergeant, you really have. I mean, sure, you usually manage to get kicked off whatever case you're working on, but this time, *this time*, you've been kicked off it twice. Holy shit! Like, just, holy shit. So, no, you cannot go back to work.'

'Really? You're suspending me?'

She makes an almost sitcom-esque confusion face, then shrugs.

'I don't know. I don't know if I can suspend you over this. I mean, I want to, but we'll see. I've got this woman, this Hamilton woman, shouting at me. I've got the super through there losing his shit. But I know if I go too far, I'll have the union people coming out your arse.'

'What do you want me to do?' I say, voice suddenly flat, deflated, wiped of emotion. The stand has been taken, for what it was worth, and now I just need to leave. The rollercoaster, bolstered by a brief burst of resistant energy, has hit the downward plummet.

'Go home, at least for today. Probably tomorrow. Maybe the rest of the week.'

Her voice too, taking its lead from mine, does the same, the energy, the urgency, evaporating.

'I'll call you, let you know what's happening.'

We hold the gaze across the table, a completely different gaze from the ones I hold with Kallas, which in turn are quite different from the looks Eileen and I share. Maybe I could write a book. A literary novel. *Gazing At Women Across A Desk.*

Hmm… that doesn't really sound like me, does it? How about *Banging Women Across A Desk*? Well, that at least sounds like the kind of book I might like to think about. Very unlikely to write it of course.

She snaps her fingers.

'Jesus, Sergeant, where do you go? Can you concentrate for, like, five minutes?'

'I'm leaving,' I say. 'You can… call.'

Another gaze, I feel like she wants to have the last word,

but really there's nothing else to add, and so instead she just makes a small chin gesture towards to the door, and I turn, and I'm gone.

Stop briefly at my desk, shut down the computer, DC Ritter not in position, Eileen out on a job, nobody home, and so I put my phone in my pocket and head for the stairs.

Passing Ramsey on the front desk, I give him a short wave.

'Skipping off early, Sergeant,' he says.

I glance over, drag my thumb across my throat, he rolls his eyes in a fuck-me-you're-incorrigible kind of a way, and I'm out of there.

*

Rain pishing down, torrential, unrelenting. Picked a perfect afternoon to come out for a run. It was this or drink. Ultimately, I will do both. But the weather was coming in, cold and grey and wet, and I thought, fuck it, get out in that. Go on, you bellend, see if you can actually *feel* something.

Have come up to Cambuslang Park. Drove here. Sat in the car for half an hour, watching the rain stoat off the windscreen. Finally, now, forced myself out into the storm. Past the war memorial, and down into the belly of the park.

Gloriously cold and wet. It's been, what, a couple of months since I last went running, and perhaps three years before that. I'm going to be stiff tomorrow morning, worse the day after. Nevertheless, of all the pains in the world, it's the best. The feel-good pain. The know-you-did-something-worthwhile pain.

Have that basic contented feeling of knowing I can drink later. Nothing to stop me. Sure, Eileen'll be round, more than likely, or Kallas maybe, but it won't matter. It'll be too late. By the time they get off work, I'll have started. I'll have had that taste. Wine on my tongue, the scourge of a too-strong vodka mixer on the throat. The thought of it leads me on through the rain.

As usual when I've been booted from a case, I just can't let it go. Wish I could. Wish I could just stick my hand into my head, grab something, grab a handful of thoughts, take them all into one clenched fist, and drop them in a passing bin. Not so easy with thoughts, though. Ungrabbable. Undismissable. They are there, good, bad, indifferent, ugly, whether you like them or not.

Thinking about Dr Thebes, and the way he shifted, the way his demeanour changed. It was slight, but perceptible, nevertheless. When I asked him about his previous life, the world he'd left behind. From that moment he was heading out the door, even though the conversation lasted a little longer. And I can't help thinking there was something there with the mention of Elizabeth Bishop. I couldn't see his face, but I felt it, as though his discomfort or his wariness or his suspicion reached out across the room, as obvious as if I'd been staring straight at him and his mouth had contorted into a snarl.

I'd been thinking of John Abercrombie, and the wastrel widower, the lesbian lover and the arrogant American gazillionaire. Now I'm not so sure. Now I'm thinking about Elizabeth Bishop, although, really, my thoughts have nowhere to go. Not enough information. No idea how to get more information, nor really, despite the feeling of being unable to let go, the desire to.

Past the old bandstand, bleak and dispiriting in the downpour. At one time a walk along here would stir memories, warm summer days in the seventies, family days in the park, music and ice cream and arguments over sun block, and once upon a time I used to be able to remember them, why they happened and who was there and what it was all about. Now there's nothing left. Just the memory that those days existed, that this was a place I used to come, a park in between hills, with steep paths and football pitches and a bandstand and a stream running through it, and too often we've been called to investigate crimes here, and so over time the old memories have been lost. Some people will recall those old days, no doubt. I just don't give a shit. It happened; it's gone.

Up the path, beneath the trees, towards the football pitches. Onwards to open ground, where the wind howls unbroken and the rain falls uninterrupted.

Elizabeth Bishop. Came out of nowhere, bringing her London values and London condescension to the provinces, the investigative equivalent of some cabinet minister announcing fifty jobs will be moving from London to Glasgow, while saying, *our staff will love it there, they'll love Glasgow, they have electricity and running water, and the people are delightful.*

Maybe I'm just projecting, choosing to be offended by her

presence. She's got a job to do, same as the rest of us. Yet, there's something there. Something with her and Thebes. Not that that should mean Thebes would be the innocent party. It could be he's thinking, uh-oh, she sees through me, and she'll make sure Hutton, and all the rest, see through me.

Feel the effort of running in my throat, less than seven or eight minutes in, as I head up to the top of the football pitches. Soaked through already, and cold, freezing cold. Anyway, I was soaked through in the first thirty seconds. Now my throat has that rasping, grasping feel, uncomfortable and scratchy, that comes with running when you're not used to it, even though I'm barely running, I'm just jogging, easing my way into exercise, this year's exercise, the final instance, even though it's only April.

There's one other person in sight, a woman in a long, bright red, vinyl trench coat, hood pulled up, head down, dog on a lead walking disconsolately at her side, not bothering to even make an effort to sniff at the grass as they pass.

Elizabeth Bishop. She was chatty enough in the car, approachable, easy-going. Drew me in. And there was that low-level flirting as well, the one that wasn't going anywhere. Maybe she was just bullshitting with all that marriage stuff. Maybe she'd have jumped me if she'd actually wanted it. Or had to. Maybe, like in real life, sex wasn't even part of the equation.

Breaths becoming heavy, legs heavier. This isn't going well. Now I'm just soaked, feel like shit, it's chucking it down and I'm a fifteen-minute walk from the car.

Guess I'm kind of star-struck by the whole MI6 thing, which is entirely Bond-related, right? Those movies, there was something aspirational about them. The women and the cars and the first-class travel and the hotel rooms. It was all such shit, as fantastical and detached from real life as a swords-and-dragons epic, yet you wanted to believe. There really were men out there doing this shit, killing people for the Queen. And whoever they were, they weren't regular police officers. The regular police stuff was just bullshit, dirty and tough and depressing and grim, and by God, if that ain't the truth. But the spy shit? Gorgeous.

Course, the Bond movies are a bit like Formula 1. It has the same glamour, aspirational thing going on, but then most of the races are boring as fuck, just like most of the Bond movies, once you look back at them, are pretty lousy. Except *Goldfinger*. *Goldfinger* is the Jackie Stewart, Monza 1969 of Bond films.

Finally stop running when I'm at the far end of the football pitches. And when I say I finally stop running, I've been running for all of twelve minutes, so let's not get carried away here. Lean forward, hands on knees. Whose brilliant idea was it to do this before getting hammered, as though one mitigated the other?

I look back across the park. The woman in red has vanished, like the evil dwarf in the red coat in *Don't Look Now*. I scan the park for her, as if it matters, but there's no sign. Not of her, not of anyone else. No one else in Cambuslang is stupid enough to come up here on a day like this.

Damn it. Fuck Elizabeth Bishop. I was trudging around here developing this stupid plan, where I was going to head into town, park down the road from the HQ, and wait for Bishop to emerge. Then I was going to follow her.

I start laughing at the preposterous, hollow stupidity of it. Maybe she's a spy, maybe she's not, I don't know. But really, *I* was going to follow *her*. Fuck off, sergeant.

And then somehow, from somewhere, the rain increases in intensity, and I start cackling with laughter, and it reminds of the times that Taylor and I would laugh stupidly like this, and that makes me want to cry as much as laugh, and leaning forward, hands on my knees becomes slumping down onto the ground, knees first, into the soft, sodden earth of the football pitch. Then I'm bent forward, head in my hands, crying-laughing, as soaked through as if I was sitting in the bath, alone in the middle of a grey downpour, the day stretching ahead of me like a long descent into drunken madness, and soon enough I'm lying in the grass, sobbing stupidly, tears from nowhere – wasn't I laughing thirty seconds ago? – consumed by the awful hopelessness of virtually every major investigation I get into, and my own hopelessness, the inanity of every thought I have, my own investigative ineptitude, where every breakthrough I ever make comes from luck and chance and the work of others. And really, I may be thinking what the fuck are you doing here, *here*, lying in this swimming pool of mud, but you know what? It's perfect for you, you fucking lowlife, useless cunt.

36

I'm in my spot. Me and my nineteenth-century confidante in lilac. I have a glass of wine. The vodka, the main course, is in the freezer.

I expect either DI Kallas or Sgt Harrison will pitch up or call or something at some point, but it won't be for a while yet. I have time.

I pause before the first drink. Lift the glass, breathe in the aroma. A mid-range Chablis, Thebes having put the idea of the Chablis in my head. First drink, a long one, enjoying the taste, straight down the throat, then leave a little sitting on my tongue as I lower the glass, close my eyes, let the taste linger and my skin tingle and my head feel absolutely glorious with it, and it feels so good, and, *and* I don't have to go to work tomorrow.

'That is perfect,' I say to Gertrude. Gertrude looks back at me like she's happy to be fucked, right here, here on the table. She's got over the slight of me not finishing her off, and she's ready for it.

'Drink up, cowboy,' she says. 'Then take me. I want to feel your tongue on me. I'm soaking already, and I want your tongue on my…'

The intercom buzzer goes.

I look at the glass.

No!

Well, my friend, we got this far.

I put the glass to my lips and down it, finishing off as the buzzer sounds again.

Jesus, that's good. And I don't care who this is, they ain't pouring the rest of the bottle down the sink, and they ain't dragging me to some AA meeting starting in the next twenty minutes.

Stand at the door, finger on the intercom.

'Yep?'

'Tom.'

Kallas. Shit. Somehow, I'm used to Eileen's disappointment in me. I can handle it better. We have it out. We argue, we fuss and we fight. There's no fighting with Kallas, of course. Nevertheless, plenty of disappointment.

I buzz the door without speaking any further, then retreat to the table, though I don't sit down. Leave the empty glass in position, but at least stop myself from filling it up.

Footsteps on the stairs, then outside on the landing, then she pushes the door open, closes it behind her, and then she's in the sitting room. She stands in the middle of the room, in a shaft of sunlight, the afternoon bright after the earlier downpour. Dark grey jacket, white blouse, jeans, shoes taken off at the door. I'm not sure she usually does that, though she is not here very often.

'You are drinking,' she says.

I look at the glass, I look at her. Impossible to deny.

She approaches, lifts the glass, puts it to her nose, breathes in the aroma, tips the glass to her lips and tastes the dregs, then places it back on the table.

'Chablis.'

I nod.

'How many have you had?'

'That's my first.'

'Did you buy anything else?'

'I've two bottles of that, and a litre of vodka. I haven't had any vodka yet. Not long in.'

'What have you been doing?'

Having a mental breakdown in the pouring rain, thank you, ma'am.

'You have showered this afternoon.'

This woman has the sensory perception of that weird fucker in *Perfume*. I smile weakly in response.

'I went for a run.'

'You do not usually run.'

'No.'

'You will be stiff and sore tomorrow.'

'Already am.'

And there we are, the preliminary conversations dealt with, and so we regress to the familiar place that is awkwardness and discomfort. And this time, by dint of her approaching the table to taste the remnants of the glass, and me taking up position by the chair I was sitting in, we are no more than a couple of feet apart.

She swallows. I swallow too. She can smell the mint of my

shower gel, the wine on my lips, I can smell the light fragrance of jasmine that clings to her from the start of the day.

Maybe she sprayed it just before she came up here.

There's a thought. She wants me as much as I want her.

Damn, of course she wants me as much as I want her. There's no explanation for it, but here we are. This isn't about that. This isn't about not being entirely sure what the other person wants. This is about it being wrong. She's married, she has children.

Neither of us moves, neither of us can think of anything to say. Or we can think of everything to say but can't force the words into the silence. I wish there'd been music playing, but I was in such a rush to pour the drink when I got out the shower, I didn't even stop to do that.

The silence is complete, the room waiting for a sound, waiting for something to happen. We look into each other's eyes. I can feel a hand on my stomach, squeezing and twisting and tightening. The ache of it. The ache of standing here like this. I wish I could make the move to her. I wish I could be the one to control the situation, even if it was just to sit down, or to go and make a cup of tea, or even just to get the wine. Anything. But I'm standing here, helpless, hoping she does something. I'm letting her, the married one, the mother of young children, take the responsibility.

I don't know how long we stand in impotent silence, then out of nowhere she says, 'You should not drink anything else.'

'I know.'

We lurch briefly back into the quiet abyss, before she manages to drag us out of it.

'I will make tea.'

'No,' I say, automatically.

'You should drink something other than alcohol.'

'I can't,' I say. 'I'm done. I'm just… I'm done.'

Another long look, our eyes never leaving each other. She swallows again, silently, I see the movement in her throat.

Finally, I close my eyes. This is just too much. She needs to leave, leave me to it, let me wallow in my own repeated failures, my own descent, let me raise the white flag.

'What can I do to stop you drinking?'

Her voice is soft and a little bit closer, my turn to swallow this time, my heart suddenly pounding and crashing, and I don't know how the sound of that isn't filling the room, bouncing off the walls, and I can't bring myself to open my eyes, can't bear the thought of her this close, this close and I cannot touch, and then her fingers rest lightly on my chest, and I feel her right in front of me.

Open my eyes. Kallas, her body almost pressed against mine, her face only a few inches away, and now there's nothing to be done. The river has been crossed, the defences have been breached, we have both crumbled, and suddenly our lips are together.

I stand still at first, we both do, as though there's nothing else we can do but kiss, her lips, soft and moist and giving, and as perfect as I've imagined them all these months. Hands at my side, eyes closed, I breathe her in and taste her, losing myself. And then I feel her hand lightly touch my cheek, running gently down my neck, I feel a thousand tiny orgasms cover my skin, and we are lost.

37

Sometime later, lying in bed, staring at the ceiling, our fingers lightly touching. We've been in bed a long time. We dozed for a while, woke up, drank some water, and then made love again. Last of the daylight still lingering outside, but the sun has vanished behind the buildings opposite, and the bedroom is in half-light.

It's been so long since I slept with someone for whom I've had this level of feeling. Jesus, it's such a game changer. Sex with added emotion is sex multiplied, gloriously, by a thousand.

I have to be cool about it, though. This is easy for me. I don't have a young family, I don't have a partner, I don't have a career I care in the slightest about. Kadri Kallas has three children under ten, a husband, and a job she's great at. There's no way I'm worth losing any of that over.

Her guilt will likely have already started. I've been in her shoes before, I know how it feels. The pleasure, and the guilt, in equal measure.

I squeeze her fingers, and she responds.

'We cannot do this again,' she says, her voice soft, but assured. Looking forward, rather than skirting around the present.

'I know.'

A moment, then she says, 'I'm sorry, I need to go. I will get up and have a shower, but first I will go to the kitchen and do as Dr Thebes did last night.'

Man, I don't care.

Wait, what? Some alcoholic you turned out to be.

'I may need to drink again tomorrow night,' I say, delivery perfectly dry.

She laughs lightly, and I look curiously to my left. DI Kallas never laughs at home.

'This has to be a one-time offer,' she says. 'You will need to go to a meeting tomorrow evening. I will ask Eileen if she will accompany you.'

She looks at me, smiles, squeezes my fingers.

'You will need to find a long-term solution. You need to learn to rely on yourself. Perhaps… perhaps once you leave the police.'

'Word's out, is it?' I ask.

'I am not sure who will be on your side. I think Chief Hawkins… she understands you and I, even if she is not sure about it. But I do not believe she will continue to put much store in my protestations on your behalf.'

'It's fine,' I say, voice low. 'You shouldn't be making them anyway. I've shot myself in the foot quite enough, and it can't be doing your career much good having to be the one who's always putting her reputation on the line to defend me.'

'I am happy to,' she says. 'You are a good officer. Now, however, I am not sure there is any point.'

A moment, I can feel her poised, about to move, and then she squeezes my fingers a last time, sits up in bed, and swings her legs over the side, before walking naked to the door. She turns.

'I will dispose of the liquor. Perhaps you could make me a small cup of coffee while I have a shower. I should not stay long.'

I nod. She stands there for a moment, a last look at her extraordinarily beautiful, naked body, and then she turns away and disappears from view. For a moment I look at the thin air, imagining her still there, and then I let my head fall back on the pillow.

*

The atmosphere has completely changed. I cannot remember the last time we were able to just sit at a table, drinking coffee, like *normal people*. Jesus. We should have had sex ages ago.

The strained atmosphere will be back, of course. How can it not be? It will be back as long as we work together, and she's married. Of course, as she said, we may not be working together for very much longer.

'Anything to report?' I ask.

'I did not come to report,' she says. 'I am more concerned that you do not follow me out, and then go and buy more alcohol. I know what the first taste does to a person.'

'You, em… It's OK, you took it away. I know, it won't

213

last, but… you took it away. You must have temporarily rewired my brain.'

'You did that to me even before we went to bed,' she says, and smiles weakly on the back of it, before lifting the mug to her lips.

'Tell me how today went,' I say. It's more about talking about something that isn't her and me and this, anything to get away from the seriousness, from her perspective, of what just happened.

'I spent some time in Dr Thebes' apartment,' she says. 'A very interesting place, and one can sense the man from the way he lived.'

'Yeah, it's a nice place. Maybe if he never comes back, I could move in.'

She smiles, staring vaguely at the window. We're both imagining being in that apartment, sitting at that table, looking out on the Clyde, as the river runs through our lives.

'I could finish off the Andrea Doria,' I say. 'Ha. It would end up like that fresco restoration in Spain.'

She smiles at that, takes a drink of coffee, still staring at the window, still imagining the view.

This is us, living our imaginary existence. Another world. And it's easy enough for me. I can lose myself in it. I can wallow. I fully intend to stay in it, at least for the rest of the evening. Kadri, however, has just committed adultery. I guess for the first time. This has the potential to rip her life apart.

'I did not see the Andrea Doria,' she says, emerging from the other life with the mundane.

'They removed it when they took all his tools,' I say.

She takes a drink, a slight furrowing of her brow.

'I had not been in his apartment before. There was a model on the workbench. I assumed they had decided to leave it in place.'

'There was a model on the bench by the window?'

'Yes. It was very beautiful.'

'You sure it wasn't the Andrea Doria?'

'It was named the Falls of Clyde.'

'The what?'

'A nineteenth-century packet ship. The real ship is permanently berthed at the museum at Yorkhill.'

I take a drink, try to begin functioning properly. After all, I've had wine, sex and coffee, all the main stimulants, I should be able to reach some sort of operational level.

'Did you see Eurydice after you visited the apartment?'

'I came straight here.'

'OK, OK.'

Stand up, hands to my head, run my fingers through my hair.

'They took the Andrea Doria model in when they impounded all his tools. I have no idea why they did that, by the way, it wasn't as though he'd killed someone with the model. I didn't go back there in the last couple of days, after he'd been back there, then left again, but I saw a report. They said the place was unchanged.'

'Yes, I saw that too.' A pause, then she adds, 'But for me, I saw the word *unchanged*, that was all. When I saw this model, the Falls of Clyde, I assumed it must have been there all along.'

'It was right in the middle of the workbench?'

'Yes,' she says, a modicum of expression, at having to repeat what she believes she's already made clear.

'So, it's got, what sails and shit?'

She smiles.

'Yes, Tom, sails.'

'There was nothing like that there when I was in the apartment. Which means…'

I pause to think about it, and she completes the sentence.

'Which means he must have been back to the apartment, possibly today or last night, and placed it there.'

'It seems unlikely anyone else would choose to do it.'

'And if he risked breaking back into his own apartment to do that, he must have done it for a reason.'

How many reasons can there be?

'He wants us to go to the Falls of Clyde,' she says.

I've got the buzz, the adrenaline of progress. Well, holy shit, this is some evening.

'How did he know we would even notice?' she asks.

'Why did you go to the apartment?'

She stares at me while she thinks it through, then nods to herself.

'I saw a minor anomaly in a report from the apartment. It seemed insignificant, about some of the tools being left in place. I wondered if someone had made a mistake. I decided to check it out for myself, rather than bother Eurydice.'

'Too small to pass on, big enough to make you look.'

'You think Dr Thebes manipulated what I was looking at?'

'Yes.'

'How did he know I would look at it?'

'Perhaps he knew what you were looking at in real time and changed it after you opened the document. If it hadn't worked, he'd have tried something else. Perhaps it wasn't the first thing he tried.'

'If he wants us to go somewhere, why not just tell us? I do not understand the subterfuge.'

Brain working overtime, but it doesn't really need to on this matter, as I'm already there.

'He doesn't trust Elizabeth Bishop. He may not trust Eurydice, I'm not sure. But he trusts *us*. Why did you come here now, and why wasn't it Eileen?'

'You sent Eileen the text. You asked to see her. She was called away and couldn't make it. She passed it on to me.' She pauses, and I give her the look, the significant look, with a shake of the head. 'You did not send Eileen a text, so we will assume he made sure she would be unable to come to your aid. A little labyrinthine, perhaps, but each individual step is plausible, and it appears that he is entirely in control of the situation.'

'Shit,' I say, another thought coming to me. 'We probably weren't supposed to sleep with each other. He couldn't have known that.'

'No. We should go to the Falls of Clyde now, but we will call it in first. There will be others who are closer.'

'No.'

She's out of her seat, heading to the door, me in her wake, grabbing a jumper as I go, pausing at the door to put on shoes.

'You think we should treat the others with the same suspicion as Dr Thebes is treating them? That is siding with the murder suspect over our police colleagues.'

She stops in the doorway, looking down at me as I tie my shoelaces.

'Shit,' I say. 'I'm sorry, I really didn't want to drag you down this path.'

'What if he wants us to call it in?' she says, as I'm out the door, closing it behind us, and we're heading down the stairs. 'We assume he is in control, that he understands everyone's motives. He made sure I was here. He would know that you would happily keep these details to yourself, but that you would at the same time want to protect me. He knows you do not want to leave me exposed in this way.'

'So, you think he wants you to call someone?'

'That is correct.'

'Who?' I ask.

'In this logic, perhaps I should call the person he trusts the least,' she says.

'To smoke her out,' I say, with a nod at her back, and she catches my look in the mirror on the landing of the second floor, and on we go, down to the ground, quickly out onto the street, and into her car.

She starts the engine, making the call with one hand as she moves away from the side of the road with the other.

'Inspector Bishop,' she says, 'I cannot get hold of DCI Hamilton. We have a situation.'

38

The ship, like the museum it stands besides, is in darkness. We park a hundred yards away, then approach and walk around the side of the museum, where the path to the waterfront is blocked by a six-foot metal gate. Kallas tries the handle, gives picking the lock the merest consideration, and then quickly climbs the gate and jumps lightly over to the other side. I, now beginning to really suffer from my abject running in the rain earlier today, follow in her path, my movements much more laboured.

A tentative walk along the side of the museum, then a glance around the building to the ship, the Falls of Clyde. No one around. No security, no one loitering. If anyone is awaiting our arrival, they are, as one would expect them to be, out of sight.

We could, of course, be making quiet fools of ourselves. We briefly talked about it in the car. Are we forcing this narrative, are we taking various talking points from the investigation, and distilling them into completely the wrong thing? Clutching, desperate to make a breakthrough that's not there to be made.

There's a covered entrance to the ship, a locked gate, that leads to a couple of steps, then the wide, solid gangplank. Kallas tries the gate, and there's the kicker. The gate is unlocked. Unlike the previous locked gate, this one cannot be clambered over.

She eases it open, turning and giving me a look as she does so.

We were right. Buckle up.

Feel it properly now, the tension of it. Creeping around in a dark and unfamiliar place, waiting for who knows what. The jump scare, the moment that arrives without the burst of music, the moment that comes out of nowhere with a flurry of unexpected movement, the shadows that materialise into shape and form out of the semi-darkness.

Onto the deck of the ship, and now we're both moving

218

slowly, feet soundless on wooden boards. She turns, she indicates with a look that we should split up. About to turn away, I squeeze her arm. The *just be careful* arm squeeze. Despite the earlier lovemaking, it suddenly feels overfamiliar, and I nod, turning away.

Read the room, genius.

There are two doors into the structure on the upper deck on this side, but neither of us go inside just yet. I head along to the bow, tension ramping up with every step. Heart thumping, ears straining for any sound.

There's nothing. Kallas has gone, her footsteps soundlessly off into the night. The river silent and still. There are the sounds of the city, behind and on the other side of the water, but it is a low, distant white noise.

Up to the bow, still nothing to see. Another door, at the base of some steps, leading to the deck below. I pass it by, walking beneath the boom of the large sail at the front. What's the name of the front sail? the question automatically in my head, and I shake it away. Focus!

Take a moment. Stop, listen. Suddenly think to look up, and I strain my neck, looking into the black, endless depths of the masts and the folded-up sails. Nothing obvious, no one poised to leap down. Look down the starboard side of the boat, the same blank canvas of river darkness, and then I start to slowly walk down the length. Aware that at some point I may well meet Kallas on the way and need to be prepared to not lose my shit over that.

As it is, she's ahead of me in her tour of the upper deck and turns the far corner when I'm still a few yards shy of it. We nod at each other, she indicates she's going to enter the cabin that's now on our right, and I jerk my thumb backwards.

Turn round, more quickly back along the deck, get to the top of the stairs, another quick look around – the bottom of these stairs next to a locked door would be a shit place to be trapped – and then down the steps, try the handle and again, I'm not in the least surprised when the door opens.

Quickly inside, close the door, and suddenly I'm standing in a narrow corridor that turns back round to the left and the right, a couple of yards either side of me. A wall in front, lined with photographs of old sailing vessels, indistinct in the dim light.

Choose left, choose right. It doesn't matter. We are being

led here, pulled forward. One way or another we're going to come to it.

Take a moment, hold my breath, take the temperature of the place, this lower deck, let instinct take over, let it make the decision, and then I turn left.

Round the corner, a door on the right, another straight ahead. The door on the right, can't be much, almost up against the hull of the ship. Try the handle, it is locked. Can be little more than a narrow cupboard. The door ahead has a small window, but it is dark behind.

Quick look, nothing to see. Fingers on the door handle. A sound from above.

Hold my breath.

A footfall. Another. Soft, the quality of detachment. Someone trying not to be here, trying to project that they are elsewhere.

Kallas and I would have walked with such attempted stealth, and so must have been as obvious to anyone already down here. Fuck, fuck, fuck.

The sound from above fades, or stops, it is so indistinct it's impossible to tell which. Fingers still on the door handle, time to buckle up and get on with it.

Open the door, slowly at first, but there is no squeak of a hinge, and so I push it open, and step quickly into the room, closing the door behind me.

Total darkness. Stand still, ease back against the wall, a little away from the door. Try to get the feel of the room. It seems large, the obscure darkness reaching into far corners. No sound. Nothing from above, nothing from in here. But then I get the sense of it. I'm not alone.

Don't move, eyes wide, letting them slowly come to terms with the dark. Muscles tensed, waiting for the rush of movement. Another noise from above, slightly louder this time, something other than a gentle footstep.

Ah, fuck, come on.

Phone out of my pocket, flashlight on, hold it forward. Anyone in here will already know my location.

The light gets lost in the room, not reaching a far wall. I step forward, movements more rapid now, turning, trying to get my bearings as quickly as possible. No one either side, step further forward. Chairs stacked at the side of the room, and tables too. In regular times, this is the café, perhaps, or an events room.

A central post, the main mast running through the room, then the light falls on the bar counter at the far end. The sense of it, of someone outside, and someone else in here with me, growing.

Another quick spin round, waiting for the rush out the darkness.

And there she is. Jesus. Thebes, you bastard.

Finola Stephens, bound and gagged in a chair. How pedestrian, how predictable, Thebes toying with the conventions of the genre, like he's playing a game.

Her eyes are wide, the whites of them bright in the light. Indicating nothing with her look, no frantic *he's over there* glances to the side. I step forward, quickly, ignoring the possibility of her being the trap. The distraction to make me turn my back. If there is anyone else here, they've known where I was from the second I entered the room.

I undo the gag, and she breathes heavily, shaking her head as she does so, eyes still wide, then I turn and shine the torch around the room. Here in the corner, the light does not penetrate far.

'Where is he?' she says.

'What?'

'Where is he?' she snaps again. 'I'll fucking kill him.'

'Who?'

'What?'

I look at her, shine the light just off her face.

'What are you talking about?' I ask.

'Jesus. Where's Crispin?'

I hold her gaze for a moment, though she will not be able to clearly see my eyes, then whirl round, shining the light so that it gets lost in the darkness of the room.

'When did you last see him?'

'Jesus Christ,' she says. 'Can you untie me?'

'When did you last see him?'

'What's the time?'

'Like, nine or something.'

'Fuck me. Sometime this afternoon.'

'You've been here the whole time?'

'Will you untie me, please?'

I try to think it through, try to think if she might be any kind of threat, but the reality is just more obvious than that.

Thebes really is a brutal bastard.

I go behind her, lay the phone on the floor, light shining up towards her bound wrists, and undo the wire that's been twisted around them.

'You must really need to pee,' I say. What a mundane thing to come into my head.

'Bladder of steel,' she says, acerbically. 'Where is he?'

'He's gone.'

'What? Well, what the fuck am I here for?'

Finish the wire, and she whisks her arms round, and starts rubbing her wrists, sucking in her breath.

'Fuck,' she mutters.

Another sense of something from outside the room, and I put my hand on her shoulder. She stops moving, and together we listen to the ship, ears straining in the near darkness, and the shallow thrust of insignificant light.

Another sound, the approach of something, and for the first time since I got down here, I think of Kallas. Fuck it. She should be in here, I should be out there, with whoever it is. Not for a moment do I think it's just her.

'Why am I here?' says Stephens, voice a strained whisper, leaning forward, undoing the ties on her legs.

'You're bait.'

Blunt. No time for anything else.

'Goddamit, I knew it. I'll fucking kill him.'

You're never finding him.

Who's coming? I need to know who's coming? Bishop? Really? Would Bishop do her own wet work?

Wet work? Listen to the bullshit from this guy.

The door bursts open, practically kicked off its hinges. Smacks off the wall. A hand in, light switch on, and then Kallas enters.

Aw, fuck.

Kallas, then a yard behind, in the bright glare of the ceiling lights, the barrel of a gun, with a silencer attachment, aimed at her head.

39

I stand impotently beside the chair. Fucking guns. I hate guns. Don't bring guns into it. Who are these people? And, of course, it's not just the gun. It's this person. Out of the blue, walking on set, a character plucked from the mire of the investigation.

Except, of course, it makes perfect sense. Just as the gun makes perfect sense.

Who was it who set the ball rolling? Who was it who had me making the connection with Thebes? Who was it who casually threw sex around, just like they do in the movies? The way they come out of nowhere, and the way they produce guns in the movies.

'See you brought your phone to the gunfight, sergeant,' says Alice Rowe, rowing club captain. Fuck me.

I give her nothing.

She indicates for Kallas to move over and stand beside Stephens and me, Kallas giving me a look of apology – all in the eyes, but I can read it just the same – and then Rowe is watching us, gun trained on Kallas, identified as the principal threat.

She holds us like this, thinking, and I take the time to quickly think it through too, how we got here, what it means.

Thebes set it up to be like this. He may not have kidnapped Stephens, but he got her to leave with him, and then did this to her. Laid the breadcrumbs for Kallas and I. We played our part. Came here, alerted Bishop. We can deduce that Bishop alerted Rowe, and she's standing there holding us at gunpoint.

Rowe is not walking away from this and going back to rowing up and down the Clyde tomorrow morning. Or, if she is, we're not walking out of here alive.

'You killed Wright and Talbot to set up Thebes,' I say. 'Finish the job with Mrs Stephens to further implicate him. You can then put the full weight of the police behind the search for him.' A pause, we stare at each other, though, to be honest, I'm not entirely sure she's even listening. 'Which means you have to kill both DI Kallas and I.'

'Stop talking.'

Something else worth being honest about is that this woman, whoever she actually is, likely doesn't give a fuck about killing anyone. This is the trained assassin, a beast far outwith the realms of the familiar Glasgow crime-scape. I think DI Kallas and I might be out of our depth here. Well, I certainly am.

I'm not sure standing here thinking about it is the best use of this woman's time. There's not much to think about. There are two options. Thebes lured us all here, got her to show her hand, and intends to take her out; or he's already a thousand miles away, and is going to let Kallas and I do his work for him, clearing his name in his absence.

It has to be option one. There's no reason why he would expect us to be able to deal with someone like this. Which means his arrival is imminent.

She straightens the gun. Her decision is made. As is mine.

Start to move. The three-yard dash. Even if it means I take the first bullet, it gives Kallas a fraction longer to do something.

The lights go out.

Fuck!

I run pointlessly forward in the darkness. Movement all round, the gun goes off, the dull thud of a bullet hitting wood, three more rapid-fire shots, then the flurry of footsteps.

I listen for a moment, then turn back, staring into the dark in the direction of the women.

'Kadri?'

'I am good.'

Relief washes over me.

'Mrs Stephens?'

'I'm fine.'

The tone! The pissed-off, *why am I even here?* of it.

I dropped my phone in the senseless dash through the dark, and now I bend to lift it, the light of it evident though it is pressed against the wooden floor.

I turn the light towards the others. Finola Stephens is standing, poised to do something, albeit she does not know what to do. Kallas is kneeling on the floor, her shoulder a mass of blood.

'Jesus,' I say. 'You s –'

'I am fine, really. The bullet passed straight through.'

I kneel down beside her, but Finola Stephens is clearly the more practical of us, and instantly whips her blouse up and off, and rips it down the middle, and then rips it again, then starts attending to the wounds.

'Do not go after her,' says Kallas. 'That is a direct order, Sergeant. Dr Thebes is obviously here. He is orchestrating the situation.' She winces slightly, face hardens. 'We know which way this will go. You will only get hurt.'

'I wonder if that phone-flashlight of yours could perform some other function,' says Stephens, 'such as, I don't know, calling an ambulance. Maybe there are other officers who could come as back-up.'

I look at Kallas. She's the boss, after all. She nods.

'And call Eurydice,' she says. 'Tell her to track down Elizabeth Bishop, if she can. I suspect she will be unable to do so.'

From somewhere on the ship a loud, dull thud. A body falling.

We all turn, looking up in the direction of the sound.

'Fuck,' I say. 'We should move. Come on. In case Rowe's coming back.'

Kallas nods, getting to her feet. We listen for it, for the sound of movement, the sound of Rowe returning quickly to finish the job, but we know already. The heavy thump of the falling corpse will not have been Thebes.

The lights come back on. We stand for a moment. Listening. Waiting.

Silence.

In the air that indefinable quality of finality. The last body has fallen.

Into the silence comes Finola Stephens' voice at a strained, raised whisper.

'I've barely stopped the bleeding. Will you make the fucking phone call?'

40

The place is a blaze of light. An ambulance sits idly by to the side of the concourse that runs along the front of the museum, its only purpose to remove the corpse of Alice Rowe when the instruction is given. The other ambulance, the one that came for DI Kallas, has already left, Kallas on board, on her way on the short trip across the river to the Queen Elizabeth.

Someone put a cup of coffee in my hand, which I'm not complaining about. God knows where it came from. Coffee just seems to be everywhere these days, which is just fine. It's better than cigarettes and alcohol being everywhere, though someone offering a vodka-tonic would not have had their hand bitten off.

Finola Stephens has also been taken away, to give a full statement, before being released into the relieved arms of her husband. If he is relieved. Could still go either way. He'll know it in his heart, after a day of wondering whether he'd ever see her again. He'll be ready to forgive her, or he'll know he was happy at the idea of her being gone. Perhaps she won't want forgiven. She was the one who went looking for something outside their marriage in the first place.

Who knows about people's lives, and I don't care either way.

Eurydice approaches, slipping her phone into her pocket, then her hands follow, and she stands in front of me, everything about her, face and posture and overall air, speaking of phlegmatic resignation.

'We got completely played, right?'

'From the start,' I say.

'Not sure how much you had to do with it.'

It's not a question as such, but still, it's a question.

'I got played on a slightly different level, that's all.'

She nods, looks away around the scene. A few cars, a few coppers, a few SOCOs. We found Rowe's body on the deck, a single gunshot wound to the head. The attending pathologist, a woman I did not recognise, reckoned a shot from distance.

Would know more, in the way of pathologists worldwide, when she'd got the body back to her lab.

'Well, Sergeant, I guess, insomuch as we will ever know anything of this matter, you were right. Thebes was being set up, and I played my part by thinking he was guilty. I'm not entirely sure how you knew which part you had to play, though.'

'I didn't. He just used me as he saw fit.'

'What'd he see in you in the first place?'

I shrug, and Eurydice nods along with it.

'The fuck knows, right?' she says. 'Sometimes these things happen, sometimes they don't. I don't suppose you'll have any special insight into where the doctor is now?'

I shake my head slowly, take a moment to look around.

'I have no idea,' I say. 'Maybe he's watching us. Maybe he's a hundred miles away. My guess, and I don't know what I'm basing this off other than it's the kind of thing you'd expect to see in movies, is that all along he's had a safehouse somewhere in the city, and that's where he'll be. Laying low for as long as it takes. If the suits in London are so keen to get him that they'll murder people just to set him up, then he may well be laying low for the rest of his life. Or,' and I take a sip of coffee, because it feels like maybe I'm talking too much, but she raises her eyebrows at me, indicating for me to continue, 'or he heads to London, and starts to exact his revenge.'

'You've no idea what this is all about?'

I smile.

'Honestly, I talked to him last night for about five minutes. I know little more than you do. I mean, presumably he knows things. He's got secrets, knows where the bodies are buried. Someone, somewhere, decided it was time to remove him from circulation. Who knows why they thought they had to set him up to take him down, rather than just put a sniper on top of Pacific Quay and put a bullet in his head one afternoon while he sat at his window?'

'Yep,' she says, 'that's about the size of it. We know little, and for all the resources we throw at it now, I suspect all we'll learn is how much we don't, and never will, know. And it'll be a lot.'

'At least you have someone, a killer, to put on display. The murderer is dead, there've been no further victims.'

'Everyone's a winner,' she says, drily.

'Except Julia Wright and Jennifer Talbot.'

'Yep. Pawns in the game, right?'

She smiles ruefully at her own cliché, turning away as she says it, to look around the scene.

'Surprised that Elizabeth Bishop's not here,' I say, and Eurydice turns back, smiling.

'Funny. I suspect we shall never hear of Elizabeth Bishop again. When I make enquiries tomorrow morning, I will get short shrift. *Elizabeth Bishop?* they'll say. *Never heard of her.* But I spoke to you about her last week. *Sorry, chief, you must be mistaken.* Jesus…'

We hold the gaze for a moment, and I realise that Eurydice is as disinterested in Elizabeth Bishop as I am. She came, she tried to influence how the story played out, she failed, she left. There are two aspects to any crime investigation. There's the catching who did it, and there's the making sure it doesn't happen again. We've achieved them both, and if it's the case that it was all done on the instructions of someone much higher up, then it's so far above our pay grade, it's barely worthwhile getting upset about.

That's just the way it is. You have to be pragmatic, and this is where we are. There are a hundred other fish to fry out there, and this means we can get on with all the other shit. Yes, Benjamin Wright and Daisy Johnson and John Abercrombie and a few others are going to want answers, and they're not going to be happy with the ones they get, but they're not going to get very far if they try to take it up with a higher authority, just as the press won't get very far if they throw the dogs at it.

'You should've slept with her when you had the chance,' says Eurydice.

Since my mind, at that moment, had turned to Rowe, I take a second, and then I realise she means Bishop.

'She blew me off,' I say.

'Really? You tried?'

Well, no, not really, but what's a pointless lie every now and again.

'Of course,' I say. 'You asked me too, right?'

'Didn't get anywhere?'

'Said she'd been married for twenty-nine years, and that I shouldn't believe everything I see in the movies.'

'Nice,' says Eurydice. 'Well, if only you'd had sex with Alice Rowe when you interviewed her, you might've had some inkling.'

There we are. Not being a complete stranger to that kind of stupid, unreal sexual encounter, I just didn't pick up on it. I didn't pick up on its total lack of realism, the where-did-that-come-from moment. The foreshadowing. I was living the joke that maybe Bishop would try to drag me off to bed, when it was Rowe all along.

We look at each other, an end of the evening kind of a look.

'Thank you, Sergeant,' she says, 'you're free to go. Probably best you report to your regular station tomorrow. I'll likely have a tonne more questions, but I'll be in touch. Need to try to unravel as much of the ball of shit as possible first.'

'Boss,' I say, and then with a nod we're done, I turn away, and start walking to Kallas's car.

*

And here's the other scene we've all seen in the movies. The hero – that's me, by the way, just in case anyone lost track – arrives at hospital to check up on the woman he loves, and there she is, at the end of a corridor, sitting up in bed, her shoulder bandaged, and the hero perks up and can't wait to talk to her, and then her husband comes into view from behind a curtain, sitting beside her bed, holding her hand.

I stop where I am. They haven't seen me yet; I can easily turn and walk. I have her car here, but she's obviously not going to be able to drive it anyway.

I hum and I haw, go back and forth, but the longer I stand here, the bigger the chance she sees me, which will make the decision for me, so I make the call, turn quickly, and walk back out of the hospital.

I sit in the car, staring at my phone, thinking about it. Thinking about what to say, and whether to say anything at all. Then quickly type:

Hope you're doing OK. I'll leave your car at the station tomorrow.

Sleep well.

Put a kiss, take the kiss away, then also remove the last two words, think about putting them back in, don't, then send the text.

Jesus.

Text angst. Fuck, man, we've all been there.

I sit and stare at the phone, waiting to see if she's going to reply, and straight away I can see she's typing a message.

Thank you. I am fine. I will see you tomorrow. Good night.

I stare at the message, I contemplate replying, I manage to stop myself.

Time to head for home. Time to head to bed. Amazingly, and God knows where this has come from, but I have no desire to ruin the rest of the night with alcohol. I want to go home, and I want to see what's left of the scent of jasmine on my sheets.

*

I walk into the apartment, dog-tired all of a sudden. Nevertheless, already decided to have a cup of tea first. I will sit with Gertrude, and she and I will pass an agreeable, if lonely, half hour, before I head to the bedroom.

I see it as soon as I walk into the sitting room. Stop, then smile, then walk forwards to the table.

There's Gertrude, face and shoulders and breasts intact, the rest of the dress dismantled, returned to, I expect, exactly the same state as she was before Thebes completed the jigsaw three days ago.

What a fucking guy.

I look around the room, although I know there's nothing else to find. This is who he is. He had done this one minor thing that he then felt he shouldn't have, and so he returned, when he knew I wouldn't be at home, and reversed it. More than likely, the first thing he did after he'd killed Rowe.

We were all wondering what had become of him, and all the while he was at the investigating officer's apartment.

I go into the kitchen, get the kettle going, stand there quietly, silently, waiting for it to boil, then make the tea, grab the last Tunnock's caramel wafer in the cupboard, and head to the small sitting room table.

'Well, Gertrude,' I say, sitting down. 'Hell of an evening, right?'

'Fucking tell me about it, Sergeant,' says Gertrude.

By Douglas Lindsay

The Barber, Barney Thomson

The Long Midnight of Barney Thomson
The Cutting Edge of Barney Thomson
A Prayer For Barney Thomson
The King Was In His Counting House
The Last Fish Supper
The Haunting of Barney Thomson
The Final Cut
Aye, Barney
Curse Of The Clown

The Barbershop 7 (Novels 1-7)

Other Barney Thomson

The Face of Death
The End of Days
Barney Thomson: Zombie Slayer
The Curse of Barney Thomson & Other Stories
Scenes From The Barbershop Floor Vol 1
Scenes From The Barbershop Floor Vol 2

DS Hutton

The Unburied Dead
A Plague Of Crows
The Blood That Stains Your Hands
See That My Grave Is Kept Clean
In My Time Of Dying
Implements Of The Model Maker

DCI Jericho

We Are The Hanged Man
We Are Death

DI Westphall

Song of the Dead
Boy In the Well
The Art of Dying

Pereira & Bain

Cold Cuts
The Judas Flower

Stand Alone Novels

Lost in Juarez
Being For The Benefit Of Mr Kite!
A Room With No Natural Light
Ballad In Blue
These Are The Stories We Tell

Other

For The Most Part Uncontaminated
There Are Always Side Effects
Kids, And Why You Shouldn't Eat More Than One For Breakfast
Santa's Christmas Eve Blues
Cold September

Printed in Great Britain
by Amazon

67190382R00144